CORBIN'S BASEMENT

CORBIN'S BASEMENT

Brette-
Wishing you the best.
With love,
Erin Yauney

LORIE YAUNEY

AVIVA
PUBLISHING
New York

For additional copies or bulk purchases, visit:
www.LorieYauney.com

Editor: Tyler Tichelaar, Superior Book Productions
Cover Design: Kerry Jesberger, Aero Gallerie
Interior Layout: Fusion Creative Works
Graphic Design: Kerry Jesberger, Aero Gallerie
Author Photo Credit: Dave Shirley Photography

Cataloging-in-Publication Data is on file at the Library of Congress
Hardcover ISBN: 978-1-950241-21-7
E-book ISBN: 978-1-950241-22-4

Aviva Publishing
Lake Placid, NY
518-523-1320
www.avivapubs.com

First Edition, 2019
Printed in the United States of America

For Michelle. May you always have two thumbs.

ACKNOWLEDGMENTS

Completing this book and holding it in my hands is a life-changing experience. From a vague idea bloomed this great story, and it wouldn't have been possible without Michelle Landrum, my dear friend, supporter, critic, and muse. Thank you for badgering me to finish the book, for all the phone calls of encouragement, for all the reads and rereads, and for all your worries about Corbin's poor thumb. I wouldn't have completed this book without you.

So many people have influenced me and made me who I am today. I wish I could list each person, so if your name isn't below, please don't be offended. You still had an impact on my life and I thank you. I would like to individually acknowledge:

Amanda Yauney Cremer for being the best daughter ever. I'm proud of you and the caring, wonderful person you have become. You are an amazing person, friend, and mother. I love you.

Katie, Corie, and Kendall, who have brought more love into my life than I ever imagined possible. When you're old enough to read this book, don't judge your LoLo—it's just a story.

My dad for making me the hardass I am today and teaching me that if you want something done, do it yourself. You can do anything you want, if you just set your mind to it.

Gaines Lanier, for being a leader I trusted, honored, and respected. I learned so much from you about running a successful company while treating people well. Thank you for all the opportunities you've given me. May your cows be healthy and prolific.

My friends who have always believed in and supported me, Lynn Yarborough, Tammy Lamb, Rhonda Usery, Kasey Dewberry, Brent and Sandra Blanks, Mercer Owens, Jerry Duke, Selena and Jim Major, and my countless JSL friends.

Tyler Tichelaar of Superior Book Productions for not just editing my manuscript, but teaching me in the process. Your edits and suggestions took my manuscript to a whole new level. You're the best!

Kerry Jesberger of Aero Gallerie for designing the amazingly perfect cover! You're awesome and captured my vision perfectly.

Some random guy named Corbin whom I met one time…and his basement. It all started there.

1

CORBIN

Hi. I'm Corbin. Welcome to my basement.

I have so many things I want to share with you so you will understand how important my basement is to me and why I am welcoming you so warmly into its depths.

I've recently taken a new job as a customer service representative at Blast, a huge internet shopping site. I thought it would be a blast working at Blast! Living in Atlanta has been a fun experience compared to living in Omaha—hated those winters there. Being in the Buckhead area gives me plenty of opportunities for good food, drinks, and entertainment. Plus, I like being a social butterfly after a long day on the ninth floor of the Peachtree Building. The work I perform five days a week from my 6'x6' cubicle covered in plum purple fabric isn't really challenging, but it does pay well, and the benefits are great. Some customers can get pretty heated up over a one-day delay in their normal two-day shipping, but for the most part, they can be satisfied with a listening ear, patience, and a bit of understanding. Not that we ever give them anything, but my job is to let them complain until they are no longer angry and then tell them how much we appreciate them shopping with Blast. Life could be a lot worse.

Spencer, my best friend, works at Blast, too. We met when I started six months ago on my first day. Spencer is kind of a dork, but I'm nice to him. I try to get him laid when we go out, but it's sometimes a hard sale to hook up a 5'5" nerdy guy who's about eighty pounds overweight, and quickly going bald. I never have a problem hooking up, although I wasn't always as pleasant to the eye as I am now. I'm 6'2" and my regular exercise habit is easily noticed. I'm also fortunate to have my father's transfixing green eyes. My mother hated that I inherited his green eyes. I guess she was reminded of his untimely departure from our lives when she looked at me. But they certainly work for picking up girls. There haven't been that many during my life, but the count has certainly escalated in the last few years. I guess it's like any other addiction—it starts with one here and there, but before you know it, you're craving your next fix and the time in between fixes gets shorter and shorter. All of a sudden, you're craving a new fix every weekend (or more if you're lucky enough to have the opportunity). However, I know to be careful and take care of myself.

So, like on every psychiatrist's couch across the country, let's start at the beginning. Hang on, it's going to be a fun ride!

Thirty-two years ago, I was born to Jessica Callahan and Franklin S. Eastman in the Great Falls Community Hospital in Great Falls, Montana. Jessica was a student at Montana State University majoring in accounting and Franklin was a handsome, small town rodeo cowboy. A long, tall drink of water, Franklin was instantly an aspiration for Jessica. While attending the Thirty-Fourth Annual Augusta Rodeo, Jessica was standing by the chutes when Franklin flew out on the back of a bucking, dun-colored mare, marking and spurring with each jump, his bright green-and-blue chaps flapping in rhythm to his spurring. Making the full eight seconds, Franklin gracefully dismounted and swaggered toward the fence, directly toward Jessica.

As the mare rounded the arena, seeking a bit of satisfactory revenge, she charged at young Franklin. He quickly leapt the fence right in front of Jessica, whose heart swelled at the twist of fate. Dropping to the ground and safe from the angry mare, Franklin smiled broadly at Jessica, his green eyes sparkling.

"What'd you think of that ride?" he asked arrogantly.

Jessica felt her face flush, and for some reason, she found it difficult to look him directly in his eyes for fear she couldn't stop looking. "It was pretty good, I guess," replied Jessica.

"Pretty good? I bet I win today's competition! Want to make a bet?"

"Sure. What'd you have in mind?" Jessica managed to say.

Rubbing his chin, Franklin surveyed his obvious prize for the night, looking her up and down, noticing her tight jeans and snug red T-shirt with her allegiance to her alma mater of MSU screen-printed over the left, nicely sized, breast. Smiling, he said, "How about this—if I win, you buy me a beer, and if I don't win, I buy you a beer?"

Smiling at her win-win, Jessica nodded and held out her hand, suddenly confident. "Bet," she said.

2
PEYTON

Peyton groaned as the blaring alarm resounded against the bedroom walls. She slammed her hand repeatedly on the snooze button, even though one time stopped the annoying sound, and fell back onto her oasis bed comprised of a Cloud Tempur-pedic mattress with 1,000-count cotton sheets and a Southern Tide comforter made from the softest, finest cotton she'd ever felt. Feeling the soft bedding cradle her still exhausted body, she remembered how she had saved her pennies for this extravagance and how her mother was typically critical. Good ol' Stella. Always count on her to be degrading and awful, even though Peyton was far nicer to her than her two brothers who hadn't seen her in years.

"Don't you think you're big shit with your fancy mattress and bedding?" Stella had said when Peyton told her about her new purchases. "You should be ashamed of squandering so much money on this frivolous stuff. You should be saving your money so you can afford to take care of me when I'm old and decrepit. I won't live forever, you know, and it's the children's responsibility to make sure their parents have a comfortable and safe retirement."

Peyton had just rolled her eyes. She was silently appreciative that her career change had taken her across the country to Atlanta.

Recently hired as the Associate Director of Human Resources at Blast, Peyton would be rewarded with not only a large paycheck, but the perfect opportunity to get out of her mother's grasp. Her old job held no promise of promotion and a recent incident with a coworker made things uncomfortable in the community. This move was a welcomed blessing.

Realizing she was lying in her new apartment, Peyton looked around in wonderment and toyed with the thought of going back to sleep.

Although it was only two days ago, it seemed like an eternity since she had been in South Dakota with the movers.

"Miss, is this all from this room?" asked the pot-bellied, yet amazingly strong mover from Two Guys Who Move Stuff.

"Yes, that's all in here. Let me take a quick look, but I think we are about done." Peyton smiled excitedly at the mover.

"Sure thing," he replied. "Let us know if there is anything else. If not, we'll lock the truck and head to Atlanta."

After Peyton found a few small boxes and a couple of potted geraniums that she put in the back of her Toyota 4Runner, the movers finished up, closed the truck, and headed down the gravel driveway toward her new beginning in Atlanta. Peyton smiled.

As the alarm sounded again, Peyton was pulled from her daydreaming about her last moment before her exciting move and the new chapter in her life. Slapping the clock, Peyton threw back the covers, stretched, and headed for the shower. After a hot, cold, then hot shower, Peyton threw on a pair of yoga pants, a faded green T-shirt, and black flip-flops with yellow sunflowers adorning the soles.

"Lots of unpacking to do today," she said while scrubbing the ears of her orange tabby cat, Molly, who looked at her questioningly and purred like a fiend.

All day, Peyton worked furiously at unpacking, and by 8 p.m., she had most of her trendy two-bedroom apartment on Southern Towers' sixth floor all in order. Living in Atlanta was going to be such an exciting adventure. Tomorrow, she started her first day at Blast. She opened her walk-in closet, excited to have one. She remembered stuffing her clothes into a two-foot wide armoire at her childhood home. A walk-in closet was quite the extravagance, and one of the reasons she had picked this apartment on her first visit to Buckhead following her lucrative offer from Blast.

Picking out a pinstripe pencil skirt, a red fitted cardigan, and her favorite three-inch Mary Jane heels for her first day tomorrow, Peyton brushed her teeth and crawled into her favorite nest of a bed.

"Tomorrow is the first day of the rest of my life." She sighed, then dozed into a happy, exhausted sleep.

3

JESSICA

Jessica rolled over and gazed lovingly at Franklin. *Oh, my God, he is simply the most perfect specimen of a man that I have ever seen.* Since that day at the rodeo, they had spent several heated and romantic nights—sometimes a little too rough for Jessica's taste, although she would never admit that to Franklin—together. She already knew she loved him completely. While Franklin was not her first sexual encounter, she had never felt this way about anyone. He was a beautiful, sexy cowboy with aspirations to join the Professional Rodeo Cowboys Association (PRCA) and have a successful career as a bareback bronc rider. Jessica envisioned their life together, traveling the country in his pursuit of fame and fortune, the two of them, together always. When his rodeo career ended, they would retire to his family's sprawling cattle ranch outside of Great Falls. While Jessica had never seen his family's ranch, the Lucky Draw and the Eastman family had always been envied by most people anywhere around the Great Falls area, or anywhere in Montana for that matter.

Franklin snorted a throaty snore violent enough to wake him from his drunken slumber. Then he opened his eyes and noticed Jessica staring at him. "Damn, baby, we got shit-faced last night, didn't we? Come here and climb on." Jessica complacently obeyed.

After a few hard thrusts and animalistic grunts, Franklin pulled out and pushed her aside. "What's for breakfast, woman?" he asked as he slipped into his faded Wrangler jeans. "I don't have much time. Have a busy day," he said as he walked from the small bedroom.

They had gotten drunk the night before. Jessica would do anything for Franklin, including losing her mind and good sense by riding dirt roads and getting completely drunk on his favorite cheap-ass beer, Lucky Draw Beer, brewed locally by a small company owned by the Eastmans and named in honor of the ranch. "Lucky Draw Beer, a tasty pilsner for the working man," the can proclaimed.

"Come on, baby; have another one; what, you a pussy? Don't let me outdrink you."

And Jessica would comply by guzzling another can of beer. It was after one of these great nights of drinking and riding around that Franklin reached under the seat of his lifted F-150 truck to pull out what appeared to be a hand grenade. Holding it out to Jessica, the pin still in place, he said, with that charming twinkle in his eye, "Wanna throw it?"

Jessica smiled and tentatively reached for the grenade. "Well, what do I do? Where do I throw it? What if I mess up?"

"Aw, you won't. As soon as you throw it, I'll gun the truck to make sure we aren't hurt. Think how fun the explosion will be!"

"But I...I...I don't even know where we are," Jessica said. "What if we hurt someone?"

"Oh, come on; we're on my ranch; we're perfectly safe."

"Really?" Jessica asked. "You're positive?"

"Yep. Just hold it right here; keep holding it down or you'll kill us both. Pull the pin; then, dear God, let it fly."

Jessica took a deep breath, and gripping the grenade so hard her fingers turned white, she screeched, pulled the pin, and held it securely, knowing she could not release it now without it exploding.

Her brown eyes round with fear, she stared at Franklin. "Are you sure I can do this?" she whispered. "I'm scared."

"Well, ya gotta do it now. If you don't throw it, you'll have to hold it the rest of your life," Franklin said.

"Okay, get ready," Jessica said, mostly to encourage herself. "I'm gonna do it."

"Well, do it already," Franklin said and drained his Lucky Draw beer. "We ain't got all night. Throw it."

"Okay, here goes." Jessica threw the grenade with all her might out the passenger window. Much to her horror, the grenade landed about fifteen feet to the right of the truck. Jessica started screaming. "Oh, my God, Franklin, get us out of here! I didn't throw it far enough. We're going to die! Please go!"

Franklin started laughing hysterically and refused to take action to remove them from impending doom. "What the fuck? Get us out of here," Jessica said, as she began hitting him on the shoulder. "I don't want to die!"

Franklin grabbed a fresh beer and opened the driver's door. He walked calmly over to the grenade lying harmlessly in the alfalfa field. Setting his beer on the ground, he picked up the grenade and tossed it back and forth between his calloused hands. "Oh, you think this little guy is going to hurt an Eastman? Silly woman. Nothing takes down an Eastman."

Her face contorted with confusion, Jessica kept a mindful eye on the grenade, watching it fly through the air repeatedly, only to be caught and launched again. "But I don't understand," she said, mostly to herself.

"Ha, of course you don't understand. It's a fake grenade. I tricked you. No woman is smart enough to figure it out. All of you fall for it, dumbass."

Giant tears instantly welled up in Jessica's eyes. Turning her face from Franklin, she managed to whisper, "Oh, I see," before popping the top on another beer from the blue cooler and taking a big swig, hoping to suppress her emotions.

"Oh, I hurt the baby's feelings," Franklin said. "Sure, now I'm the bad guy for wanting to have some fun." He climbed back into the truck, slammed the door, and turned the key.

"I'm sorry," Jessica said while touching his arm softly. "I should have been smarter."

"Yeah, but you're just a woman. You're only good for a couple of things." Franklin grinned at her. "And we're about to take care of one of those things," he said, while grabbing the back of her head and pulling her into his lap.

See, he does love me, Jessica thought as she undid the brown leather belt clasped with a shiny gold trophy belt buckle displaying a bucking horse and engraved with his name.

He'd not said that he loved her, or given her any insight into his feelings, but he did want to see her every time he was in town. Franklin was dedicated to his rodeo career, so Jessica understood he needed to travel a lot to make that happen. Sometimes she didn't see him for a couple of weeks, but when he was in town, he always called her for at least a quick visit, and if she was really lucky, he'd spend the night so she could stroke and admire his strong, muscular body while he slept.

The thought of birth control never entered Jessica's sheltered mind. Growing up, her strict Catholic mother didn't even discuss the reproductive life cycle. Jessica remembered when she had got her first period. Terrified and embarrassed, she had made pads by wadding up toilet paper and using safety pins to affix it to her underwear. More times than she cared to remember, the blood flow would leak and cause an embarrassing stain on her pants at school.

She started wearing a sweater or two shirts, so she had an extra to wrap around her waist and cover any unfortunate accidents. Her boobs became quite large and obvious before her mother came into her room one day and scolded her for having her shameful tits hanging out like that.

"I guess you need to get a bra. What size do you need?"

"I don't know," Jessica replied.

Her mother grabbed Jessica's boob and said, "You know, what size is it?"

Humiliated, Jessica cried softly when her mother left, but she was thankful when she finally got a bra to hide those odd, growing things on her chest that all the kids at school made fun of. At least they wouldn't flop around in gym class now. Jessica was sure the teasing would not end because of the introduction of a simple bra, but at least it wouldn't get worse, hopefully.

And, now, she had Franklin. He loved her tits. So, maybe they weren't such a horrible thing after all.

Jessica grabbed her robe and headed to the kitchen to make Franklin some breakfast. She needed to make sure his every need was met so he would never leave her. After some scrambled eggs, bacon, and white toast with raspberry jam, Franklin pushed back his plate and let out a hardy burp.

"Thanks, babe. Gotta go."

"Call me later?" Jessica asked.

"Yeah, sure," he said as he headed for the door.

It was several weeks before she heard from Franklin again. By that time, something was wrong. Her monthly period had not occurred in a while. She was too embarrassed to buy a test. She had gone to the corner CVS and walked the aisles. She had walked past the pregnancy kits and pretended she was looking at other medications on the shelf. She touched it one time and then grabbed a package of Band-Aids next to it and quickly exited the store. The next day, she returned to the CVS, threw the pregnancy kit in the basket, and immediately covered it with a bag of Hershey's Kisses, Lay's BBQ potato chips, and a pack of athletic socks. At the checkout, the nosey cashier rang up the items, paused at the pregnancy kit, and then looked Jessica in the eye and said, "Oh, if you think you are pregnant, you should see a doctor."

Jessica was humiliated and just nodded. She tossed some money on the counter and felt the blood flushing her cheeks. "Okay, I will, but I gotta go."

At home, she drank a few beers—Franklin's brand because if she did everything he liked, he would approve of and love her. After mustering up her drunken courage, she peed on the stick from the kit and paced the trailer's narrow hallway while the results processed. Positive. Oh, holy hell. Positive? No way. Suddenly, rid of all embarrassment, Jessica jumped into her 1964 Ford Pinto and drove to the corner CVS to purchase another kit.

Twenty minutes later, same result. Another beer slammed. *Oh, wait*, Jessica thought. *I shouldn't be drinking!* Putting down the empty and crushed beer can, Jessica picked up the phone and called Franklin. No answer. Ten minutes later, still no answer. Another ten minutes, still no answer. "I'm sure he's traveling," Jessica said, trying to console herself. It was Saturday—the third Saturday since she'd seen him. She might be naïve about most things, but she knew better in her heart. He'd been home in the last three weeks. She was certain he had. He loved the family ranch.

4

PEYTON

Peyton walked into the office on the ninth floor of the Peachtree Building and approached the receptionist's desk. "Hello. I'm Peyton Alexander. This is my first day at work," she told the receptionist and then immediately felt silly for her choice of words.

The receptionist, an attractive redhead in her twenties with a beautiful smile, said, "Let me call Mr. Sanderson."

A few moments later, Peyton was ushered through the cubicles into the oddly decorated office of Paul Sanderson, CEO of Blast. Her interviews had been conducted in the conference room, so this was her first visit to Paul's office. Because Paul was an avid hunter, his office was home to many of his stuffed victims. Peyton noticed a large moose head, a duck mounted in a flight pose, a red fox with a bushy tail, two skunks, a raccoon, and a huge black squirrel. Walking to the guest chairs, Peyton stepped cautiously on the bearskin rug. While a dazed-eyed, twelve-point buck stared blankly at Peyton from behind Paul's desk, he expressed his excitement over her arrival.

"Peyton, we are happy you decided to join our team. Our strategic initiatives this year necessitate an expansion of our human resources team, and we hope your addition will result in exponential results unsurpassed by our previous attempts."

After a long conversation with Mr. Sanderson, Peyton was introduced to her direct supervisor, Lois Hutchinson, Vice President of Human Resources. Lois, a round yet welcoming woman, made Peyton feel instantly comfortable, somehow like the supportive mother Peyton had never had. Lois called her "dear," which Peyton found most endearing. *I love the South*, she thought. After spending some time with Lois discussing job expectations, Lois stood up abruptly and said, "Well, let me introduce you around the office, my dear."

Peyton smiled and rose to follow Lois out of her office. They walked down a short hall and then stopped at the first cubicle in a large room full of cubicles where a handsome young man sat.

"Peyton, this is Corbin," said Lois, dramatically gesturing toward him. "He is our top customer service representative and such a delightful colleague."

Peyton shook Corbin's hand confidently and smiled. "Hello, Corbin. Nice to meet you," she said as she gazed into the most piercing green eyes she had ever seen. She felt her cheeks warm slightly, feeling as if Corbin were somehow able to see her standing naked and vulnerable in front of him.

"Why, hello. Nice to meet you as well," said Corbin in a tone that made her think of Molly's happy purr this morning as she scratched her ears before leaving for her first day at the office. "Welcome to Blast. I hope you will find it a rewarding career. I look forward to seeing you around the office."

Peyton smiled and said something pleasant she could not remember later in the evening when trying to recount the incident over a large glass of Merlot with Molly snuggled in her lap purring. Peyton smiled again and let her mind drift into the nonsensical comedy on television. Why did she watch this stuff?

5

CORBIN

I will never forget the first time I met the perfect Peyton Alexander. She was the most beautiful woman I had ever seen. I noticed the flush in her cheeks when her eyes met mine. My mouth was literally watering at the possibility. I hoped I was able to keep things in check, but how could she not have detected my desire? I simply have a hard time controlling my emotions and expressions at times. I wanted her from that first moment, but I needed to play my cards more carefully on this one.

My lightning-fast evaluation of Peyton concluded she was much more intelligent than my other conquests. I needed to have more than my physical charm to draw her in. Even though that flush in her cheeks was quite encouraging. Funny. With all the cards I've been dealt, I'm lucky I have my looks to help me with my hobby.

How could I have accomplished all these intricate achievements if I had popped out of ol' Jessica's vagina as an unattractive, boring, round guy, similar to my friend Spencer. I know it's wrong to be that demeaning of Spencer, but let's be realistic. Poor guy. I'm not sure he's ever been laid. Sure, I've helped him land some girls who were drunk and willing to go home with him, but I'm not confident he actually did anything with them. He always gloated and bragged the next day about what a performer he had been, but the level of detail he gave caused me to doubt him.

You know, when a liar is covering a lie, the first giveaway is the complicated and detailed story they tell. When I strike out with a girl, I smile at Spencer the next day and say, "It was awesome." He thinks I scored even when I didn't. I sometimes feel bad for lying to Spencer, but at the end of the day, it's probably best for him that he doesn't know the truth. I assume he thinks I'm a player since I never have a second date, but that's okay, and well, Miss Peyton Alexander may be the first exception to my "Only One Date Rule."

6

JESSICA

Finally, Franklin knocked upon Jessica's door. "Oh, hi," she said, trying to sound cavalier. "What's up?" Franklin, obviously drunk although it was only 7:00 p.m., wrapped his long arms around her. "Hey, babe. How are you? I need some of that pussy."

After a short stint of thrusting and grinding on the couch, Franklin stood up. "I need a beer." Jessica jumped up to get him a cold Lucky Draw from the fridge. She kept an abundant supply always available for him. Upon her return, she said, "Hey, I need to talk to you."

"Oh, what the hell! You know I don't like talking."

"Well, I'm sorry." Jessica looked down and felt ashamed. "It's just that, well…." She bit her lip.

"Spit it out!"

"Well, I'm…uh…pregnant."

"Hmm. Well, whose is it?" Franklin asked.

"Yours, of course!"

"Oh, really?" Franklin said. "How do you know that? We just fuck, but I don't know who else you're fucking."

"No, Franklin. You don't understand. I only make love to you."

"Make love? Make love, you say?" said Franklin before guzzling the rest of his beer and slamming the empty can on the coffee table. Then, he laughed the most degrading and sarcastic laugh Jessica had ever heard. "Oh, Jessica, that's priceless. When did we start 'making love'?"

"Well, I do love you."

"Ha-ha-ha. That's hilarious. Do you really think you are anything more to me than an easy lay?" Franklin asked. He pulled on his green and brown cowboy boots.

"But, Franklin, I really haven't had sex with anyone but you. Please have another beer and let's talk about this."

"Hell, no," Franklin said while jamming his wallet into his jeans' pocket. Heading toward the door, he said, "That baby ain't mine, and you ain't getting shit out of me. Don't you ever try to pin this one on me. You made your bed; now *lay* in it."

Although Jessica was crying, scared, and embarrassed, she softly said, "Lie—it's lie in it; not lay, you dumb fuck," but Franklin was already out of the trailer and slamming that cheap, ugly, sun-faded door behind him.

Jessica crawled on the couch and sobbed unmercifully. What would she do now? She was in college; she had no one she could turn to. Her life had just been shattered by Franklin. Her hopes, her dreams, her plans for the future—all gone, all destroyed. No husband, no traveling the rodeo circuit, no ranch in Montana. She would have to tell her parents, but she couldn't even consider that conversation yet. My God, she remembered as a child lying in her bed, listening to her mother talk to her father about how her oldest sister, who was getting divorced from an abusive man, was going to burn in hell for the cardinal sin of divorce. What in the world would happen to her in the afterlife by having a child out of wedlock? Not only was her future compromised, but so was eternity! Her mind reeling, Jessica finally cried herself to sleep, all alone on the blue couch her mother had dragged out of her basement after Jessica had moved out of the dorms and into her rented trailer. It smelled vaguely of dog pee, but Jessica no longer cared.

Jessica stood naked before the mirror and rubbed her bulging stomach. She knew she was supposed to feel love for the baby growing inside her, but each day, her resentment grew. Franklin had not visited her again or returned any of her phone calls.

Her thoughts wandered to the day she had told her mother the news.

"You're what? You're having a baby?"

"Yes. I'm sorry; I really thought he was the one," Jessica said.

"Well, who is he? Do I know him?" her mother asked.

"It's not important, Mom. No, you don't know him, and he wants nothing to do with me, so I'll just handle this myself."

"It will ruin your life. You need to get rid of it right now. Trust me; get rid of it."

"Mother! Are you saying kill it? It's a baby and we're Catholic. You know that's a sin."

"Well, you don't have to put it like that. Plus, God is forgiving. But, mark my words; if you don't, you will regret it every day of your life. It will ruin you."

Jessica would not give in to her mother. Besides, she hadn't given up on Franklin yet. In her heart, she believed he needed some space. He'd come to his senses. He had to know she loved him and that this baby was his. He would do the right thing. He just had to.

But weeks turned into months with no contact from Franklin. As Jessica's hope of his return waned, her anger toward the baby softly kicking against her uterus intensified. Now that it was too late to have an abortion, Jessica realized her mother was right. She would regret this for the rest of her life.

7

CORBIN

Growing up, all I ever wanted was my mother to be happy. I only asked once who my dad was. We had moved from Great Falls to Omaha because my mother obtained a position—well, let's call it what it was, a job—as a waitress at the Quick Pick Diner in Omaha. She could have gotten a waitress job anywhere, but I think she chose Omaha to get away from Great Falls and the bad memories it held for her. She never said that, but that was my impression. Oh, and I guess we shouldn't overlook that her new boyfriend also lived in Omaha. Earl was a long-haul trucker with a bulging beer belly and receding hair line. Although I was quite young when she was seeing him, I never got the impression that Earl was really that into her.

I observed from an early age that my mother was a man-pleaser. Anything any guy wanted, she did. They quickly became her first priority, even over me, and that was expected. Earl would show up at our cheap, seedy apartment above the Quick Pick Diner at the corner of Fourth and Mulberry every couple of weeks for a home-cooked meal and fucking. I could always hear them grunting through the paper-thin bedroom wall.

I was six years old, and Mother had returned from her second shift at the Quick Pick Diner. I was waiting on her arrival in my

Jetsons pajamas with a bowl of Kraft Macaroni and Cheese freshly prepared for her dinner. As soon as she walked in the door, smelling of greasy hamburgers and chicken fingers, I smiled broadly, pulled out her chair at the gray Formica table with the silver metal trim, and said, "Ta-Dah! Mother, I've made you dinner!" I was so proud of myself that I then bowed to her.

"Mac and cheese? Are you kidding me?"

"But, Mother, you have to be hungry." This evening was already off-track and would not end well for me.

"Whatever," she said and went into the dingy bathroom with the toilet that always wobbled when you sat on it. I sometimes feared the toilet and I would fall through the floor and land in the diner below, on a table, right in the middle of a customer's cheeseburger and fries.

When Mother came out of the bathroom, she was wearing her pink chenille bathrobe, and a freshly lit Winston Light hung from her lips. She went immediately to the futon and plopped down with a heavy sigh. "Why the hell am I burdened with you?"

I looked at the floor, noticing that the linoleum was cracked and peeling where our two ripped kitchen chairs constantly rubbed and slid across it. "I'm sorry, Mother. I know I should have prepared you something better for dinner."

"Oh, fuck, kid, I'm not even hungry. It pisses me off that you look so much like," she paused awkwardly and looked away, "him."

This was the opening I had been waiting on for the last six years—well, as many of those years as I could remember. "Who is 'him,' Mother? Who is my father?"

In one quick movement, my mother leaped from the futon like a Siberian Tiger pouncing on an unsuspecting gazelle, grabbed my throat, and slammed me into the wall. Pinned to the wall and choking, I was terrified as she stared into my green eyes with pure hatred.

"You have no father, you fucking bastard! You are a mistake! You should have never been born! Never ask about 'him' again or I will fucking kill you!"

She dropped her chokehold on me, grabbed my ear, and pulled me into the tiny kitchen where she grabbed a black plastic spatula, pulled George Jetson off my ass, and proceeded to spank me so many times I lost count. Following the beating, she pushed me into the closet by the front door, slammed it shut, and screamed, "If you come out of there, I will beat you until you can't walk!"

I stayed in the closet. My buttocks hurt too much to lie down. I stood beneath our shiny yellow rain jackets and among our black rain boots and smelly sneakers. I stayed away from the mousetrap set and baited with peanut butter. I stood all night, and I don't even know how long. I was only six and didn't have the luxury of a watch, and there was no clock in the coat closet. At some point, I peed and soiled myself, and then the pain in my buttocks became less than my exhaustion from standing. I took down the shiny yellow rain jacket I wore outside when thunderstorms struck, stomping in puddles and laughing as the rain hit my face, and covered myself as I curled into a tiny ball as far away from the peanut butter mousetrap as I could, and finally slept.

I don't know how long I stayed in the closet. At some point, the door opened and another beating ensued because I had soiled my pants and made a mess. After that beating, my mother threw me in a tub of cold water and scrubbed my body with a Brillo pad. I wanted to cry, but that would make it worse. I took the pain as that Brillo pad scraped my flesh and made me bleed in several places, leaving the other places bright red and stinging. Following the cold bath, my mother put me back into freshly laundered pajamas. Then we went to bed in the fluffy pink bed, my mother cradling me to her breasts and singing, "Hush, little baby, don't say a word." At that moment, I ceased caring whether my mother was happy, and I wanted to vomit at the suffocating scent of her lavender body lotion. The beatings became more and more frequent, with quite a variety of kitchen implements used to deliver the pain. I hate lavender…and pink.

8

SPENCER

Spencer pushed his purple plum-colored task chair away from his computer, rolled into the tiny cubicle entrance so he could see Corbin's back, and said, "Hey, man. Let's do something tonight."

Corbin spun around in his chair, smiling, and said, "What did you have in mind?"

"Well, I know you are going to think this is dumb, but I'd really like you to come over. We'll order a pizza, and work on my model train scene," said Spencer. "And, wait, before you say anything, there is this big video competition coming up, and I could really use your help."

Corbin rolled his eyes while grinning at Spencer. "Hell, man, you are lucky to have a friend like me 'cause that sounds oh, so much better than going out and picking up girls. But for you, my friend, I'm in. *You* buy the pizza and the beer."

Spencer threw him a thumbs-up and went back to work.

Spencer had known Corbin only since he joined Blast last year, but he seemed like a solid dude. He never fully understood Corbin's desire to try to hook him up with women. He recognized that he wasn't at the top of the list—hell, he wasn't even in the middle—so the chance of him finding someone he was interested in was unlikely. He had strong requirements these days for a woman he would date.

She needed to be thin, shorter than him—which already ruled out a lot of the population—brunette—don't even consider any other color—with no kids, but the desire to have children, and a great job. Unbeknown to Corbin, Spencer had actually been married twice.

The first marriage had happened about three months after Spencer met Olivia. He had been head over heels in love with her. He had catered to her every whim and wish, bought her extravagant gifts, and took her to the social events he was invited to, which was only a few dinners with his stodgy parents and one birthday party for his three-year-old niece. He had only kissed her peach, lipstick-laden lips a few times before he proposed. Olivia did not fulfill all of his requirements because she had three children, but Spencer was willing to overlook that undesirable burden. And Olivia was likely the reason he had developed his current dating criteria anyway.

It was a stormy, windy evening, with the heavy, horizontal rain soaking them as they burst into the dark entrance of the Welcome to Dinner Murder Mystery Theater in downtown Atlanta to celebrate Halloween. Spencer had big plans for the evening, and with nervous, shaking hands, he helped Olivia out of her pink-and-black-striped raincoat. After being escorted to their round table, draped with a black tablecloth and with a twinkling flameless votive candle on top, Spencer ordered a whiskey sour, which surprised Olivia since he rarely drank in front of her. But tonight was a big night for them, as Olivia was to find out.

To ensure the evening went perfectly, Spencer had called the manager of the Welcome to Dinner Murder Mystery Theater and begged (that is, paid handsomely) to be selected as a volunteer for the cast so he could deliver his life-changing question to Olivia.

Spencer had never been to the Welcome to Dinner Murder Mystery Theater or he would have known he could have volunteered to play a part. But he likely wouldn't have taken that chance. Tonight needed to be perfect.

After taking a hefty swallow from his whiskey sour, the ice clinking against his recently whitened teeth, Spencer slipped his sweaty hand into his black dress pants pocket and was comforted by the feel of the small velvet box contained there. *Tonight will be perfect*, he thought, smiling.

"What are you smiling about?" Olivia asked.

"Oh, just happy to be here. I'm excited about the show, and you know Halloween is my favorite holiday. Oh, and to be here with you makes it complete."

Seemingly unaffected by his admiration, Olivia said, "I sure hope I don't get picked to play a part. That would be humiliating." Spencer smiled because of his intricate plan. His mind wandered to the near future as he pictured the handsome Mr. and Mrs. Spencer Davis walking down the front steps of the First Community Baptist Church in his hometown of Blue Ridge, Georgia, then heading toward the waiting white limousine while being sprinkled with white rice as the just-released doves flew into the sunny sky.

A cackling witch dressed all in black except for her neon green stockings dragged Spencer from his daydream with a loud and throaty, "Good evening and thank you for joining us at the Welcome to Dinner Murder Mystery Theater! We have a great event for you tonight, but remember, audience participation is the key to great success!"

Spencer heard Olivia groan. "They damn well better not pick me."

"Don't worry, honey," he replied. "I'm sure you have to volunteer. Come on; try to have fun. This is going to be great!"

"Okay, I'll try, but I'm going to need more wine." She held up her glass as a scraggly werewolf with bright red, fake blood dripping from his stained fangs suddenly appeared and poured more red wine into her skull-shaped wine glass. "At least all the wine is included with our tickets," she said, trying to sound a little positive for Spencer's sake.

I wonder, Spencer thought, *how much of that fake blood has already dripped into people's wine. Oh, and I hope he's not also our food server. With that mange-ridden looking costume, we'll be sure to get some hair in our chicken Alfredo.* But, as fast as it came, the thought vanished, and he was back in the moment as the scariest vampire he had ever seen stepped through the groaning wooden door with screeching, rusted metal hinges as the fog machines whirred and billowed fog around the imposing character.

As promised by the manager, Spencer was selected to play in the show. Spencer's character was I. M. Nosey, a pushy and inquiring reporter from the *Atlanta Herald* who had heard rumors of the multiple, horrific murders that had taken place in the Foggy Hollow Mansion. By pulling strings and blackmailing the mayor with pictures of his latest indiscretion, a young busty assistant working her way up in the mayor's office, I. M. was able to secure an invitation to the exclusive holiday party hosted each Halloween by the eccentric millionaire, Count B. Positive.

Olivia, relieved she had not been selected to participate, found Spencer's performance surprisingly good. Well, not famous actor good, but he seemed to really get into the role and effectively read his lines from the 3x5 cards at the proper times. As she sipped another glass of wine, she noted that Spencer really looked like he was having a good time as he bounded around the stage acting like a goofy reporter. She wasn't sure where this relationship was going. On one hand, there was no denying that Spencer would do anything for her. He had a good job, and he would pay for anything she or her kids needed, even if it meant pulling money out of his 401k. On the other hand, she wasn't strongly attracted to him. When he kissed her for the first time, it was awkward as he jerkily wrapped his hand around the base of her neck and pulled her to him. No emotion came with the ill-timed kiss, other than pity at his awkwardness. But she did have three kids to take care of, and she couldn't rely on their deadbeat dad. Last she had heard, he was back in the slammer for yet another petty drug deal.

On stage, Count B. Positive was rapidly pursuing I. M. Nosey and threatening to drink his blood, even though everyone knew if the tall and somehow handsome vampire really wanted to catch I. M., he would have no problem overcoming him. As Count B. Positive got closer and closer, Spencer could feel his hot breath on his neck, and while it was not real, it still made the hair on the back of his neck prickle. But he wasn't sure whether it was Count B. Positive's chase or what was about to happen with Olivia that made adrenaline surge through his body.

As he headed toward the little table, Spencer saw Olivia drinking her wine, and as he and Count B. Positive moved closer and closer to her, Spencer noticed her beautiful blue eyes opening wider and wider in shock, becoming two round beacons glowing in the dimly lit room. Three short feet from his target, Spencer was spun around by Count B. Positive, who laughed devilishly before crying out, "You cannot escape me! I shall now drink your blood!" and then clamped down on Spencer's throat. Much to Spencer's relief, the fangs collapsed instantly upon contact, leaving only the warm feeling of fake blood running down his neck. In a final heroic effort, Spencer pretended to elbow Count B. Positive in the stomach, causing him to gasp and release the life-draining fangs from Spencer's neck.

Weak from the blood loss, Spencer crawled to Olivia and managed to push himself up on one knee. With Count B. Positive at bay, as instructed by the manager earlier, Spencer held out his hand, opened the black velvet box with one flip of his thumb, held it up to Olivia, and gasped, "My love, the only thing that will save my life is for you to accept my hand in marriage; will you be my wife?"

A shocked Olivia, feeling awkward and uncertain if this was real or part of the show, said, "Uh, I guess…."

Count B. Positive had returned to the stage. Wild with enthusiasm, the audience clapped and whistled until Count B.'s voice boomed throughout the room. "Congratulations to the lucky couple! The Welcome to Dinner Murder Mystery Theater and our entire crew thank you all for coming tonight. We hope you had a hauntingly good time! Please remember to post your review to our website. Thank you and good night!"

9

PEYTON

Peyton grabbed her brand new, buckskin leather Coach briefcase, stuffed her Surface Pro 4 into the secure section designed to fit it perfectly, and headed to the door. Molly blocked her exit by rubbing on her leg and purring loudly as a reminder that she had not yet been served the proper breakfast of white albacore tuna packed in water, not oil.

"Oh, my God, baby. I'm sorry. I am so anxious about work that I completely forgot to take care of you." Putting her briefcase down, Peyton entered the spacious kitchen she loved with the black and silver granite countertops and prepared the proper breakfast for Molly. Purring in gratitude, Molly gobbled up the meal and allowed Peyton to exit the apartment.

After parking her 4Runner in the Blast parking garage and walking next door to the Peachtree Building, Peyton entered and flashed her employee badge at the security officer on duty. After passing through the metal detector, she approached the elevator bank. She truly did have claustrophobic tendencies and dreaded the tiny space on the jerky ride to the ninth floor. Granted, it only took a few seconds to ascend that height, but it still made her uneasy. Whenever she was confined in a small spot, it brought back harsh memories of when she had been trapped in the corn silo at her grandfather's farm outside of Mitchell, South Dakota, when she was six. Her ridiculous cousin, Max, had dared her to climb the ladder on the outside of the twenty-foot-tall silo, open the tiny 4x4 door, and drop into the pile of corn awaiting below, promising her it would be like how Scrooge McDuck rolled around in his basement of money in the Donald Duck cartoon.

"Peyton's a scaredy cat. Peyton's a scaredy cat," Max had said. Max was two years older than Peyton, and she saw him once a year in the summer when her aunt and uncle came to visit. She didn't really like Max because he was mean to animals and once tried to bury a batch of newborn kittens in an old purse from her playhouse by throwing them in a freshly dug post hole. Peyton remembered their tiny soft mewing as they sought out the comfort of their mother, their baby eyes so new they were still tightly closed. When Max started stuffing them in the yellow and green paisley-printed purse with the worn brass clasp, Peyton ran crying to her father.

"Dad, Dad, help me! Max is going to kill them! They are just babies! Please help!" Thankfully, her dad was quick to derail Max's devious crime before it could be executed.

But now, Peyton was faced with being called a baby or climbing the corn silo. She mustered her little six-year-old courage, and thankfully, or not thankfully, didn't have the common sense to consider how she would get out of the corn silo after rolling around in the corn, pretending it was her multi-billion-dollar fortune.

Determined not to be a baby, she hitched up her OshKosh B'gosh overalls, railroad conductor striped like her grandfather's, and made sure her Justin Roper boots were tight on her feet. With a deep breath for confidence and a flashback of Scrooge McDuck, Peyton started up the tiny metal ladder with the white paint chipping and peeling from years of baking in the hot South Dakota sun, followed by the harsh winds and freezing temperatures of a typical Midwest winter.

Focused on not looking down for fear of the terrifying and paralyzing panic, Peyton took one rung at a time, looking only toward her goal, that little door. Climbing and climbing, she finally reached the top and took one ill-advised moment to glance down at Max, now a tiny figure in the distance, standing at the base of the silo, his hand raised above his hairy black eyebrows to protect his eyes from the sun. The moment she looked down, the sudden realization of how high she actually was hit her like a perfectly timed baseball into her stomach. She wanted to cling desperately to the metal ladder and cry until her dad saved her. But she had to do this to prove she was not weak. With a deep breath, she grabbed the metal handle and pulled the door open with a rusty creak. One quick look to confirm there was corn for her to roll in, and without a thought of how to get out, she lifted herself off the small platform at the top of the ladder and leaped into the pile of corn.

While the fall was much longer and faster than she imagined, gravity quickly delivered her with a poof onto the side of the corn pyramid, and then she rolled over and over again until slamming into the side of the silo with a loud clank. As she stood up gasping, the tears started and the yellow dusty corn began shifting under her feet, pulling her deeper into the pile of corn. Luckily for Peyton, and probably the only reason she didn't suffocate, the corn was not deep in the spot where fate decided to deliver her tiny body. Her boots made contact with the concrete floor when the corn had just begun to tickle her chin. She had kept her arms free, but she was too scared to move for fear the giant mountain of corn would come avalanching down upon her. She remained still as a statue, staring at the interior ladder that would lead her to freedom, had it only been within her reach. Hours later, or so it seemed, her father and grandfather finally came to her rescue. While she was punished with a weak spanking that mostly just hurt her feelings, Max was given a well-deserved beating by her uncle Pete. She was glad. He deserved it for what he had tried to do to the kittens that one day more than for what he had done to her.

Putting that memory as far from her mind as possible, Peyton pushed the up button and concentrated on the work awaiting her on the ninth floor at Blast.

10

JESSICA

In the Great Falls Community Hospital, a terrified Jessica was in the painful throes of labor, giving birth to her first and only child, alone. No family was there. No friends. No spouse. No mate. Not even a sperm donor. Only Jessica dealing with whatever was happening to her swollen and painful body. Rarely seen by a doctor, Jessica had no idea what an enema was. Shortly after being administered the fluid, Jessica felt the strong and urgent need to shit—the completely uncontrollable urge. Extremely embarrassed because the nurse was still in the room, Jessica apologized repeatedly for defecating in her presence, even as the contractions continued to increase and become more severe.

Dr. Crawford came into the room. An older man with a nice bedside manner, Dr. Crawford was calming and somehow made Jessica feel she might survive this ordeal, at least this part of it.

"Jessica, you are healthy and the baby is healthy. We are going to get through this just fine," he said before leaving the room.

Jessica lay on the bed, trying to control her panic. *This is happening. A baby is coming out of me. I have no idea what to do. Dear God, please let me get through this.*

As the contractions became more and more severe, Jessica overcame her typical shy, accommodating personality by demanding pain killers. The patient, middle-aged nurse—Jessica didn't know her name—said, "Oh, dear, you are too far into labor for pain killers. You will have to buckle down and get through it."

Jessica clenched the nurse's hand and said in a demonic voice she didn't recognize, "No, you will give me something, and I mean right now!" The nurse complied, but the shot in Jessica's left buttock did nothing to alleviate the pain.

In the delivery room, Jessica pushed when told to push and tried not to push when told not to, but at times, the urge was too much to resist. "Stop pushing, Jessica; it's too early for you to push; just breathe through it," Dr. Crawford said.

"I can't help it," Jessica replied. The nurse patted her arm and held her hand. "Please, you have to listen to him. You can do this."

Thirteen hours later, Jessica finally felt relief as the baby came sliding out. "Oh, thank God," she sighed.

"Oh, wait, you aren't quite done yet, Jessica," Dr. Crawford said. "This will be easy, but you have to push for me a little longer. The placenta is next."

A couple of pushes later—and thankfully, Dr. Crawford was correct, it was much easier—she was finally done. When they held the bloody baby up for her to examine, all she saw were those damn green eyes. "Jessica, you have a healthy baby boy! Would you like to hold him?" asked the nurse.

"Do I have to?" Jessica said without thinking. Then, getting her manners back, she added, "I mean, is it safe? I don't know what to do with him."

"Of course it's safe, dear," the nurse replied. "And don't worry; being a mother is natural to all women. You two are going to be fine." Jessica knew she would survive, but "being fine" sounded a bit too optimistic.

When the nurses asked about her level of pain in recovery, Jessica lied so she could have more of the wonderfully strong pain killers that made her sleep. She had been through a lot and deserved to rest. She vaguely remembered being gently awakened at some point during the night by another nurse. "Jessica, we need to bring your baby to you. He's crying and disturbing the other babies in the nursery."

Jessica, still under the influence of the pain medicine or she never would have replied so rudely, said, "Well, I don't know what to do with him. Aren't you supposed to take care of him? That's your job, right?" and then fell back into a deep sleep.

Somehow, the nurses must have figured it out because they didn't bring that green-eyed evil creature to her that night. However, she was forced to spend time with him the next morning. The nurses delivered his now cleaned little body to her arms. For their sake, she pretended to be the proud mom, and because all the medicine had worked itself from her system, she was able to pull off the act.

The regular nurse was back in the morning. "We were wondering, are you planning on breast-feeding?"

Horrified at the thought, Jessica replied, "Oh, no, I won't be doing that. I don't have to, right?"

"Oh, of course not. Many women don't. It's completely up to you."

Well, that's a little piece of good news, Jessica thought.

Left to bond with her baby for a few moments, Jessica looked down at the bundle, now asleep in the crook of her arm, wrapped up in a blue-and-green-striped hospital baby blanket of soft flannel. "What the hell are we going to do, kid?"

He gurgled comfortably in his sleep. Jessica knew she would have to figure it out—one step at a time. "Well, I guess we have to think of a name." She didn't know if she was having a girl or a boy before the birth, and well, quite frankly, she hadn't fully accepted the reality of the situation until now.

She was not close to her family, so a family name was out of the question, especially after the shameful act of her becoming pregnant out of wedlock became common knowledge. Growing up, she'd had a favorite uncle, Calvin, whom she'd absolutely adored. Calvin was married to an older, mean, spiteful woman named Diane who would never agree to bear him children. Jessica didn't know why, but she had always liked Calvin. She would crawl up into his lap when he visited the family. Every year, Calvin had sent her birthday cards with a crisp $5 bill enclosed. When he found out about her pregnancy, Calvin wrote her an extremely hurtful letter, stating that Jessica would never hear from him again, and he hoped she burned in hell for disgracing the family.

Brought back to reality by the baby waking and crying, Jessica grabbed the remote and quickly pressed the "Call Nurse" button. A few minutes later, the nurse arrived and asked, "What's the matter?"

Jessica held the crying baby out awkwardly toward the nurse and said, "Uh, he's crying. Do something!"

The nurse smiled. "Well, dear, you are going to have to figure this out sooner or later, but I will take him for now."

Relieved, Jessica fell back to sleep, vaguely remembering that she needed to name that kid.

11

PEYTON

Upon arriving on the ninth floor, Peyton made her way to her office, greeting those faces she recognized from her initial visit yesterday with a hearty "Hello" or "Good morning" just to keep things mixed up. Settling into her office, she clicked on her computer and began answering emails. Realizing she hadn't yet had her regular cup of coffee, she pushed back from her desk, stretched her arms over her head, and started toward the breakroom.

Rounding the last corner before entering the generous breakroom with fashionable décor focusing on smooth lines with muted tones of gray and white, Peyton practically collided with Corbin, who held his freshly brewed coffee high above his head to avoid splashing it all over the both of them. "Whoa! Slow down there, girl," Corbin said, laughing.

"Oh, my God, I am so sorry!" Peyton apologized while holding her hand to her chest. "I didn't even see you."

"Hey, it's fine; my coffee was saved." He laughed while motioning to his white Styrofoam cup without a drop of brown liquid running down the side. "Crisis averted."

"Again, I'm sorry," Peyton said, quickly walking around him to avoid further eye contact. She couldn't stand looking at those green eyes. She was lying to herself, she realized as the Keurig brewed her mild blend roast coffee; the problem was she was quite interested in this man and his eyes.

Paul Sanderson interrupted her intriguing thoughts of Corbin. Peyton smiled politely and greeted him. "Good morning, Mr. Sanderson."

"Oh, please call me Paul," he replied. "How have your first experiences with Blast been?"

"Great. Mrs. Hutchinson is a very good mentor, and I think I'll learn a lot from her years of experience," Peyton said.

"If you can keep her from gossiping." Paul grinned. "That woman sure likes to tell stories, which is odd for someone in Human Resources. I hope you don't fall into the same habit. HR knows a lot of secrets that need to remain in the closet."

"Oh, certainly, Mr. San…uh, Paul," Peyton said. "You don't have to worry about that with me. These lips are sealed." She made that gesture of locking her lips and throwing away the key.

"Good to hear," Paul replied before walking from the breakroom.

Oh, my God, that was such an odd thing to do; really, Peyton? The key and lips thing? Way to be professional. She was picking up her coffee to leave when Corbin returned.

"Hey, glad you're still here," he said. "A couple of us are going out for drinks after work. There's a cool place around the corner that serves ice cold beer and gator bites. Would you like to go with us?" he asked, flashing that beautiful smile at her.

Flustered by how his smile created the cutest little dimple on his right cheek, not his left, only his right, and those amazingly straight, white teeth, Peyton tried to remain professional. "Is that allowed here? We both work for the same company, so isn't there a policy against that? And, I'm sorry, did you say 'gator bites'?"

Laughing heartily, Corbin answered, "So, no gator bites in South Dakota, huh? I remember being surprised when I first got here, too. It's just alligator that's battered and fried. Quite delicious. And, regarding policy, uh…no. It's not against the rules, Madam HR," he joked while bowing slightly.

How did he know I was from South Dakota? she wondered. She had barely even spoken to him. "Bad idea, Peyton; no socializing at work. This is a bad idea!" the angel on her shoulder screamed into her ear.

"Well, thanks for the invitation, but I'll have to think about it. I guess it depends on what Lois has in store for me today."

"Okay, well, I hope you'll be able to join us. Like I said, just a couple of beers. It'd be a good chance for you to meet some of your coworkers. And you can't live in Georgia and never experience gator bites." Corbin smiled.

"Sure, I'll think about it. Thanks; I gotta get back to my office." She grabbed her steaming coffee and quickly walked out past the vending machine.

Not until Peyton sat down at her desk did she allow herself to take a deep breath and let it out slowly through her mouth. How could she possibly have drinks with Corbin? She was attracted to him, and he was probably a total player anyway. She opened her top desk drawer and pulled out her crisp new employee manual. She had read every page last night, but she could not remember anything about a fraternization policy. Looking through the index, she found Corbin was likely right. It would not be against the rules to go, but…that other problem still remained.

Stop it, she scolded herself for the second time today, *Get back to work; quit thinking about it, and do not go tonight."*

Opening her human resources software, Peyton began entering a new employee's information into the system. She had a lot of work to accomplish today, and because she was still learning, she was not as efficient as she liked to be.

12

CORBIN

I remember my first. So tasty, such a delicious quest. I think her name was Marcella. While I am not entirely certain that was her name, we will call her that for this story. She was a beautiful little bird who was trying to find her way in Denver, meet the right people, and prove to her doubtful father that she could be successful despite his criticism.

It was years after Mother's and my stint in Omaha. I found myself in Denver working at an electronics store in a crappy strip mall peddling laptop computers and other electronics to fools who wanted the latest and most trendy gadgets. The work was easy and gave me access to burner phones and other devices used to erase online activity.

Considering my awkward childhood, it was ironic that I somehow learned to master the skills necessary for impeccable manipulation of the human psyche. Maybe it was all the craziness I'd been around my entire life.

I met Marcella for drinks and possibly dinner. She was young and hungry, not nearly as hungry as I, and quite fetching. She had a lot of potential—if only she hadn't met me. Poor girl. But again, I'm getting ahead of myself.

Sweet Marcella and I met for drinks on the patio of the Rusty Nail Steakhouse, a classy choice on my part for a first date. Marcella and I initially started chatting on BestSingles.com and quickly moved from the initial emailing through the app, to the texts, to many phone calls before she agreed to set up an actual meeting. Finding the perfect first one required the utmost patience on my part, but I was prepared for the task. I wasn't even sure if it would actually happen after our first encounter. I would have to make the final decision depending on how the evening progressed. Regardless, though, I was quite excited. I had been waiting for this moment a long time.

Luckily for me, it progressed very well.

Giggling and blushing like a school girl, Marcella finished her vodka martini and smiled brightly while the beautiful words of, "Oh, Corbin, you are such a delightful surprise" slipped from her brightly painted and full lips as she picked up the olive-laden toothpick and seductively sucked the olives into her warm, inviting mouth. *Definitely going well*, I thought.

I had also finished my gin and tonic, which was actually only tonic. I confirmed this on my first trip to the restroom. Stopping our beautiful Latino server, who was wearing the required too-short uniform that exposed an equal amount of strong, muscular thighs, and perky young cleavage, I said, "Hey. This is my first date, and I'm a recovering alcoholic. I don't want to be too heavy on my first date, so I'm going to order gin and tonics all night, but will this tip guarantee I only get tonic?" I smiled and slipped her a fifty-dollar bill.

She smiled brightly. "Yes, sir. It will definitely take care of that."

Reassured, I returned to the table prepared to become a pretend drunk with the beautiful and engaging Marcella.

"So, Marcella," I said, "I know you have two small children. Are they with their grandmother tonight?"

"Oh, no. I put them in bed before I left and told them not to cry. They're used to it." She tipped her martini glass back, sucking the last few drops into her indulgent mouth.

"Oh." I tried to sound casual. "So, they're old enough to stay alone?"

"Sure, I gave them fresh diapers, and they are locked in their rooms. What are they going to do? But don't bring this night down by talking about them," she said, her heavily lipstick-lined lip curling up.

"Sure, of course not. Tonight is about you and me. Would you like another drink?"

"Oh, yes, I would like another," Marcella replied. "Well, if you want one. I don't want to be presumptuous that you are having as much fun as I am." Her big brown eyes glanced down and her fake eyelashes quickly fluttered open and shut. I didn't have the heart to tell her I could see the adhesive stuck solidly above her lash line when she blinked.

I took this opportunity to gently put my strong, warm hand on top of her ridiculously adorned fingers, shining with purple polish accented by some sparkling design that vaguely resembled spiderwebs. "I'm glad to hear that. I am having a great time! Better than I could have ever imagined."

And that was all it took. Vodka martinis kept appearing as well as fresh "gin" and tonic for me. We ordered an appetizer of Calamari with spicy mustard and fried jalapeño slices delivered with an avocado ranch dressing. I would have been willing to buy her anything from the menu, but Marcella was fine with some snacks and more vodka martinis.

"Whatever the lady wants," I said, getting up from my seat to go to the restroom. I bowed slightly and intentionally staggered as I stood. "Ha! Forgive me. Guess those gin and tonics are starting to hit!"

"Oh, no worries," Marcella said. "Wait until you see me try to stand up," which I did witness upon my return. Marcella pushed back her chair with a bit too much enthusiasm, screeching it across the tile floor, causing several patrons to look up, surprised by the sound. Laughing loudly, Marcella said to the room, "So sorry, everyone! Nothing to see here." She then proceeded to wobble her way to the lady's room, leaving her fake, oversized, Louis Vuitton bag, hell, almost carry-on luggage size, occupying the adjacent chair. Waiting until she had rounded the corner and knowing she would look back to make sure I was looking, I accommodated her shallow expectation.

As soon as she was out of sight, I grabbed her wallet, also fake Louis Vuitton, and checked her driver's license for her home address. Quickly calling 911, my eyes on the hallway to the restroom, I waited anxiously for the call to be answered.

"Thank you for calling 911. What is your emergency?"

"I wish to remain anonymous, but I know there are small children left alone at 1581 Shallowford Circle, Unit 4. Their mother is at a bar and won't be home for hours. Please help them. They are young and still in diapers." I quickly ended the call.

Sliding Marcella's ridiculous wallet safely back into her giant handbag, I was calmly dipping a jalapeño slice in the avocado ranch dressing before popping it into my mouth by the time the intoxicated Marcella returned to the table, her cheeks glowing red and eyes starting to haze. This was all working out perfectly.

Carefully maneuvering the chair on the tile floor and finally managing to sit down with a thud, Marcella took my hand and looked directly into my eyes. "I have a confession to make," she said. "I told my friend to call and save me if she didn't hear from me by ten. You know, as insurance. No offense, but a girl can't be too careful these days. Well, I just called her from the bathroom." Marcella was already slurring her words. "I told her she didn't need to worry because things were going great!"

I smiled at my fortunate luck. "Well, I feel the same. I'm curious; what all have you told your friend about me?" I also noted that Marcella had left her phone at the table, so it was likely she had told no one of her date tonight.

"Oh, I told her you were a sales rep I met at work. I would never admit to her that I've started online dating. I know it's supposed to be okay, but it still seems kinda desperate to me…not that I'm desperate. Sorry—or that I think you are desperate. Just saying that some people aren't used to the idea yet. She thinks you are a printer salesman named Steve."

"I completely understand, Marcella," I said, slurring my words a bit to continue the charade. "I don't admit to anyone that I'm online dating either."

"Oh, I'm glad to hear that! I would never tell a soul I'm online." She let out an ear-piercing screech.

Feeling I had enough information to make my move, and all guilt removed since hearing that annoying screech—icing on the cake after her complete disregard for her children's safety—I leaned in close to Marcella and stroked her cheek softly with my right index finger. "Shall we get out of here?"

She quickly agreed, and whipping her head toward the counter, said, "Check, please!"

Smiling at how easy this evening had been and how every detail had fallen into place, I tossed some cash on the table before standing up and taking Marcella's elbow to escort her toward the door.

The drunken Marcella slid into the passenger seat of my gently used Honda Accord, shoving her ridiculous Louis Vuitton bag to the carpeted floorboard. Turning her overly-done face toward me, she smiled, her recently applied red lipstick lingering on her two front teeth. "Where to now, Mr. Eastman?"

Even though I would never see my conquests again, I didn't use my real name. I chose that of my father. I found it humorous and a bit ironic that if someone ever started poking around, the trail might lead to him. I was careful to cover my tracks, though. I only accessed BestSingles.com from a burner phone I grabbed from work. My profile was completely fake except for my one picture. Also, I had secretly followed Marcella prior to our meeting. I learned where she worked, her standard routine, where she lived. She had no friends who visited her. She ate lunch alone in her car.

"Oh, you leave that up to me." I patted her hand that was resting on the center console.

"I can't wait! This is the best date I've had in I don't know how long! Are you sure you're okay to drive? You're as drunk as I am!"

Marcella was far too excited for my taste, but that would be over soon enough and I'd have my first victory. "Oh, yeah, I'm fine to drive. I know the way. Nothing to worry about." I smiled, then threw in an adorable wink before I pulled the lever into drive and accelerated toward Marcella's, or actually, my dream ending to the perfect first date.

Marcella babbled the entire drive, more reassurance for me that this was the right thing to do. My guilt had long been gone. Leaving the city behind us, I drove down the winding country road toward Eldorado Canyon State Park, taking us deeper and deeper into rural Colorado. It never crossed Marcella's radar to wonder where we were going as she continued to babble on and on about some creepy guy named Alexander who had once dated her and given her a pinecone as a symbol of his love for her. I was not even vaguely interested in her story, but why would someone deliver a pinecone as a symbol of love? And, why would that act be worth repeating?

I maneuvered the Accord into an obscure position beside the abandoned barn. The lights of Denver were a small smudge of light in the distance of the dark Colorado sky.

"Wait, we're at a barn?" Marcella looked around, suddenly confused and alarmed about where she was.

"Did you miss the part where I told you I live on a ranch?" I asked. Even though I had never mentioned that, I simply didn't want her nervous yet.

"Oh, yeah, right. Sorry. I forgot that."

"Well, you sit right there and allow me to get the door for you. A beautiful lady like yourself deserves only the best treatment," I said while getting out of the car, leaving a giggling Marcella inside, anticipating a night of sex and fun, while her abandoned children lay crying for their mother or, hopefully, in the safe custody of Child Protective Services by now.

Opening the passenger door, I held out my hand, and bowed graciously. "Come, my lady; let me show you my ranch." A willing and actually greedy hand latched onto mine as Marcella stepped from the Honda, her stiletto heels sinking into the soft soil.

"Oops." Marcella laughed. "I guess these were the wrong shoes to wear to a ranch; sorry."

"Oh, no worries. Take them off. Something has to come off first."

Smiling broadly, Marcella slipped out of her pink, pointed-toe heels and tossed them back onto the Accord's carpeted floorboard. God, I hate pink.

"Wait," Marcella said. "Can I at least have a kiss before going further?"

Stepping close to Marcella, I looked deep into her eyes. My hand reached up and gently held her chin between my thumb and forefinger. "Oh, you want a kiss?" I asked with impeccable feigned desire as I moved my face closer and closer to hers, noticing her increased heartbeat and dilated pupils as she gazed into my green eyes. Her red-colored lips parted in anticipation of my kiss. With bile suddenly swirling in my throat, I was reminded of Jessica's seductive expression when she thought of my father. It was time, finally. Slowly drawing my other hand behind my back, I slid the seven-inch boning knife from its sheath and quickly plunged it into Marcella's panting abdomen, pushing it underneath the ribcage and angling it to penetrate her left lung, then jamming it into the right one.

A shocked Marcella realized her destiny and searched my eyes for answers as she gurgled and panicked from the recent deception. I held her solidly by the neck as she flailed and gasped for air. I watched excitedly as I saw her losing the battle, giving in to the defeat, accepting that she would soon be dead. Her eyes, asking a question that would never be answered, locked with mine as her last shaky breath left her body and she went limp in my arms.

The most amazing feeling of complete satisfaction rushed over me. I started laughing uncontrollably at how easy this was. Why had I waited so long for my first? I had known the desire was there for years, but why hadn't I been enjoying this sooner? I dragged the unresponsive Marcella into the abandoned barn and laid her in an empty stall that still smelled of horse shit and sweaty leather, even though the horses had been sold at auction when the Parker farm went bankrupt over a decade ago.

After spreading Marcella out in the smelly stall, I removed the boning knife from her bleeding stomach. *Hmm, I need to make sure I am more prepared for all the blood next time.*

Holding the boning knife, I grabbed her left hand and sliced off her thumb. After wrapping it in a piece of feed sack from the barn, I stuffed it into my pocket. Then, I slit open her stomach to reveal her still-warm organs, waiting for me. My excitement escalated, and digging around a bit, I found the liver. I carefully carved off a healthy section of the steaming organ. Examining it closely and relishing the copper smell, I thought, *Oh, I hope there isn't too much alcohol in this guy*, before shoving the warm, bloody mass into my drooling mouth. That first bite tasted better than my vivid imagination could have ever anticipated. My fate was sealed.

13

CORBIN

I leaned against the counter and watched the frazzled Peyton Alexander quickly exit the breakroom. I enjoyed the view of her black-and-white, herringbone pencil skirt as it hugged her toned and perfectly curved butt. She moved gracefully, her posture straight as an arrow, head held high, her reddish blonde hair swaying slightly back and forth, softly.

Oh, this is going to be a delightful adventure and the success will be so sweet. When I first started, I wasn't picky with my prey. It was more a matter of safety and willingness in the beginning, but as I perfected my craft, I realized I not only liked reaching the goal, but also greatly enjoyed the hunt. Now, I prefer them to play hard-to-get, and it doesn't hurt when they are as pleasing to the eye as Peyton Alexander.

On my way back through the maze of purple cubicles, Pam from Accounting stopped me in the hall by the loud copier that was always jamming and beeping.

"Hey, are you still up for helping with Saturday's event at Pet World?" she asked. "It's supposed to be hot, but we need the help." Pam loved animals and volunteered every moment of her spare time at the Furry Friends Animal Rescue Shelter. I imagined her home to be filled with cats since she usually had white and black cat hair stuck to her sweaters. This Saturday, the shelter was having an adoption event at Pet World in the hopes of finding forever homes for its growing population.

"Oh, you bet I'll be there. Eight o'clock, yes?"

I have always been a lover of furry friends. My mean-spirited mother would never allow me to have any, but the owner of the Quick Pick Diner was a kind old Jewish man, Sam. He enjoyed feeding scraps to the scruffy scoundrels who frequented the garbage dumpster behind the diner. Sometimes allowed to sit quietly at the counter while my mother worked, I noticed Sam kept the food scraps in a separate blue five-gallon bucket.

"Say, Sam, why do you keep that food? Are you hungry?" I once asked.

Chuckling and putting a weathered hand on his stomach, bulging from years of eating his own diner food, Sam said, "No, son, I'm not hungry. Look at this belly!" Then, holding out his other hand, he said, "Come with me and I'll show you."

I hopped off the red plastic stool at the bar and willingly took Sam's hand as he grabbed the blue bucket. We made our way toward the gray metal back door, past the stacks of boxes of napkins, paper cups, and drinking straws. Stepping out into the bright Nebraska afternoon sunlight, I squinted as Sam dropped my hand and began softly whistling. After a few minutes, they started arriving. Six scruffy, mangy street dogs, rough from living in the street, eagerly made their way toward us like a pack of wolves. I shrieked with fright, but Sam calmly said, "No, son, no need to be alarmed. If you are nice to them, they are nice to you. Never let them see you scared."

Sam proceeded to feed them all the partially eaten burgers, pieces of country fried steak, and even the ketchup-soaked fries from the blue bucket. Much to my surprise, each dog waited patiently for its turn to eat, tails wagging, or in lieu of a tail, a stubby nub where a tail once had been. Sam also showed me the makeshift shelter he had made, hidden behind the dumpster, for the dogs to use during the freezing winter months.

"It gets too cold out here for them sometimes," he explained. "Even with their fur, they can't take the cold. I know they are mutts, but each one of them deserves to be loved."

I started feeding the dogs with Sam. Sam was a good, kind man, and I enjoyed our time together.

Back at Blast, Pam said, "Wonderful. You are the best person ever, Corbin. There is a special place in heaven for you. Thank you."

Special place in heaven, indeed. I smiled to myself. Do you suppose there is a piece of heaven with an entrance sign that reads, "Enter only ye who are kind to animals and despise people"?

Well, that's not completely true. I don't despise all people, I don't despise Spencer, or he would have been gone long ago. Stacy at my gym, Fit Bodies, doesn't make the despised list either; she makes my pity list. I try to hit the gym before coming to Blast. Every morning as I push open the fingerprint-smudged glass door and walk to the registration desk to sign in, Stacy smiles shyly and, without making eye contact, asks, "Would you like a towel today, Mr. Callahan?" She refuses to call me Corbin.

I smile brightly at her and say, "I brought my own today, but thank you so much, Stacy. I hope you have a great day." It makes her blush, but also makes her smile. Stacy is about seventeen, and my guess is she's had a pretty hard life. She has to wear a Fit Bodies uniform at work, so I have no idea of her personal style, but her hair is mousey brown, long, and uncut. No makeup adorns her freckled face or accentuates her dark, long eyelashes. Timid and jumpy, she often falls prey to the rude and arrogant patrons of Fit Bodies, a trendy, expensive gym where all the eager young professionals and middle-aged Stepford wives come to network and perform the ridiculous charade of the rich and successful. I come here for different reasons. There's prime picking at this place.

One day after finishing my thirty minutes on the Bowflex Trainer, an evil beast of a machine, and working through my routine for arms, chest, and back, I was walking toward the door to head back to my place and shower. Ellen, a loud, obnoxious divorcée, who obviously screwed over her husband in the divorce and made out like a bandit, was screaming at poor little Stacy.

"What do you mean you don't have any coconut water? I get one every day, and if you were any good at your job, you would have one waiting for me when I finish my workout! You know I'm thirsty after working so hard!"

I've only seen Ellen walk slowly on the treadmill, focusing on gossiping with Jenny about whose kid messed up in school and whose husband is cheating.

"But, ma'am, I've tried to tell you; we simply don't have any today. The truck didn't deliver."

"Oh, so now you're being rude to me? Is that it? I need to see your manager. Get him *now!*" Ellen's face was now bright red, and I noticed a bulging blue vein poking out of her botoxed forehead.

Stacy's big brown eyes brimmed with tears, and her bottom lip quivered as she picked up the phone to call Russell, the manager. Swooping to her rescue, I said, "Oh, Stacy, it's okay. I don't think you need to call Russell."

Putting my hand on Ellen's forearm, which was not sweaty at all from her "workout," I dialed up my charm. "Oh, I know you must be exhausted after that workout in there. You were on the treadmill forever!" To myself, I added, *Forever standing there, running your mouth with Jenny.* "I tell you what—there's a Starbucks right next door. Would you please honor me by letting me buy you a refreshing beverage there? I'm worried that you are so upset and dehydrated, you simply may pass out if you try to drive right now."

"Oh, finally, someone who understands my dire situation," Ellen said, her Southern accent stronger than ever as she held the back of her hand against her forehead. "I would be delighted. Shall we go, my kind sir?"

She wrapped her arm in the fold of my extended elbow, and we headed toward the door. Glancing back at Stacy, I smiled and said, "Have a good day, Stacy." That day, Stacy smiled at me and made eye contact. The rude Ellen became a priority for me and would join my collection within the month.

I gave Peyton some space and didn't speak to her again until the end of the day. Then, tapping lightly on the doorframe to her window office, I said, "You look like you are ready for a cold beer and some gator bites to me!"

"Oh, I don't know. It's kind of been a long day, and I should probably get home," Peyton replied.

"Whatever; you're coming. Admit it and log off your computer."

"Who all is going?" she asked.

"Well, considering you have been here two days, and I have seen you out of your office exactly four times, I'm guessing you won't know anyone's name if I told you. So, the best way to find out is just to come. I'll meet you downstairs at the elevator, and we can walk over together," I stated, making the decision for her, and sounding more confident than I felt. Then I walked out of her office.

It seemed an eternity before the elevator beeped and slid open to reveal the beautiful Peyton Alexander smiling at me. "Okay, you convinced me, Corbin. But I can only have a couple of drinks," she said, her hazel eyes shining under the harsh fluorescent lighting. "Lead the way."

Success. Step one.

14

SPENCER

It was official. Spencer would marry Olivia. Regardless of the less-than-enthusiastic reply, she had accepted the platinum, square-cut ½ karat diamond that night at the Welcome to Dinner Murder Mystery Theater, and she had been sporting it on her perfectly man-icured hand, with the standard French manicure style that he had come to love, ever since. Although, he was slightly bothered by how thick her nails were after all that acrylic, or whatever material they used, he never mentioned it. They seemed unnatural. Olivia also had this annoying habit of tapping her fake, thick nails on the table when she was trying to deliver a point or debate a position. No, not tapping them, but clacking her nails and moving them side to side like creepy spiders galloping across the table, marching and tapping in time to the rhythm of her words. But, no matter, she had said yes, kind of, and he loved her.

After extensive research, Spencer booked the River Falls Plantation near Blue Ridge that included an exclusive ceremony in the chapel overlooking the serene lake (no kids would be peeing in the murky lake that day), a grand reception in the Magnolia Hall, which would easily accommodate their 125 guests, and managed to ensure all the floral arrangements contained only red roses and white magnolias. Olivia loved the smell of magnolias, and she needed to have the symbol of his love represented by the red roses. Spencer thought the smell of it all was a bit nauseating, but he would do anything to please Olivia.

Olivia's parents were pretty much—well no, were—trash who lived in a dirty, rundown house next to the projects. The disgusting house was filled with outdated copies of *Hollywood Stars*, a trashy gossip tabloid; they covered the floor, scattered among needles, bongs, and other drug paraphernalia.

Who the hell reads Hollywood Stars, *and if you can't afford to buy groceries, why are you buying* Hollywood Stars? Spencer thought as the headline of "Caroline Kennedy's Exclusive Untold Story" grabbed his eye. *Wait,* he thought. *If it were untold, then the article wouldn't exist.* "Caroline's Exclusive Never Before Told Story" *would have made more sense. And does anyone care about Caroline Kennedy at this point? I guess some people do or the magazine wouldn't exist.*

But her parents somehow found the funds to accommodate their next fix. When Spencer was first introduced to Olivia's mother, she gave him an almost toothless grin, her few remaining teeth black with decay. "Hey, baby, we should party sometime. I'll do most any-thing," she bragged as she put her hand on the hip of her sagging acid-washed jeans, which only accentuated her emaciated body, the result of severe drug usage. At tops, Olivia's mother maybe weighed eighty pounds, her face gaunt, wrinkled, and looking much older than her actual age of forty-five. But Spencer knew Olivia wasn't like them. They were going to have the perfect life together. He was con-fident he could learn to love Olivia's children, little Buck, Trudy, and Lil Bit, whose name was actually Lolita, but she answered to Lil Bit.

Spencer was excited and nervous on their wedding day. Not nervous that he was making a bad decision or because he doubted Olivia was the right one. He was nervous because he hoped Olivia would be pleased with the wedding. He was excited to finally be man and wife.

The expensive wedding went off without a hitch. At the last minute, Olivia's parents declined to attend, which caused relief for Spencer, but did cause a momentary bout of panic until someone could be found to walk Olivia down the aisle.

"I don't mind doing it," Spencer's father, Brad, volunteered, "unless she has someone else she'd rather have do it."

Olivia didn't have anyone else and was grateful for Brad's generosity. Brad was a pompous little man with a shiny bald head and jittery, beady eyes. He worked at Ray Daughtry Mobile Homes where he attempted to sell homes on wheels to credit-unworthy customers. The office of Ray Daughtry Mobile Homes consisted of a used, single-wide trailer that Ray had moved to the front of the lot the day before their grand opening. As the manager, Brad had two other salesmen on staff and a smoking hot receptionist, Mona, who was willing to do anything for raises or bonuses. Brad told his wife, Elizabeth, that Mona was an overweight, middle-aged woman with an annoying laugh. Luckily, Elizabeth hated Ray Daughtry and refused to step foot on the lot. Elizabeth and Ray had a history, and Brad didn't care enough to find out what that history was. He was simply relieved he didn't have to worry about Elizabeth showing up at Ray Daughtry Mobile Homes to bitch at him for not taking out the trash that morning and then seeing the attractive Mona.

Olivia felt a bit sleazy walking down the aisle with Brad, his cheap cologne applied far too liberally, but thankfully, the regularly exposed gold chain that usually encased his fat neck was hidden beneath his coat and tie. While she did appreciate him volunteering, she wondered if he was a bit too excited to be that close to her. Nonetheless, the walk was quickly over, and then she was standing beside Spencer, who was beaming like an idiot.

For Spencer, the ceremony was but a blur, except for the fond clear memory of kissing Olivia passionately as the minister proclaimed them man and wife. He barely saw Olivia during the reception as she flitted about from old friend to distant cousin, hugging them and shrieking her gratitude at their attendance. Spencer spent most of the night at the bar with Brad, whose face was bright red from the many whiskey sours he had consumed. Spencer kept his alcohol consumption at a minimum because he had a big night ahead of him and wanted to be focused the first time he and Olivia made sweet, precious love as man and wife.

Finally, as the night was drawing to a close, Spencer went searching for Olivia. He was barely able to contain his physical excitement about the next events of this evening when he saw Olivia leaned up against the bar, talking to a dowdy, round girl he didn't know. He planted a sloppy kiss on Olivia's cheek as he walked up. "Hey, honey, it's time to throw the bouquet," he said.

Olivia rolled her eyes at the dowdy girl and said, "Sorry, Nat; duty calls." Then to Spencer, she said, "So, where is it? Let's get this over with."

Undeterred by her lack of enthusiasm and noting her slurred speech and glossy eyes, Spencer produced the bouquet from behind his back with a hearty, "Tah-dah!", which generated an eye roll and giggle from the dowdy girl. Wobbling and staggering, Olivia made her way to the front of the room and miraculously managed to toss the wedding bouquet over her head without falling down. Dropping to one knee, Spencer attempted to lift the white toile to search for the elusive garter.

"What are you doing?" asked Olivia. "Not here, you fool! You can't fuck me until we're at the hotel."

Humiliated, Spencer stood up and whispered softly in Olivia's perfectly formed ear, adorned with outrageous silver earrings that dropped from her earlobes almost to her neckline, "Shh, honey; it's okay. Let's go."

"Whatever," Olivia slurred as Spencer took her hand and led her gently outside. She was oblivious to the white rice falling around them and the romantic release of the elegant doves as they flew into the orange-and-red-streaked Georgia sunset.

Spencer's anger was brewing, but he contained it. *How dare she get so drunk at our wedding? Hell, she missed most of it. She better snap out of it because I will make love to my wife tonight.* Spencer seethed as they rode the short distance to the River Falls Plantation Inn and Resort. Watching Olivia's head begin to bobble as she struggled to keep her eyes open only intensified his anger.

With check-in finally complete and following several apologies by Spencer for Olivia's rude behavior toward the front desk clerk, they made it to their bridal suite. The pre-ordered champagne sat in a bucket of melting ice; the chocolate-covered strawberries were covered in beads of sweat from being out of the refrigerator for so long.

Olivia headed directly to the granite-tiled bathroom and began vomiting violently into the white porcelain toilet. *Thank God she made it to the toilet, 'cause I'm not cleaning that shit up,* Spencer thought while pouring himself a glass of champagne. Leaving Olivia to take care of herself, the angry Spencer slid open the glass patio door and stepped onto the tiny balcony overlooking the lake.

"Happy wedding night to me," he toasted dramatically into the night sky. His anger increasing with every flush of the toilet, Spencer continued drinking and waiting for his lovely bride to emerge so they could consummate their recent marriage. Olivia finally appeared, looking quite weak, her hair in a ponytail, and the hotel bathrobe wrapped tightly around her body. Olivia's face had been scrubbed clean and her usual heavy makeup removed. She looked nothing like Spencer's bride of a few hours ago.

"Are you finally finished?" Spencer asked as she approached.

"Wow, thanks for your concern. I could have used some help in there getting out of that damn dress."

"Seems you managed. Plus, I wasn't the one forcing drinks down your throat at the reception when you should have been with your husband."

"Oh, forgive me for not performing my wifely duty," she replied, "and if you weren't so socially awkward, you wouldn't have spent the whole night standing by your pervy dad!"

She was still drunk, and Spencer was getting close after drinking most of the tepid champagne. Grabbing her arm, Spencer jerked her to him and heavily breathed into her face. "Well, you are going to perform your wifely duty right now or this won't end well for you."

Shoving him hard in his fat, untoned chest with her fisted hand, Olivia's eyes flared and she said, "You will not fucking touch me, you creepy little troll."

Spencer, shocked by her aggression and words, released her arm. "What? A creepy troll? You said you loved me. I spent a fortune on this wedding; what the fuck?"

"You dumb fuck," Olivia said. "I was looking out for my kids. They need a daddy, and I need someone to take care of us. But as I got deeper and deeper into this, I realized you are gross and I can't do it."

Spencer stood there a moment, soaking in the most hurtful words he had ever heard. He felt his pulse increasing, felt the color rise to his face, felt the anger churning in the pit of his stomach. Picking up the empty champagne bottle and lifting it over his head, he slammed it into the tan stucco wall behind Olivia's head. The bottle shattered into a million shards that fell around Olivia.

"You crazy mother fucker!" Olivia screamed. "You stay the hell away from me."

And Spencer watched his lovely bride, the future mother of his children, jump back in the room to avoid the broken glass, quickly gather her things, and leave the room, where the chocolate-covered strawberries, still untouched, sweated in the silver dish.

The following Monday, Olivia filed for an annulment.

15

JESSICA

If Jessica could have left Great Falls Community Hospital alone, she certainly would have. But fear kept her from finding her fat pregnancy clothes or simply walking out of the hospital in the white and blue gown, open in the back. Oddly, she questioned where she'd put her keys to that piece of crap, rusted, old Ford Pinto that had surprisingly made it to the Emergency Room without breaking down. So Jessica stayed.

"Honey, you are going to have to pick a name before you can leave with your new baby," the nurse said.

How can anyone be that genuinely nice? wondered Jessica. To the nurse, she replied, "But I don't know what to call him."

"Well," said the nurse, "is there maybe a special family member or an actor or someone you look up to that you could name him after?"

Jessica thought long and hard, scanning the last twenty years of her sheltered life to try to come up with anything. Glancing around the room, Jessica spied a copy of the *Great Falls City Herald* resting on a small table tucked in the corner. Skimming through the pages, she made her way to the page that announced the recent arrests in the Great Falls area and outlined their alleged crimes. Her eyes were drawn to the arrest of Corbin Joseph Bailey, who was caught after a recent home invasion in the Peaceful Park Apartments where he allegedly crashed through the door and passed out on the living room floor.

Jessica smiled and spun around to the nurse. "Corbin Joseph Callahan, that will be his name."

The nurse smiled, wrote down the name, and said, "Jessica, I think that is a beautiful name for such a beautiful baby. You and he are going to have such a great time together. I do have to tell you something. Even though we are supposed to remain neutral, your little Corbin is the favorite of all the nurses. He's such a sweet and cuddly little guy!"

Inwardly, Jessica sneered and thought, *Well, why don't you take him then?* But outwardly, she smiled and said, "Thank you."

Then Jessica was sent home with this new, crying, pooping creature that had somehow been created in her body. Every time she looked into that baby boy's green eyes, she hated him. Hated Franklin, but more so, hated that baby boy. How dare he have those eyes that would torment her the rest of her life? She never heard from Franklin again, and she was happy his name never appeared on the PRCA national standings. She liked to think he was a sad, miserable failure, crawling back to his parents' ranch in Montana. But she would never know. And she had this Corbin kid to deal with now.

Life at home now became more complicated. Corbin woke several times during the night. The first time in their cramped space, Jessica didn't even recognize the sound until his crying became desperate screams. Reaching into the stained bassinet she had obtained from Goodwill, Jessica wanted to slap the round little face that continued to cry and scream, demanding imperceptible things. She didn't slap him, well at first, but she had no problem letting him scream, while his soiled diaper burned deeper and deeper into his bright-red bottom. Jessica didn't care. This kid was going to have to figure out that this life was not about him. She had to do what she needed to do, and right now, that was to find a man to take care of her.

Leaving baby Corbin crying in his crib, Jessica dressed in her tightest jeans, pulled on her favorite royal blue tank top, which made her milk-filled breasts look amazingly large, and grabbed her fringed leather boots from the tiny closet. "I'll see ya later, baby," she laughed as she walked out the door. "Mama has to go get us a man."

Corbin cried for another hour before he fell asleep, exhausted and alone.

16
PEYTON

Peyton walked next to Corbin as they left the Peachtree Building on their way to Mahoney's Bar & Grill for the touted cold beer and gator bites. She wondered who else would be joining them, but quickly dismissed the thought because Corbin was right; she didn't know anyone yet. She resisted her urge to cut sideways glances at him as they walked.

"No office romance," the shoulder angel reminded her.

No, I'm going so I can meet people, Peyton lied to herself.

Upon arrival, Peyton was surprised by the table of people welcoming them. *Okay,* she thought, *this is legit and it's not a pretense for a date,* even though the thought secretly disappointed her a bit.

The two available seats put Peyton and Corbin at different ends of the crowded table, which was fine, she told herself, because this wasn't a date.

Peyton tried to ignore Corbin as he recounted story after story; clearly, he was the most popular person at the event. Pam from Accounting stared at him with doe eyes, even though she was twice his age. Sally from Customer Returns looked as if she were undressing him with her eyes, while her boyfriend, Jed, looked sullenly into his beer.

Peyton had a few drinks, experienced the gator bites, and was looking for her exit move, when Corbin said, "So, anyway, I wanted y'all to meet our new HR lady, Peyton. She started a couple of days ago, but I think she is going to be such a great addition to the Blast team!"

The group cheered and welcomed her to the company. Peyton smiled appropriately, a bit embarrassed by the attention, and thanked them all for the big welcome.

"Well," Corbin intervened, "we are like family at Blast, so, Peyton, welcome to the family." While he spoke, he gestured to the group. Peyton noticed that he didn't point his finger, but rather cupped his hand slightly, almost like the royal wave, and held it open, low, and inviting, with a comforting sweeping motion as if welcoming people into the fold. She also noticed that he kept his left hand in his lap most of the time. In one of his more animated stories about working with a rescue dog and being dragged down the sidewalk, she caught a quick glimpse of his left hand. Was he missing a thumb?

Peyton smiled and said, "Thank you, Corbin. I had no idea what to expect tonight, but I must be going home. It was great to meet everyone. I look forward to working with you all." Sliding her uncomfortable chair across the sticky tile floor, Peyton grabbed her purse and, in her final announcement, declared, "I'll catch the waiter and pay my tab," although they had returned to chatting, including Corbin.

Relieved to be out of the spotlight, Peyton paid her bill and exited the building. Walking across the street and toward the Blast parking deck, Peyton expected Corbin to appear at her side and make sure she made it back safely. He did not. Sliding behind the wheel, safe and secure, she patted the black leather dash and gave it a little, "Hello, girl."

Arriving at home, Peyton greeted Molly and apologized for her tardiness. Molly rubbed against her leg and then retired to her fluffy, yellow cat bed, kneading it thoroughly before curling in a ball to sleep.

"Well, clearly she isn't too worried," Peyton said as she made her way to the master bedroom to change and snuggle into her favorite comfortable jammies. After changing, taking out her contacts, and washing her face, Peyton wasn't quite ready for sleep. It was only nine o'clock, and while she should go to sleep, her mind wasn't ready. Climbing on the couch, she clicked on her flat screen TV and accessed Netflix.

"Recently watched by Peyton" appeared, and she selected the next episode of *Jane the Virgin.*

When her iPhone beeped its new text message chirp, Peyton rolled her eyes. *Has to be my mom,* she thought. Picking up the phone, Peyton typed in her code only to find a message from an unknown number.

"Hey, this is Corbin. I hope you had an okay time. I'm sorry I couldn't sit by you."

How does he have my number? Peyton wondered. *Maybe Blast has some open communication thing about phones? It's like a family, right?* And even though she had not been provided anyone's personal phone information other than Lois', she decided to reply with, "Oh, hey. Yeah, it was fun. Thanks for inviting me."

A few seconds passed before Peyton received another chirp. A little too eagerly, she grabbed her phone to view the message, "Please save my number."

Smiling, she complied, adding him to her contacts as Corbin From Work because she needed to be reminded he was off limits. *Oh, but those amazing eyes,* she remembered.

As Peyton was losing interest in Jane's dramatic role, her phone chirped again. "I'd like to get to know you better," Corbin had sent.

"Well, thanks, but I don't think that is appropriate," was her return.

"I understand, but give me a chance," Corbin challenged. "I'm a little more than I present."

"LOL, okay, no judgment here," Peyton replied. "We are cool."

"Good deal," was the response, followed by, "Have you tried Rioja red wine? It's quite delicious."

Quickly googling Rioja wine, Peyton investigated, having no idea what it might taste like sliding over her welcoming tongue. *Well, maybe Corbin is more than he seems,* she thought as she turned off *Jane,* and scrubbed her teeth with her Colgate soft bristle brush.

As she crawled into her dreamy Tempur-pedic bed adorned with soft white 1,000-count sheets, Peyton smiled. *Corbin is into me,* she thought as Molly joined her in the bed. *And he's pretty hot,* she finished before drifting off into a cloud of pleasant dreams, her delicate hand draped over Molly's purring and comforting body.

17

CORBIN

I looked at my phone and expected a reply from the beautiful Peyton Alexander. Maybe I had waited too late to text. Maybe I didn't give her enough attention. But, maybe, I gave her the exact amount of distance needed. I couldn't come on too strong. I recognized that she was different from the rest of them. Yes, I had an impressive collection now. A meaningless collection of hurtful people who had already succumbed to my desires, but a collection nonetheless. However, she had not returned my text.

The weeks flew by; I lost count of how many, but no return text from Peyton. I focused my attention on other conquests to soothe my hunger, and while I saw her across the office, I was never able to accidentally run into her. Something big was going on, though, from a corporate standpoint. A lot of suits I didn't recognize were around the office more than usual, and the glass doors of trendy offices kept all the conversations happening inside safe from nosey ears and office speculation.

I felt my pulse race as I saw her toned body walk boldly across the office, weaving her way confidently through the purple cubicle maze. Always dressed above the required business casual attire requirements of Blast, she was especially amazing in the baby blue sheath dress with the cap sleeves that closely, yet appropriately, hugged her body, her neutral heels completing the look as she headed toward the breakroom where I was starting to prepare my first morning cup of coffee.

"Hello," I said.

"Oh, hello," Peyton replied with a polite smile. "How are you, Corbin?"

I was a bit displaced by her change from the naïve South Dakota girl to this now professional, confident woman. I had watched her blossom from a shy, quiet, reserved girl to a strong, confident, beautiful woman. I liked the transformation.

I was a little surprised about Lois' quick resignation, but then remembered how the old woman liked to spin gossip around the office. Although I had nothing to confirm details, I had a sneaking suspicion Lois had used some inappropriate gossip against Paul Sanderson, which had led to her swift resignation.

"Don't fuck with people above your pay grade," may have been the conversation between Lois and Paul that I never heard, "'cause bitch, I'll bury your ass and humiliate you beyond reproach. Write your resignation," is how it played out in my mind. Whether or not it was true, that's the story I'd created.

I had never liked Lois. She had always been a bit too joyful, and told people explicit details of her personal life. Everyone heard about her heartbreak when her husband of fifteen years, Albert, an awkward CPA who dedicated his life to Tramell and Tramell, although his last name wasn't Tramell, came home one day, looked her squarely in the face, and said, "I no longer love you. I've been struggling with my sexuality since high school and am ready to be open about who I am. I met someone, a man, and have started a new relationship with him. I'm finally happy, and I'm going to need you to pack your shit and leave."

Lois did exactly what Albert had asked.

Back in the breakroom, I smiled charmingly at Peyton. "I'm doing well; how about you, Madam HR?"

I was comforted by the slight flush to her cheeks. "I am well," she said, smiling. "I really could use some more gator bites soon." She paused, leaving the door open while diverting her eyes to the gray and black tile lining the breakroom floor.

Oh, she is still shy, I thought. *Play it cool, Corbin.* "Well, we can go get gator bites anytime you like."

Much to my amazement and delight, Peyton smiled slyly and said, "I'll take you up on that," before spinning around elegantly and exiting the breakroom. I smiled broadly and chuckled to myself, *"And she didn't even get anything from the breakroom."*

Later that morning, Haley, our receptionist, ushered in a group of executives, who looked around curiously as they walked toward Paul's office. Paul's door swung open, and he greeted the visitors. "Gentlemen, welcome! I'm glad we're wrapping this up. Please come in."

"Shit," Spencer said. "I wish someone would tell us what's going on around here. This has been going on for weeks. All these secret meetings, and visitors we've never seen before. They need to tell us something!"

"I'm sure they will when they can. Paul's usually up-front with us, even when we don't like the message," I said, trying to calm Spencer down.

Born into a wealthy family, Paul was an arrogant, tough businessman originally from Dallas. Of average build, he wouldn't stand out in a crowd except for his full head of wild blonde curls. He was fond of black turtlenecks with blazers, expensive sports cars, and women. Although he was married, many beautiful women had appointments in his office. They could have been sales reps on legitimate office visits, but I had my doubts. It didn't matter to me.

What Paul did behind closed doors was his business. But now, we were curious what was going on. Spencer was right. The excessive meetings and strangers in the office made us all wonder.

Around noon, Paul and the group of strangers came out of Paul's office, laughing and smiling. I heard Paul say, "Let's go get some lunch to celebrate." As he walked past Peyton's office, he said, "Peyton, wait to send it until I'm gone. Then, get busy with that list. I want it all done this afternoon."

Peyton nodded and said, "Yes, sir."

Her face was white; her eyes looked tired and heavy. She turned to her computer and started typing. As soon as Paul was safely gone from the office, I received the email with the subject line, "Exciting Company Developments." It had been sent to all Blast employees from Peyton Alexander, on behalf of Paul Sanderson. I opened the email anxiously.

To All Blast Colleagues,

It is with great excitement that I send this important announcement. For the last several months, I have been working on a business venture with Worldwide Fulfillment Services, Inc. (WFS) and am happy to announce that today negotiations have ended, and we have executed the contract to sell Blast. Effective tomorrow, you will be an employee of WFS. I will remain as your CEO and your direct supervisors will not change at this time.

We will continue to operate as Blast for the foreseeable future. You should experience few immediate changes. Human Resources will be meeting with certain individuals this afternoon to discuss future plans.

I am excited about this new venture because it will provide many exciting financial opportunities for the Blast organization. Thank you.

Sincerely,
Paul Sanderson, CEO

Employees gasped and whispered throughout the office. Rob stormed to the breakroom and said, "I need some chocolate!"

"Is this true?" asked Heather.

"How can this be happening?" Ryan asked.

"They sent it as an email! An announcement like this and he can't even tell us himself?" asked Pam.

"What does he mean HR will be meeting with *certain* people?" asked Melissa.

I looked at Peyton, sitting in her office. She was rubbing her neck and then ran her hands through her hair a few times before sweeping it up into a ponytail. Wiping her face with her hands, she picked up the phone and spoke. I noticed a stack of folders on her desk. Moments later, Haley walked into her office and closed the door. Peyton rose and shut the blinds.

All eyes were glued on Peyton's office. We waited silently for what seemed hours before the door opened and Haley emerged, her eyes puffy from crying, mascara streaks under her eyes. She gripped a manila folder to her chest and bolted from the office as fast as her high heels allowed.

The scene repeated itself over and over. Melissa was next, then Debbie, followed by Andrew. An audible sigh was heard after each person started the walk to Peyton's office—relief that the rest of us were spared one more time. While it was an agonizing afternoon, I wondered how Peyton was holding up. This had to be one of the toughest things she'd ever had to do.

After taking a call from an angry Seattle man whose shipment of feather boas had been lost in shipping, causing a problem for the opening act of Kitty LaClaw at the Rainbow Room later this evening, my iPhone chirped.

"Up for gator bites tonight?" My heart raced as I read the message from Peyton. "I could really use a drink after today."

Resisting the urge to jump on my desk and do the happy dance, I simply typed, "Sure. Sounds good. I'll meet you at the elevator after work."

The last hour of work was the longest hour of my life.

18

JESSICA

Jessica somehow managed to address the basic needs of baby Corbin, other than love. She applied for Welfare and WIC, so it was a bit easier to live when the regular checks started coming in. The ample amounts of cheddar cheese, Cheerios, and gallons of milk were a blessing, not to mention the multiple cans of baby formula and Gerber baby food.

She lived in a smelly, single-wide trailer with cheap rent of $200 a month. She had dropped out of college and gotten a job waitressing at the Country Kitchen off Highway 415. She was thankful Corbin could stay home alone. She had always left him alone at times, even when he was a baby, but now he was two and plenty old enough to be left home alone regularly. Locked in his tiny bedroom, he couldn't hurt himself. His entire bedroom ensemble consisted of a urine-stained twin mattress lying on the dirty brownish/orange shag carpet that was once likely the same orange color as the rest of the house, a velour Bugs Bunny blanket, and a brown cardboard box containing his few clothes.

The windows in the dilapidated trailer hadn't opened in years. Jessica had purchased a lock for the outside of his door so he was perfectly fine when she had to leave him for work. Because her shifts were usually eight hours or more, she would give him a bowl of macaroni and cheese, or a box of Cheerios, and leave him a bucket to use as a bathroom. She did acknowledge that he was a pretty easy baby, rarely crying, and quick to be potty trained. If she was lucky enough to pick up a truck driver from the Country Kitchen, she left Corbin in his room until they were finished. He never let out a peep.

Jessica praised herself for raising such a self-sufficient boy. She felt certain the only reason he was quiet and complacent was because of her early behavior of leaving him alone. Sure, it was sometimes difficult to peel the dried-on shit off his butt after he'd been sleeping in a soiled diaper for a day or so while Jessica partied with whomever was willing to buy her drinks and fuck her, but hell, that's what made him stronger.

They successfully survived a few years in Great Falls. Jessica hadn't yet met Earl, the truck driver who convinced her to move to Omaha, which was yet another poor decision typical of every decision Jessica had made.

Tonight, Jessica walked down the narrow hall of the single-wide trailer, wrapped in her faded pink robe, her hair turbaned inside a thread-bare towel, to see Corbin standing at the Formica countertop. He'd pulled a chair up to the counter and was deeply focused on his task at hand.

Hmm, when was the last time I changed that shit bucket? Jessica wondered absently, but the thought quickly dissolved as she observed Corbin's behavior.

Horrified, she watched, hand over mouth, as Corbin ripped open a package of raw hamburger and stuffed it into his tiny face. She stood in shock while he consumed the entire package of raw meat. He didn't notice her initially, but by the end of his feast, he turned and saw her.

Jessica acted fast. Flying across the room, she grabbed his arm and pulled him violently from the green vinyl kitchen chair.

"What the hell are you doing, you little freak?" she shrieked. "You are the only reason I can't find a man. Who would want to put up with a freaky sideshow like you? You are such a fucking creepy kid. I wish you had never been born."

Dragging him down the narrow hallway, across the orange carpet, she pushed him into his room and quickly locked the door. "Fucking freak," she murmured as she let herself collapse onto the floor. *What kind of monster eats raw meat?* She detected his silent sobbing, and suddenly, she had an idea.

Allowing the calmness of her new plan to wrap itself around her body, Jessica walked down the worn shag carpet to the living room, grabbed the pack of Winston Lights off the laminate side table, lit the tip of the cigarette with the purple lighter, and sucked on the cigarette until the glowing cherry sizzled. With a satisfying exhale, Jessica returned down the hall and deftly flipped the lock open on Corbin's door. She noted satisfactorily that Corbin's soft whining had immediately stopped.

Jessica smiled softly, encouraged that her new plan would definitely cure Corbin's unexplained raw meat fetish. Gently opening the door to his tiny, smelly bedroom—Whoa! She needed to empty that shit bucket soon—she called to him quietly, "Corbin, Mommy is sorry. It's okay, baby; come to Mommy. Your mommy knows all the right things and only wants the best for you," she said, even though it was a complete lie. The best thing would have been for the little freak never to have been born. He had ruined her life, just like her mother had predicted.

Corbin, still too young to understand the deceptive manipulation and wanting love, slowly approached Jessica. "Mommy," he said, "I'm sorry. I didn't mean to do bad. I was so hungry."

"Oh, come here, baby," Jessica replied. She held out her hand, drawing him in. Corbin approached slowly, and when he was close, Jessica grabbed his thin arm and jerked him to her swiftly and painfully. Screeching, Corbin knew this was not mommy being remorseful about her behavior.

"You shut the fuck up, you bastard!" Jessica dragged him from his solitude into the narrow hallway and onto the green vinyl-floored kitchen. "You like raw meat, eh? Well, I know how to cure you of that!"

Holding Corbin's arm and grabbing the meat cleaver that Aunt Debbie had given her as a house-warming present when she dropped out of college to live in this hideous trailer, Jessica placed Corbin's slight little left hand upon the counter, fanning it out so all his digits were vulnerably exposed. With one quick slam of the cleaver, Jessica quickly severed Corbin's tiny left thumb.

Screaming in pain, Corbin wrestled against Jessica's adult frame, but he was no match for her. With blood spewing around the kitchen, Jessica hollered, "Oh, Jesus, look at this mess you are making! Let's fix this. Haha, I guess I didn't think this through."

Then, flipping on the electric stove, Corbin watched in horror as the eye grew to a brighter and brighter red. Jessica grabbed his severed stump and quickly pressed it into the glowing red heat of the electric stove. Corbin only remembered a brief smell of burning flesh before passing out from the pain.

He awoke some time later, alone in his room, the shit bucket still full, and his cauterized thumb throbbing in pain. His best course of action was to be quiet, so he was, the silent tears streaming from his beautiful green eyes, brimming the long dark eyelashes, and flowing down his soft little toddler cheeks.

19

PEYTON

As Peyton stepped out of the elevator, her claustrophobic feelings overcome by her excitement, she saw Corbin on his iPhone with his back to her. She took a few moments to appreciate the tall, handsome man with the gray, lightly pin-striped suit pants; the stylish, square-toed, matte black dress shoes; and the light pink, long-sleeve dress shirt. As Corbin ended his call and turned around, Peyton detected a darkness in his eyes that she had not seen before.

"Everything okay?" she asked. "We can reschedule if we need to."

In the blink of his beautiful green eyes, the darkness vanished, leaving that incredibly sexy sparkle that she was accustomed to seeing.

"Oh, no; I'm sorry. Just talking with Spencer. You know, I try to help the guy out—honestly feel sorry for him—but sometimes he gets on my nerves."

Peyton laughed, even though she knew she shouldn't. "Oh, I get it. I'm surprised you two are friends."

"Well, I try to treat people how I like to be treated," he continued. "So, ready to go?"

"Sure. I really need a beer."

Upon arrival at Mahoney's Bar and Grill, they were disappointed that all the tables were taken.

"I'm sorry," the hostess with a nametag labeling her as Ashley said, "I don't know what's going on tonight, but we've been slammed. It'll probably be a twenty-minute wait, or you can sit at the bar."

Peyton looked at Corbin and said, "I vote bar. After today…man!"

Corbin grinned at Ashley. "Bar it is."

Ashley batted her eyelashes and gestured with her open hand, indicating the direction of the bar. "Help yourself."

Peyton was happy they found two open barstools at the corner of the bar, so Corbin sat on the end and Peyton on the front. She was glad she would be able to look directly into his face as they talked.

"I know you can't talk about what happened today, and I promise I won't ask you about it. It had to be a stressful day for you. I hope all the firings are over and tomorrow is better," Corbin said.

"Thank you for understanding. Yeah, today was rough. Lots of tears and anger. I hope everyone knows I was just the messenger," Peyton replied.

"I'm sure they do. But let's forget work," he said . "So, how did you get from South Dakota to Buckhead?"

The bartender, a handsome young man, except for the giant black gauges in his massive earlobes, asked, "What can I get for you two?"

Peyton quickly replied, "I've had a hell of a day, and I need a big draft of Miller Lite."

Corbin chimed in. "I'll have the same."

The bartender quickly exited to pour their icy draft beers into tall frozen beer glasses, which were delivered back to them within seconds. Peyton did not answer his question until she had her ice-cold Miller Lite and took a giant draw from the frosty glass.

Sitting her delicious beer back on the bar, she looked at Corbin and said, "Wait a minute. How did you know I'm from South Dakota?"

Corbin's green eyes danced as he smiled and raised one eyebrow. "Well, Madam HR, you aren't the only one who has information. I have a lot of spies at Blast."

Laughing, Peyton said, "Yeah, I bet you do. Is that how you got my personal number, too?"

Corbin looked a little more serious than she expected. "Oh, I'm sorry; was that too bold? I don't want to come across as creepy or anything."

"Oh, no, it's fine. I actually assumed there was a personal phone log around the office somewhere. No, don't worry; I was happy you texted me that night."

"Whew; glad to know I didn't cross any boundaries with HR and get a black mark in my permanent file!"

The evening continued with pleasant, witty banter. A few more big drafts of Miller Lite were consumed, and the promised gator bites did not disappoint. Peyton was having a great time, even though getting involved with someone at work was not a good plan. But he was charming, and his sense of humor was spot-on to hers, a little dry and sarcastic, but well-timed.

They talked and laughed into the evening. The day's events vanished from Peyton's memory. Corbin never asked her a question about work or all the terminations.

"Oh, wow. Look at the time," Peyton said while finishing the last of her beer. Was it the fourth? She has lost count and knew she needed to go. "I have to be getting home. I could sit here all night talking with you, but we both have to drive home and work tomorrow."

"I know. I wish we didn't have to. I had a great time. I hope you were able to put the stress of your bad day behind you."

"Yes, it was just what the doctor ordered," Peyton replied, while unzipping her distressed-leather crossbody to retrieve her wallet.

Peyton had no idea how she didn't jump through the ceiling when Corbin put his hand on her arm. "Don't you even think about it," he said. "I got this. Consider it a late 'Welcome to Blast' gift."

"Oh, no, are you sure? I don't mind," Peyton later remembered saying, but she was completely unsure at the time.

"I insist. Next time, you can buy."

"Well, okay then," Peyton replied and tucked her wallet back into her bag. "Then, I guess I'll see you at work tomorrow. Thank you so much for the fun evening."

Corbin stood, bowed ever so slightly, and said, "Have a safe journey home, Madam HR."

Peyton didn't want to leave.

20

SPENCER

Spencer ended his call with Corbin, his distaste for Peyton building in his throat.

"Having drinks with the new HR lady. Sorry, man. Can't hang out this evening," Corbin had said, declining Spencer's invitation to come over to his place—well, his parents' place—but he did live in the dank basement and had his own private entrance. It was almost like living on his own.

Spencer became agitated and tried to convince Corbin to change his mind. "Come on; not that Peyton woman; she's a bitch. You see how she struts around the office like she's better than us. Plus, there is a huge contest going on right now for the best model train and scene layout. The deadline is in just a week. I need your help."

"Any other time, but she's had a rough day and really needs a drink. You saw what happened in the office today," Corbin replied.

"Yeah, yeah, whatever. I'm sure they got what they deserved," said Spencer. "Fine, be that way. Have fun with your new little girl-friend. It's supposed to be 'Bros before hos'." He ended the call.

Spencer went to the mini-fridge his mom had bought him and grabbed a Mountain Dew, ripping it open and guzzling most of it before taking a deep breath. *I'll finish this train station myself,* he thought as he walked across the room and picked up the half-built train engine. Then, on second thought, he tossed it on the table. There was no point if Corbin wasn't going to help him. He flipped on his Xbox and started playing *The War of the Worlds*.

The next day at Blast, Spencer tried to ignore Corbin. He even turned down a glazed jelly-filled donut, which Corbin knew was Spencer's favorite.

"I got you your favorite donut as an apology for not hanging out last night. Come on; we've been friends since I started here."

"Yep, until you got distracted with the HR lady," Spencer said without turning around. "I don't want your pity donut."

"It's not a pity donut. I'm saying I'm sorry."

But Spencer had put in his earbuds and was no longer listening. He was glad when Corbin left his cubicle.

Spencer sat stewing, trying to focus on his computer screen. *I thought Corbin was better than this*, he thought. *Seriously, he's into this woman? I can't believe it. It's so deceitful. He was supposed to be my friend.*

I am glad that Lois woman is gone, though, thought Spencer, changing to a more pleasant topic. *She needed to go*. He smiled slyly, recalling his involvement in her unfortunate future.

Lois had called Spencer one Thursday afternoon. "Spencer, I need your help. My computer is frozen, and I can't do anything."

"Oh, no problem, Lois; I'll be right there," Spencer had replied, smiling inwardly. Finally, the malware he had installed on her last supposed emergency—he had actually calculated that visit as well— was paying off. She only had her work computer, and she kept all of her personal information on it. He'd seen her meager bank account information and her profile on BestSingles.com. Not that impressive. Spencer felt certain Lois was not getting a lot of likes because of her lengthy profile listing demand after demand of any prospective match. But Spencer didn't care about little details such as that. He was after the good, nasty dirt that could shake things up around this unappreciative company. He'd only gotten a little 3 percent raise for the last five years in a row. If they weren't going to pay him better than that, he might as well have a little fun, and who knows? He might be lucky enough to find the juicy leverage to secure the now-vacant Information Systems Manager position.

Before leaving his purple cubicle, Spencer checked his HP laptop to make sure it had successfully downloaded Lois' entire hard drive. With one quick glance, Spencer was assured by the comforting message of "Download Complete" blinking at his gleaming eyes, which caused him to jitter with excitement. Smiling broadly, Spencer stood up, adjusted his khaki pants, hitched his black leather belt over his protruding belly, and swaggered a bit as he walked into Lois' cluttered and disorganized office.

"Hello, Lois," Spencer said. "What seems to be the problem?"

"Oh, my God, Spencer! I can't get into anything! Please help."

"Of course," Spencer replied. "I'm here for you," silently adding, *Or to make sure no one can trace things back to me when this blows up.*

"Oh, thank you, Spencer. I have no idea what I would do without you."

Spencer tapped and clicked on Lois' computer, creating the appearance that he was fixing things. He was actually removing the incriminating evidence of his tampering. The tiny hairs on the back of his chunky neck, deep with white rolls of fat, stood at attention as he anticipated later carefully scrutinizing the details of her confidential information that had remained safely protected until this moment.

"Okay, Lois," Spencer said. "I think you are good to go. You shouldn't have any more issues."

"Oh, thank you so much," Lois replied. "I hope you didn't see anything you weren't meant to. I am Human Resources, and I can't risk a breach of personal information."

"No, ma'am. It would be an ethical violation for someone in IT to look at confidential information. I turn a blind eye and forget anything I may have accidentally seen." He smiled at Lois, while thinking, *Ethical violation, my butt. She will regret not promoting me sooner. I'll show her.*

"Thank you. I can't imagine my life without you. You are the best," Lois replied as she returned to her cherry-finished desk covered in stacks of paper that should have been eliminated years ago.

"You're welcome," Spencer said to deaf ears since Lois was immersed in her now functioning PC.

Wow, Spencer thought. *She only cares about herself. Ungrateful bitch. This is going to be so much fun.*

21

PEYTON

Peyton stared dreamily out of her large ninth floor office window with beads of water splattering against it and forming small rivers as gravity pulled them toward the already-soaked brass sill. She loved the heavy pelting rain, but she much preferred to be in her baggy sweat pants, complemented with an oversized T-shirt, and snuggled into her new burgundy leather couch with the tufted back. While she enjoyed her professional attire, especially beautiful heels, which she always maintained at Blast, in her natural environment, she was drawn to her tomboy roots.

"You can take the girl out of the country, but you can't take the country out of the girl," her dad, Bill, had said as he hugged her warmly before placing a lasting kiss on her forehead to wrap up her last visit with him before her big move. "I'm proud of you, Peyton. Follow your dreams and knock 'em dead in Atlanta."

"Thanks, Dad." Peyton held back insistent tears. *Wait until you are in the car, Peyton; be strong*, she encouraged herself. "I guess I better get going. I have a big day tomorrow with the move." She knew tears were imminent. "I love you, Dad." Then she turned and walked toward the waiting gray 4Runner that would deliver her to the next exciting stage of her life.

"I love you, too," her dad replied, waving in big dramatic swoops that made Peyton giggle.

She was going to miss him, but this move was the best decision. And she wouldn't have to deal with the meddling Stella. She supposed most teenagers were upset when their parents announced their upcoming divorce, but Peyton had actually been happy at the news. She wanted to say, "Good for you, Dad; you can finally escape her unrelenting nagging," but instead, she had played it off with a dramatic emotional performance as an excuse to escape to her loft bedroom.

Less than a week after the divorce announcement, her dad had loaded the last brown cardboard carton into the backseat of his red Dodge truck and slammed the door. Peyton was his only girl and her brothers, Josh and Jeff, had already left home to attend the University of South Dakota. Stella, who could no longer tolerate the man she'd shared a bed with for the last twenty-three years, arranged to be away on a shopping trip with her best friend, Beverly, leaving Peyton and her dad, Bill, alone for moving day.

Bill and Peyton's relationship back then was strained, perhaps due to his unhappiness from living with Stella all those years. Peyton never truly understood the reason for the final split, but she honestly was not upset. Bill had not been a good father, and he was never supportive of Peyton, other than providing the financial contributions that allowed them to live in the beautiful log home nestled in the grove of cottonwood trees scattered along Dry Run Creek, their roots reaching thirstily toward the softly babbling water that refreshed them during the long, dry summers.

Peyton loved to climb the rickety ladder Josh had built and nailed to the massive cottonwood trunk as the grand entrance to their poorly built treehouse. She and her brothers had nabbed the scrap wood Bill had left over when rebuilding his small shed. The shed was where Bill retreated to tinker with his woodworking tools when Stella became too aggravated about whatever Bill had done to annoy her that day.

Funny, Peyton couldn't recall any actual projects that resulted from the hours Bill spent in his private shed. After Bill's departure, Peyton, in an attempt to retrieve a hammer and nail to hang her framed poster of James Van Der Beek, was shocked when she yanked open a warped wooden drawer revealing a large stack of *Horny Asian Women* and *Black Slut* magazines.

Ah, Peyton remembered thinking, while rolling her eyes in disgust, *that explains the hours in the shed.*

Looking out the roughly cut opening in the poorly constructed treehouse, Peyton could look for miles and daydream about Prince Charming riding his powerful white Lipizzaner stallion across Dry Run Creek, arriving at the base of the cottonwood tree, looking up lovingly at Princess Peyton and romantically bowing to his fair lady, who only smiled wryly as the fire-breathing dragon, whom she named Baby, slowly approached, holding his breath so as not to alarm Prince Charming. Waiting until he was close enough to quickly torch Prince Charming, who would be defenseless at that proximity, Baby sneaked cautiously before releasing a fierce and deadly torch, then devouring Prince Charming and the tasty, now-charred Lipizzaner. Baby would then bow his massive head to allow the laughing Princess Peyton to climb deftly from the rough opening, onto his ugly scaly head and then down his heavily muscled neck to settle in on his broad back. With her little legs barely able to span the width, they flew away into the puffy white clouds floating on the South Dakota horizon.

It wasn't until after Bill's heart attack scare that he finally figured out his children mattered. While it was a horrible event, and Peyton would never admit that she was glad it had happened, at the same

time, it was the turning point in their otherwise non-existent relationship. Peyton remembered arriving at Avera St. Luke's Hospital
to visit Bill, now living in Aberdeen.

"Hey, Dad," she had said awkwardly. She always felt awkward
around him, even though she was now twenty and should no longer
be intimidated by his presence or seek his approval that she had
never experienced thus far.

"Hey, thanks for coming," Bill had replied.

The stint had been successfully placed into the clogged artery
and the surgeon reported that he expected a full and speedy recovery. Although Bill's lifestyle would have to change if he ever expected
to live past sixty. Bill's dad, George, had not been so lucky, falling
prey to a massive heart attack a few years after Peyton's silo experience. Stan, the farm helper, found a stone-cold George lying dead
among the small sprouts of corn popping their eager heads toward
the warming sun.

"Yeah, sure, Dad," Peyton replied. "You did just have a heart attack."

"That has been made abundantly clear by that bastard surgeon,
Dr. Packard," Bill laughed. "Apparently, this is my wakeup call."

"Well, would it be that bad if it were? I mean…."

"You mean I haven't been a good father to you or your brothers,
and maybe it'd be nice if I showed a little interest in your lives? Is
that what you wanted to say, but didn't know how?" he asked.

Shocked, Peyton sunk into the blue, oddly stained chair positioned by his bed. "I guess, kinda. I don't want to be mean, Dad,
but you don't even know us." She hoped she sounded bold, but she
doubted it came out that way.

"Come here," he said, holding out his hand.

Peyton stood and put her shaking hand in his. She wasn't sure
what was happening exactly or how a simple heart attack could
result in a personality transplant.

"Look. I know I have been a horrible dad," he said. "I never wanted you involved in school activities because I was selfish. I still feel guilty about the time you came to me so excited because the Brownie lady had been to your first-grade class asking kids to join. When you came home, you were excited about being a Brownie. I remember you went on and on about the vest and how you could earn badges for things you did, and do you remember what I said?" he asked.

"Yes." Peyton felt a giant unexpected tear brimming over and sliding down her right cheek. "You said it was dumb and the other kids would make fun of me for being a Brownie and the badges were for dorks. Did I want to be made fun of for being a dork?" Her tears now gushed out. "And then you said I'd already be picked on enough because I had a big nose."

"Exactly," Bill replied. "That is a horrible thing to say to a child. I didn't want to add anything to my schedule, but that is an awful thing to say. Look at you, Peyton. You are a beautiful woman on your way to completing your degree, and I know you are going to be successful. And you were the cutest little girl. I'm very sorry for how I treated you."

"And you never used your woodworking tools."

Spraying the tepid water he'd just sipped through his clenched lips, Bill laughed louder than Peyton had ever heard him laugh and finished with a snort.

"Oh, my God, Peyton; don't kill me. I just had a heart attack. So, I guess you cleaned out the shed for your mother, huh? Sorry about that. But can you blame me? You do know your mother, right?"

"Well, Dad, I think it's great that you have this new realization in life, but don't think you can erase twenty years with one conversation."

"No, Peyton," he said, still holding her hand and squeezing it a little more firmly. "I don't expect that at all. It's a journey, and all I can hope is that you are willing to let me try. So, will you? Will you give me a chance to mend the last twenty years?"

"Yeah, I will. I kinda always wanted a dad," Peyton said, smiling; then she quickly added, while wagging her index finger in front of his face, "But this is step one. You have a long way to go, buster!"

Peyton was snapped back to the present with a light tap on the maple doorframe to her office. Jumping in surprise, she spun around in her chair to see Corbin. "Oh, hi," she said.

"Sorry; I didn't mean to startle you." He smiled at her.

Man, that smile, she thought. She quickly assessed his casual Friday attire. Today, he was sporting a stylish turquoise and pink plaid, long-sleeved shirt, perfectly untucked above his Diesel jeans, with slight fading in all the right areas; he completed the look with those stylish matte black, square-toed shoes.

"Oh, no problem," she replied while shuffling papers on her overly organized desk. "What's up?"

"Nothing as serious as you're acting, Madam HR. It's just, well, it's Friday, and I don't know if you are aware, but Friday nights, you really have to indulge in Piero's pizza. It's kind of a tradition and requirement."

"Oh, is that right?" Peyton asked. "And pray tell, what is this Piero's pizza?"

"Only the best fucking pizza you've ever had!" Corbin replied. "Sorry. Didn't mean to say the F word."

"That's no problem," Peyton said. "I cuss worse than a sailor. So, why is this pizza so amazing?"

"Piero is from Chicago, and he continues the tradition of the Chicago deep-dish pizza. Have you ever had it?"

"Well, no, I haven't," Peyton replied.

"So, it's settled then," Corbin said while stepping in front of Peyton's highly organized desk and pulling a Post-It note from her black dispenser. He held it out. "Write your address on this, and I will pick you up at seven."

"Oh, I don't…." Peyton stalled, but wanted desperately to give it to him. "Corbin, I'm not sure this is a good idea."

"You mean we shouldn't hang out because we work together," he replied. "It's not like I'm asking you to marry me. It's pizza. And they have freezing cold beer. Nothing heavy or scary from me, I promise. Just two coworkers enjoying some amazing Chicago pizza."

Even though it was far more than two coworkers enjoying Chicago pizza, Peyton snatched the yellow Post-It from his extended hand and quickly jotted down her Southern Towers address.

22

CORBIN

I was six when we moved from Great Falls to Omaha. Why anyone would want to give up the views of Great Falls in favor of Omaha always eluded me, even at six. I suppose the introduction of Jessica's regular fuck buddy prompted that move.

We showed up at the Quick Pick Diner where Jessica boldly walked in the door, proclaiming her expertise at handling the waitressing duties of a greasy spoon diner and reciting her experiences at the Country Kitchen in Great Falls.

Sam, the owner, turned a sympathetic ear to the desperate Jessica and agreed to let her prove her worth to his clientele.

We didn't have any money, and, Earl was no support at all. After Jessica closed up the diner and Sam went home for the night, we would retire to the parking lot and our rusted-out Ford Pinto. We slept in it just fine, and Jessica gave herself a whore's bath in the tiny bathroom of the Quick Pick before starting her shift each day.

I'd lay in the front passenger seat, my fuzzy Bugs Bunny blanket nestled near my heart, holding the severed thumb Jessica had decorated like a little doll for me. She had soaked it in iodized salt for months to preserve it, and then one day presented it to me. She drew a happy face on the top of the thumb with a black Sharpie, and glued denim fabric around the base to hide the cauterized bottom of my detached thumb. I welcomed that it was somewhat hidden, although I must admit there were many nights I would lift the denim skirt of my non-functioning thumb and place it lovingly on my little stump, wishing it could still waggle and move at my command. I never let Jessica see me perform this act. I was young, but I wasn't stupid. And no matter what happened in my life, I was certain to protect my little doll thumb. It was a part of me that could never be replaced or lost.

In Jessica's defense, she did exert a lot of productive energy to make sure Sam appreciated her efforts at the Quick Pick. We had probably been there a couple of months before Sam approached her and said, "Jessica, I don't need to know any details or even to know that I'm right, but I suspect you and your little boy are living out of your car. I notice it's always parked here."

"Oh, I'm so sorry, Sam; I didn't know that would be a problem. I try to keep it out of the way so it won't interfere with customer parking. I'll find another place to park it," Jessica replied.

"No, no, no; please calm down," Sam said. "It's not a problem that your car is parked here; it's that, well, that's not a great way to live or to raise a son."

"Well, I don't have any other choice," Jessica replied.

"Tell you what; there is a small apartment above the diner. Now it's not much, but there are two small bedrooms and a working bathroom. You can use the kitchen down here to cook if the diner is closed. You can live there free as long as you work here," Sam offered.

"Oh, my God! Sam! Are you kidding me? That would be terrific of you! Thank you so much!" Jessica was practically leaping up and down with excitement.

Chuckling, Sam said, "Well, glad that I could make your day. And you know, I don't mind if Corbin hangs out down here while you work," he added, wagging a finger at Jessica, "as long as he be-haves himself."

"Oh, Sam, you are so good to me. Thank you."

After clocking out, Jessica and I toted our meager belongings up the rickety back stairs, splintered and gray from the harsh Nebraska weather, but still strong enough to support our weight. Jessica pulled out the silver key Sam had presented to her earlier, looked at me, and said, "Well, let's see what we got."

Once inside, Jessica was pleased to discover that although it was indeed small, Sam had taken great pains to make sure it had been cleaned and scrubbed well, as evidenced by the slight Clorox smell lingering in the air. Each of the tiny bedrooms had a twin bed with freshly laundered, worn, and faded bedding, but still quite functional and clean. Beside each bed was a brown, wooden three-drawer nightstand; one with a pink, dancing ballerina lamp and the other a chunky, blue Papa Smurf lamp. In the living area was a brown, striped futon that looked like it had survived the '70s and a bright-yellow beanbag chair. Walking into the bathroom, Jessica noticed a stand-up shower, a basic white toilet with a small crack in the bottom where the bolt attached it to the floor, and a small vanity holding a spotlessly clean sink with a 12" x 18" mirror, missing some of its silvering, hanging above.

In celebration of something good finally happening in our lives, Jessica counted out her tips from the busy day in the diner and or-dered a pepperoni pizza with extra cheese from Pizza Palace. "Things are looking up for us, Corbin," Jessica said while cramming a giant piece of cheesy pizza into her mouth without noticing the bit of grease that landed on her chin.

But things were not looking up for us. It was only a short time before Jessica returned to her abusive and depressed state, and Earl was not a positive influence.

We'd been living above the Quick Pick a few years. Earl would visit occasionally, which was of no importance to me. I slept comfortably and safely in my tiny bedroom with the uneven, worn wooden floors, while Earl and Jessica grunted and sighed in the neighboring room. Their behavior never affected my life since I had become quite accustomed to my mother's need for male attention.

I was sleeping soundly one evening in late July, the window unit air conditioner humming quietly and soothingly, while attempting to battle the Nebraska heat. I woke to shouts in Jessica's room, slurred shouts because she and Earl were both drunk, based on the number of beer cans and wine bottles deposited on the coffee table with postcards from around the United States decoupaged to its surface with a thick shiny coating. "See Rock City," proclaimed one. "15 miles to Wall Drug," boasted another. "Get your fix at Route 66," was another, published with a picture of a green alien holding a sweating glass of some unnamed dark soda.

Suddenly, the bedroom door flew open and Earl stomped into my bedroom. "Hey, kid, your mom's pussy ain't no good. Gonna need your help."

Confused, I scrubbed my eyes, then was horrified when Earl grabbed me and flipped me over, snatching my pajamas down in one quick swoop. I struggled and screamed, but all I heard was Jessica's drunken slur of, "At least lube him up, Earl; I need to sleep and he's makin' too much noise."

23

CORBIN

I carefully removed the Post-It from the beautiful Peyton Alexander's soft, white hand, resisting the urge to kiss it affectionately, and simply said, "Cool. I'll see you at seven. Casual place, like jeans casual," I said as I turned to leave her office.

Proud that I was able to control my broad smile, I visualized giving myself a pat on my back as I returned to my purple—I guess we are supposed to call it plum, but let's be honest, it's purple—cubicle. Spencer was still mad at me, but he'd get over it sooner or later; it wasn't like he had any other friends.

Friends. That's a funny thought to me. I've never had a true friend. I had thought Sam was my friend, but like with everyone else, the moment arrived when I realized Sam did not truly care about me but had his own selfish interests.

When we lived above the Quick Pick Diner, Sam took me under his wing early on. Aside from his love for the stray dogs, and letting us live above the diner for free, Sam also took an interest in me. When Jessica would allow, Sam liked to take me trout fishing at Standing Bear Lake, west of Omaha. Sam didn't have a boat, but we'd stand on the shore and throw our line in the murky water all afternoon. He'd laugh as I grabbed giant night crawlers and threaded their writhing bodies onto the penetrating hook and watched the excitement covering my face when the red and white bobber disappeared under the cloudy, dark water.

"Snap it now!" he'd yell. "You got one!"

Sometimes, I was rewarded with a tiny trout, but my favorites were the fat, whiskered, yellow-bellied bullheads. I appreciated their spunky fight before succumbing to their eventual fate and tiredly allowing the nylon line to pull them into the oxygen-infused air that immediately ripped through their large gills.

"Oh, throw it back, boy," Sam would say. "We don't need them for food, and they have families."

It always made me smile as I released the squirming and grateful bullhead back into the shallow dark water. Sam was such a good person; well, at least I thought that until he showed his true colors just like everyone else.

We had lived above the Quick Pick Diner for ten years, so at least it took him longer than most to turn on me. It was my sixteenth birthday, and Jessica, I never liked calling her "Mom," had arranged for my birthday party at the Quick Pick Diner. Admittedly, I was excited that day in school, knowing I was well on my way to manhood, and Jessica actually seemed a bit more stable these days.

Part of me wondered if the turning point in her life was when, during a particularly difficult beating of me with a cheese grater, I simply turned to my mother, looked her in the eye, and smiled. The look of horror in her eyes was likely one of the most satisfying events of my life. Or at least the start of those moments. Clearly, things have progressed in my life beyond that now, but I think that was the beginning because she never touched me again.

At any rate, she did seem to be more settled and the free home combined with the steady, although small, income was also helpful. She loathed the pink waitress uniform, and her hatred for it always made me smile, considering her obsession with pink.

I vividly remember my sixteenth birthday celebration at the Quick Pick. It was a sunny Thursday, and I arrived after attending a full day of boring classes at Elkhorn South High School. I was always bored in my classes. While I don't know if I am genius level, I am confident I can process information at a much higher level than most. Granted, that process may be for my own benefit, but regardless, I have that unique ability.

I arrived at the Quick Pick Diner around 4:30 p.m. after donning my blue and tan bookbag and walking the short few blocks through likely the poorest area in Omaha to push open the greasy, fingerprint-stained glass doors of the Quick Pick. Sam waved and smiled broadly. "Well, happy birthday, Corbin!"

"Thanks, Sam!"

And then Jessica appeared, holding an opened bottle of red merlot. "Hey, son. Happy birthday!"

In that moment, I already knew my sixteenth birthday would not turn out how I wished. Over the course of the evening, I sat quietly in a red plastic booth with a black Formica table in front of me while my mother, excuse me, Jessica, consumed bottle after bottle of merlot, sharing with Sam and the other male customers. A moderately cold burger and fries arrived at some point, while I watched Jessica sit seductively on the laps of the many loyal patrons, her pink uniform revealing more and more cleavage as the night progressed. The tiny pearl buttons were released one by one.

In an attempt to divert my attention to anything else, I grabbed the cold burger, took an angry bite, and quickly spat it from my mouth as the bloody red meat appeared and oozed onto the whole wheat bun. Pausing for a moment before my natural instincts kicked in, I split open the bun and devoured the bloody spirals, pretending not to enjoy its juicy deliciousness. I had lost a thumb over these tendencies; I didn't want to lose another. But more importantly, today, like every other day, was about my slutty mother, Jessica.

Having had enough of this circus show, I pushed the remainder of the food away and stood up. *Fuck it*, I said to myself. *What did you exactly expect, Corbin—a birthday cake? How could you have expected this day to have turned out differently? You are the one to blame. You're a dumbass.*

Retiring to my small bedroom above the Quick Pick Diner while listening to Garth Brooks blare out "I Got Friends in Low Places" from the jukebox below, I pulled the faded, worn comforter over my head and finally fell into a light sleep.

Waking up at 2 a.m. and famished, I assumed Jessica was passed out in her tiny room next door. I slipped quietly from my bed and tip-toed down the creaky stairs to hopefully nab some soda crackers or maybe a slice of Sam's cherry pie to soothe my growling stomach. The jukebox was still playing, but now much lower in volume. Celine Dion was singing "Power of Love." At sixteen, that did not trigger any alarms in my head. I pushed through the back door of the Quick Pick Diner and walked past the stacked cartons of napkins and plastic straws. Then I rounded the corner into the typically clean kitchen, even though it should have been splattered with grease from the always busy fryers.

Instead of the neatly organized island efficiently arranged to provide quick access to all needed utensils and spices, I saw a disaster. I first thought a small tornado must have ripped its way through the kitchen, but then I came to full realization of the situation. Jessica was bent over the island, her voluminous boobs sprawling freely on the stainless-steel countertop, while a sweating Sam thrusted violently into her welcoming body from behind. As I surveyed the scene, both were too sloppily drunk even to notice my presence. Disgusted and feeling the heaviest betrayal yet in my pointless life, I quickly spun around and crashed through the backdoor onto the gravel, where I violently vomited the acid from my empty stomach.

My favorite three-legged mutt—I had named him Hamilton—slithered over, his matted black tail wagging furiously as he whined quietly, seeking at least a bit of affection. I'm not sure why I landed on Hamilton as the name for that scruffy mutt. Maybe I was trying to give him a bit of dignity in his homeless life since no one cared much what happened to the three-legged fella. Hamilton seemed like a distinguished and respectful name.

"Not a good time, Hamilton." He slipped quietly away.

I returned to my twin bed but was unable to sleep the rest of the night. Eventually, I heard the stairs creak and Jessica stumble through the tiny apartment, trying to find the now-pink door, recently painted by her in her efforts to transform her tiny nest into a bubble-gum oasis.

"Fuck, I'm drunk," was all I heard her say.

I laid sleeplessly in my lumpy twin bed and realized what must happen after this devastating betrayal—both Jessica and Sam needed to die, and I was the one to do it.

"Hey, man," Spencer said on the ninth floor of the Peachtree Building, bringing me back from sixteen years ago, "I'm sorry about the other day. I was having a bad day."

I spun around in my ergonomically correct black leather chair. "Hey, no problem, man. You're my friend, but you can't blame me for wanting some of that," I said, gesturing toward Peyton's office and attempting false bravado because my intention with Peyton was much deeper than I'd first imagined. She was so different.

"Yeah, I guess," Spencer replied. "Anyway, I'm sorry. We cool?"

"Sure thing. Let's grab some dinner next week," I said.

Spencer's eyes were darting back and forth rapidly. I hadn't noticed them doing this previously.

"Yeah, sounds good," Spencer said. He then retreated quickly to his cubicle.

24

CORBIN

When I realized Mother was fucking Sam, I was completely devastated. Sam was supposed to be my friend, but turns out, he was like all the other men Jessica chose to surround herself with. My God, Earl, for example. I was happy when that prick had had a heart attack and died in Mother's bed. Not only was I thankful he was dead, but also that he had died in Jessica's bed instead of mine.

After my great birthday party, Sam acted as if nothing odd had happened that night, but I would never forget that horrific deceit from my supposed best friend. I also tried to pretend things were fine between Sam and me. I had to carefully craft my revenge so neither one of them would be suspicious or wary. I thought about somehow getting a gun and blowing their cheating, deceitful heads off, their brains splattering against the fryers lining the back wall of the Quick Pick kitchen. I also considered running away, but I'd need a car and money, and I was only sixteen. And, well, that revenge issue surged in my veins too strongly to ignore.

Over the next several weeks, I worked out many scenarios in my mind, carefully calculating the worst possible outcomes and creating plots that would avoid police attention. It took a couple of months, mostly because I wanted to be respectful of Sam. I'd worked it out in my head, over and over, and I was comfortable with my plan.

Anxious to initiate Phase 1 of Operation Revenge, I was stuck in geometry class listening to Mr. Campbell's droning voice. Finally, Mr. Campbell's endless, boring chatter ended, and I was able to escape the sweaty, gym-sock-smelling halls of Elkhorn South High School. Tossing my navy-blue backpack over one shoulder, I trotted quickly down the front steps and headed toward the Quick Pick Diner. Today was the day, and my heart raced with excitement. Today, I would finally be free and justice would be served. I'd be a little easier on Sam than Mother, but the result would ultimately be the same for both of them.

As I pushed through the front doors of the Quick Pick, Sam was coming out of the kitchen carrying a steaming plate of freshly fried chicken fingers and fries. Holding the white plate in one hand, he waved the other to me and asked, while smiling broadly, "Hey, Corbin, how were classes today?"

Returning the smile and fulfilling my recently acquired pretend role, I replied, "Oh, just great, Sam. Thanks for asking." And then, I actually felt a wave of refreshment flow over my body as I thought about what was soon going to happen right here at the Quick Pick. Every detail was perfectly worked out, including my quick and safe getaway.

With a happy smile and toss of his head, Sam delivered the plate of chicken fingers to a rotund patron sitting at the Formica counter who was almost drooling in anticipation of its quick delivery.

Going about my regular duties of scraping plates and washing dishes, I continued to watch the trash can, wishing it would hurry up and need to be emptied into the green metal dumpster in the back. The dinner rush was coming to an end before the wilted lettuce, soiled paper napkins, and discarded tomato ends were finally brimming toward the top of the black, fifty-five-gallon trash can. Excitedly, I turned off the warm water from the sink and grabbed the black trash bag, pulling the corners up and tying them quickly to conceal the discarded junk even the stray dogs wouldn't enjoy.

Hauling the bulging trash bag through the warped, metal back door, I saw Hamilton standing, peering at me, his tail wagging wildly and thumping like a beating drum on the side of the dumpster. "Aw, hey, boy," I said. "Poor guy, are you hungry?"

His tail wagged even harder as if to say, "Yes, Corbin; please feed me. I've been very patient today."

Throwing the heavy bag into the green dumpster, I paused and scratched his black forehead. "Sorry, buddy; nothing in there that would be good for you. I promise you'll be fed well, though. You can trust me," I said, while immediately wishing I could trust someone in my life. I wondered what that would even feel like—to trust someone, to never worry they would betray you. I patted Hamilton again and smiled. "Don't worry, boy. I will never hurt or betray you." I knew that was a true statement and also that I would never have the same reassurance from anyone in this world. I could never trust another person after what Sam had done to me.

Well, no time to pontificate the future, I happily thought. *Let's get this done.*

Walking past the smelly dumpster, I crossed over the back parking lot, my feet crunching on the pea gravel Sam had replaced last summer, and popped open the rusted Ford Pinto's trunk. Jessica rarely drove the old clunker these days, what with Sam providing her everything now, literally everything, much to my dismay. However, it did provide a safe hiding place for the objects I'd collected over the past few weeks and hidden in a small, black gym bag I'd picked up from the clearance bin at the local Thrifty Mart. Grabbing the gym bag and the solid black tire iron next to it, I returned to the now closed back door of the Quick Pick Diner.

Screaming wildly and pounding on the gray metal door that separated me from the Quick Pick Diner interior, I shrieked, "Sam! Help me! Please come quick! They're attacking me! Get back! Please, Sam, HELP!"

Then, I strategically placed myself to the right of the door, hugged up closely against the painted cinder block wall where he would never see me. As predicted, a few seconds later, a panicked Sam burst through the warped door, his eyes quickly surveying the back lot as he yelled, "Corbin? Corbin! Where are you?"

A calm, confident smile spread across my face as I raised the cold metal tire iron over my right shoulder and kicked the gray metal door shut with my foot. "Oh, Sam, I'm right here," I said as the undeterred tire iron smashed into Sam's yielding skull, splattering blood across my smiling face. I laughed as I saw Hamilton poking his head out again from the rear of the dumpster and licking his lips.

Not sure if Sam were dead, I quickly grabbed the silver duct tape from my gym bag and bound his wrists and ankles. I added extra protection with a piece of sticky adhesive across his non-responsive mouth. I hated him for having let Jessica seduce him; if he had been a better person, he would have resisted. If I had meant something to him, he would not have allowed Jessica to manipulate him. I hoped he hadn't suffered; Sam was the closest thing to a father I'd ever had, but he had betrayed me. It had to be done.

Regardless of my personal emotions, I couldn't take any risks. After making sure Sam was rendered helpless, I dragged his unresponsive body out of the way, creating a trail of deep dark red blood from the contact site to the left side of the dumpster. *Heck, this ol' fella is heftier than I would have imagined,* I thought.

Once Sam was out of the way, Jessica was next. Before calling her out to meet her fate, I wiped the blood from my face with the sleeve of my black Grateful Dead T-shirt that I'd picked up on the same trip to the Thrifty Mart where I had purchased the gym bag. I thought black would be the best color to hide blood. I walked quickly around the side of the Quick Pick and peeked into the front parking lot. There was only one car in the lot, and it belonged to old Mr. Hoffert. Smiling, I returned to the back door and retrieved my deadly tire iron.

Mr. Hoffert came in almost every night for dinner. He was quite senile or had pretty advanced Alzheimer's. His wife had passed years earlier, and with no children to take care of him, he managed the best he could. Sometimes he ranted about his dog, Alex, who had long since died. Sometimes, he called me Eleanor and asked how my mother was doing. His presence in the diner would present no problem at all.

Rounding the corner of the Quick Pick, I saw Hamilton licking the bloody matter from Sam's bashed-in head. Pushing him away gently, I said, "Not yet, buddy, not yet." He retreated quickly to his hiding spot behind the smelly dumpster.

Assuming my position beside the warped metal door, I beat the tire iron against it and screamed, "Mother! Help me! Sam just passed out! Help! *Hurry!*"

In my mind, it was a boring rewind of the first incident, but much more satisfying. Jessica came running out of the back door, I assumed worried about her new lover, and more likely, worried that her future housing might be in danger. I thought I delivered the same crushing blow to the back of her hairnet-covered head, a requirement of servers at the Quick Pick, but she somehow came through it in a bit better shape than poor old Sam. She stared at me, unable to speak, but fully aware. Lucky me.

As I had with Sam, I quickly bound her small wrists and chubby ankles. I placed the guaranteed security blanket of silver duct tape over her mouth. Her wild eyes darted from side to side, looking questioningly at me, with no apparent understanding of why this was happening to her. "Oh, Mother," I said, laughing. "You can't truly be surprised this is happening. You were always the fool. Don't fret. I'll be back to explain more. Don't you go and die on me before I'm ready!" I giggled while patting her hand playfully.

Leaving Mother and Sam bleeding onto the pea gravel by the dumpster, I went inside to ensure things would develop according to plan. My first stop was at the restroom to wash any telltale signs of blood from my splattered face and hands. I pulled the Grateful Dead shirt over my head and used it to take the first pass at cleaning my face, neck, and arms. "So much blood." I laughed excitedly.

Fully eliminating all signs of any wrongdoing, I dried myself with several brown paper towels before grabbing a lime-green shirt from the dusty rack displaying Quick Pick Diner shirts that were never purchased. "Get Your Fix at Quick Pick" in 48-point font, Comic Sans in black across the chest. As I pulled the shirt over my head, I chuckled and thought, *Oh, Sam, fix and pick do not rhyme. It only works with Route 66.*

Luckily, no new customers had entered, and Mr. Hoffert sat in booth #3 carrying on a lively conversation with his imaginary companion for the evening. There was no point in trying to rush Mr. Hoffert out so I could lock the door. But reassured that no new customers were waiting, I took the opportunity to return to the pea-graveled back of the Quick Pick.

Leaving Jessica lying there on the blood-soaked pea gravel, I clumsily dragged Sam into the walk-in freezer. I wasn't sure whether he was dead or not, but I needed time to tie up all the loose ends. I didn't sentence Jessica to the freezing depths of the cooler yet; I deposited her near the back door by the boxes of straws and paper napkins. Whenever asked about the availability of a restroom, we denied having one, so there was no worry of someone wandering back looking for a place to relieve their full bladder. She didn't seem to be in such good shape, falling in and out of consciousness, but I wanted her to be fully aware of what was going to happen. I even took the time to wrap my bloody Grateful Dead shirt around the gaping wound in her skull. "Hang with me, Mother! Don't miss the fun that's about to happen." My green eyes twinkled as I spoke.

Next stop was Sam's small office next to the bathroom. I grabbed a piece of paper from his laser printer and rummaged around in his tiny desk to find a black Sharpie. Quickly, I wrote, "Closed for death in the family," chuckling at the irony. "Just have to close out the night," I encouraged myself. "Can't raise any suspicions yet." Leaving the handwritten sign on Sam's desk, I returned to the dining room.

I easily took care of the clientele for the rest of the evening since it was after the dinner rush. Cail came by for his regular country fried steak. Troy got his chicken fingers with fries, even though his doctor told him he'd die of a massive heart attack if he kept eating that shit. Liza showed up drunk around eight o'clock, hoping someone would take her home and fuck her. Dan ended the evening with his usual slice of strawberry pie. I didn't notice when Mr. Hoffert wobbled out without paying, which was normal, but no one ever cared.

Finally, after Dan tossed me a ten for the slice of pie and said, "Keep the change, Corbin," I was able to turn the deadbolt on the front doors and finish what I had started earlier. Taping up the handwritten sign, I flipped off the lights and went to check on Sam.

As I cracked the door on the walk-in freezer, there was no movement from his middle-aged body lying next to a stack of boxes containing frozen hamburger patties. To be certain, I pressed my first two fingers to his throat to check for a pulse. With none detected, I placed my cheek, covered with sprouts of black whiskers as evidence of my quick journey to adulthood, near his mouth to detect even the softest breath. Satisfied that he was certainly dead, I dragged him from the freezer and left him lying in the hallway by the bathroom. I was glad Sam had passed quickly. I was angry, but more hurt by his betrayal. At some level, though, I felt he was a decent human; he had just been manipulated by the evil Jessica.

Grabbing Jessica by her duct-tape bound feet, I dragged her into the kitchen. As I hefted her body onto the stainless-steel island, I was reminded distastefully of the night I had caught her and Sam fucking in this very spot. "Ironic, isn't it, Mother, that this would be the exact place of your final demise?" I happily saw her closed eyelids twitch and then open with fright.

"Well, hello, Mother. I'm so glad you are still with me. I want you to understand exactly what is going to happen to you."

My adrenaline surged as Jessica attempted a scream, her eyes wild and terrified. *Oh, she's very much alive,* I comforted myself. *This is going to be better than I ever imagined.*

25

FRANKLIN

Franklin arrived home determined to review the second quarter financials before his meeting tomorrow with the Spargur Oil Company, but he was greeted by a chatty Emily wanting to share all the details of her day and some nonsense her mother had called her about earlier. He was quite relieved when she tired of his occasionally muttered, "Uh, hmm," and retired to her personal bedroom, bottle of Chardonnay in tow. He loved her deeply, more than he ever thought possible, but sometimes she used too many words.

Won't have to worry about her the rest of the evening, he thought with a smile before draining his Pappy Bourbon and pouring another.

Pappy Bourbon was difficult to come by, regardless of the price, which Franklin cared nothing about. Years ago, he had established a lucrative relationship with a liquor dealer in Lexington, Kentucky. While the Pappy was supposed to be distributed first to those dedicated admirers of the brand who had waited outside the store all night, in anticipation of the unlocking of the freshly cleaned glass doors at nine o'clock promptly, the dealer always put a few bottles aside for Franklin. The power of money.

Remembering his and Emily's first encounter, Franklin smiled warmly. The Eastman Cattle Company was changing locations and erecting a new building from ground up. He arrived at the job site and surveyed the progress. Things seemed to be going well. The foundation was poured, outlining the final building location, and framing was beginning with several steel beams already in place. Franklin looked around for the foreman, Kyle, but he was approached by a young woman wearing a yellow hard hat.

"May I help you, sir?" the woman asked.

"Where is Kyle? Why isn't he supervising his crew?"

The woman laughed. "Well, the thing is Kyle was arrested last weekend. Seems a party got a bit out of hand and it didn't turn out favorably for Kyle. So, he's no longer employed, but I'm the new supervisor overseeing this job. May I help you?"

"You? You are in charge of this job?"

"Yes, I am. Is there something you needed? And, by the way, you are?"

Shocked at being questioned, Franklin replied, "Well, I am Franklin Eastman, the man who is paying for all of this, and I don't appreciate the foreman being switched out without notification."

"Sir, you hired Pinnacle Construction. We are a national firm with locations all across the United States. It isn't our priority to keep our customers informed when we experience personnel changes. Imagine the number of phone calls you would receive if we did! However, I assure you that you are in good hands and your job is on schedule. I'm Emily Fitzgerald," she said while extending her hand.

Tentatively taking her offered handshake, Franklin said, "But, you're a wo—"

"Astute observation, sir. I am, in fact, a woman. Now, I have a lot of work to do today, so if there's nothing else." She turned to walk away.

"Wait—Emily, was it?" Franklin asked. "So, can you give me an update on the project? You said we are on track?" Franklin was intrigued by this woman.

"Yep, just like I said."

"And, may I ask, what is your background?"

"You can ask anything you want, but did you ask Kyle about his? My guess is no. So, quite frankly, Mr. Eastman, my background is irrelevant to you. Pinnacle hired me because I am a capable, trained professional. If you have an issue with me being the supervisor on this job, please call our home office." Emily walked confidently away, leaving Franklin feeling slightly embarrassed, greatly aroused, and uncharacteristically speechless. He returned quietly to his truck and drove off to consider what had happened.

This Emily Fitzgerald was quite different from the women Franklin was used to. They swooned too easily, laughed too quickly, and complied too effortlessly. They were fake and shallow. But this woman…. She wore no makeup and yet was one of the most attractive women he'd ever seen. She seemed to enjoy putting him in his place. And she was a construction supervisor who seemed unaffected by his presence. Most men cowered to him, which he disliked, but used to his advantage even while scoffing at their weakness. But this woman. This woman he needed to have in his life. The following months had been committed to the seduction of Emily Fitzgerald.

Franklin finished his drink and picked up the financials. He had a lot to review before morning.

Roaring his silver F-250 diesel into his reserved parking space in front of the Eastman Cattle Co. office building, Franklin cut the ignition and grabbed the manila file folder that held the positive financials of the second quarter he'd reviewed last night. Pushing through the front door to the cattle company office, Franklin was immediately greeted by the overly perky and annoying receptionist, Janet.

"Good morning, Mr. Eastman," she said, then jumped up quickly to thrust a packet of envelopes, tightly-bound by a fat rubber band, toward him. "Here's your mail. Can I get you anything? Anything at all?" She asked a little too loudly, then realized it and added a quiet, "I'm sorry."

"Nothing to be sorry about," Franklin muttered as he stomped into his office, slamming the heavy door to make sure she couldn't follow and bother him with more trite conversation.

Sitting down at his massive desk, passed down generation to generation since God knows when, Franklin made a mental note to update his office, but then he quickly dismissed the thought because he had more important issues to deal with today. The Spargur Oil Company executives were coming to discuss future drilling and lease plans for the well-established drilling fields on the eastern corner of the Lucky Draw Ranch, aptly named when his great-great-great-grandfather, the original Franklin S. Eastman, won the deed to the massive acreage from a drunken, boastful, and woefully inept poker player in Deadwood, back when Deadwood was beginning to boom.

"I hate dealing with those mother fuckers," Franklin said. "All they want to do is rape the land. I wish I could just run the cattle and not mess with them."

But he would meet with them and listen to their bullshit because the oil money was far more profitable than the cattle business, even though they had increased profitability of the Eastman Cattle Company by 8 percent over last year by diversifying in small grain crops and alfalfa.

Grabbing the stack of today's mail, Franklin snapped the fat rubber band from the tight bundle, spreading his incoming mail across the well-worn desktop. As he quickly sorted through the various envelopes and tossed them into identifying piles, a plain white envelope caught his eye when he saw his name handwritten in a perfect cursive script. Picking up the envelope, Franklin felt his pulse increase and an uneasiness develop in his stomach when he saw the address of Omaha, Nebraska.

Jessica had lived in Omaha at one time—he knew that from the return address on the dozens of her letters he had returned unopened. He had never seen her after that day she had announced she was pregnant; nor did he want to. As easy as she had been, there was no way she had only been fucking him. She was after his money.

But this handwriting was different. Grabbing his letter opener, formed in the shape of a Bowie knife, and quite likely as dangerous, Franklin ripped through the seal and pulled out the handwritten letter, noting the narrow-lined notebook paper with three holes punched in the side.

As he slowly unfolded the pages, a 4" x 6" photograph fell on top of the second quarter financials. Gasping, Franklin looked at the familiar face staring back at him.

"What the fuck!" Franklin said. Dropping the written pages, he slowly picked up the photograph and stared at a mirror image of himself at sixteen, the piercing green eyes meeting his. The same tousled mass of black hair topped the handsome face. Slowly turning the unexpected photo over, he saw the tidy cursive writing spell out "Corbin Callahan, Age 16" before the untimely Janet opened his door.

Franklin dropped the photo in surprise as she said, "Mr. Eastman, Mr. Oliver and Mr. Tillman are here to see you." Then, noticing Franklin's white face and look of shock, she asked, "Oh, Mr. Eastman, are you okay? You look like you've seen a ghost!"

"No, no, I'm fine. Tell them I'll be right out," Franklin said, then quickly added, "Wait, Janet; ask them if they want coffee or anything. I'll be right out."

"Sure thing." Janet shut the door.

Franklin jerked open the pencil drawer, rusty rollers squeaking in protest. He quickly concealed the photo that reminded him of a time in his life he wasn't proud of and wanted to keep a secret, especially from Emily. Pushing back from his ridiculously large desk, he wondered why his ancient predecessor had needed such a bold display of power. Wishing there was some way to cancel this oil meeting, Franklin resigned to dedicate the next hour to Spargur Oil bullshit and attempt to put the disturbing photo out of his mind.

"So, that is the final point we want to make today, Franklin." Jason Oliver finally finished, even though Franklin had been giving him little attention. "We'd really like the opportunity to expand the oil drilling to more of your acreage, and we are confident you will see exponential revenue growth, which no one minds. Am I right?" He laughed at his attempt at humor, then snorted nervously. "You know, oil is a better investment than cattle."

"Yeah, sure. Well, I'll take your proposal under consideration and get back with you," Franklin said, even though he planned to give their proposal little thought.

"So, when do you think that will be?" asked the overly anxious Lance Tillman. "We want to get started on this."

"Of course you do," Franklin replied. "But it's my land, my company, and my decision. You'll hear from me when I want you to hear from me."

"Oh, oh, oh, yes, sir, Franklin," Jason said. "We completely understand. Lance didn't mean to push. We'll wait for your lead." As he finished, Lance shot him a scowl.

"Great," Franklin said, standing up. "I assume we're finished here?"

"Yes," the two said in unison. They quickly gathered their papers and shoved them into their matching burgundy briefcases, clicking the brass locks to protect intruders from viewing the confidential contents. "We look forward to hearing from you soon," Jason said, but the final comment fell on deaf ears since Franklin was already four paces past the conference room door.

What a couple of douche bags, Franklin thought as he quickly settled into the privacy of his office.

Jerking open the squeaky pencil drawer, he tentatively removed the narrow-lined notebook sheets, ignoring the photo that was thankfully upside down. Franklin slowly unfolded the crisp paper to read:

Hi, Mr. Eastman. I'm Corbin, and I think you knew my mother, Jessica Callahan. Well, she's dead, but I was going through her stuff. I found several letters she had written to you that were returned. So, I don't know if you know or not, but I think you are my father. I know that may be a bit of a surprise to you, and I promise I don't want anything at all, like money or whatever. I'd just like to know my dad.

My life hasn't been easy growing up with Mother. And now that she's dead, I'm on my own. Oh, don't worry; I have a car and some money, so I'll be fine for a while. I always wondered who my father was, and well, I couldn't ask Mother about you, but that's a long story.

So, a little about me. I'm sixteen years old and was going to Elkhorn South High, until well, Mother died. Then, I had to hide from Social Services, so I quit going to school. It's over-rated anyway, yeah? I used to work at a diner, but now I work wherever I can. Everyone thinks I'm eighteen, and I have a fake ID I got from a guy in Omaha, so I think it's fine. At least Social Services hasn't nabbed me yet.

Anyway, like I said, I don't want to be a bother to you, and I don't know if you were even told that I existed. I read my mother's letters, but it looks like they were all returned unopened. So, I'd like to hear from you. I hope that I do.

Sincerely yours,
Corbin Callahan

Franklin read the letter over and over, his calloused hands shaking more and more each time. Bravely, he retrieved the mirror image photo from his desk drawer and stared at it in amazement. There was absolutely no denying this kid was his.

"Holy shit," he said to the empty office. "She wasn't lying."

He carefully folded the letter and slid it with the incriminating photo under the black, rubber desk protector. No one ever came into his office when he wasn't there, other than Emily, who popped in from time to time for surprise sex. But she would never snoop.

Grabbing the receiver of his office phone, he said, "Rod, I need you to check on something."

26

PEYTON

It had been the longest week of Peyton's life. She was sure of it. She had tried to avoid Corbin the entire week because the sight of him drove her into a frenzy of anticipation about their date on Friday night. *Not a date*, she lied to herself. *Two coworkers going for pizza, nothing more.*

Finally, Friday rolled around and Peyton was able to work through lunch and meet all of her deadlines for Paul by 3:30 that afternoon. Relieved, she replied to emails for the rest of the day and was able to grab her purse and head for the elevator right at five. Seeing Corbin's tall frame waiting by the elevator, she took the opportunity to say, "Hey, so we're still good for grabbing some pizza tonight? You know, just two coworkers eating some great pizza."

Corbin turned his handsome face toward her, those green eyes twinkling. "You bet. I'll pick you up at seven, yes?"

"Yeah, that's great," Peyton replied. "You have the address and my mobile if you get lost or if anything comes up, right?"

"I sure do, but I can't imagine anything coming up that would keep me from Piero's on a Friday night!"

"Ha ha. Well, I can't wait to experience this amazing pizza."

Pam from Accounting walked up and said, "Oh, Corbin, thank you for helping out at the animal shelter the other weekend. We were in a bind. You saved us."

Handsome and an animal lover, too, Peyton thought as she watched them chat. *What do you suppose is wrong with this guy? There has to be something.*

And then she remembered the missing thumb on his left hand. She had forgotten seeing a glimpse of his hand at the bar until she saw him expressing his frustration with the copy machine repairman. He waved his hands dramatically, and she clearly saw his thumbless hand. She was surprised that this confirmation was emotionally concerning to her. She didn't consider herself shallow, but what the hell was going on with this guy's thumb? Allowing herself to delve into her introspective side, she created multiple scenarios about how one could not have a thumb. Was he not born with one? Did he lose it in a sporting accident? Or maybe an unfortunate encounter with a table saw? And did she think it was creepy? Could she get over this one thing? As these things rolled through her mind, she wanted to know what had happened to his thumb—well, only for the friendship to advance, but she decided she would at least give him the opportunity to explain.

Pam and Corbin continued their small talk about rescue animals. When they reached the first floor, Corbin walked off with Pam, then looked back at Peyton and said, "Seven. Casual."

Peyton walked briskly to her 4Runner parked deeply in the parking deck next to the Peachtree Building. *Should I shower? Did I shave my legs this morning? Do I have anything to wear?* Her mind raced. *How casual is Atlanta casual? Do I wear heels or boots or flip-flops?*

By the time she had reached her sixth-floor apartment, Peyton had worked herself up to the point of grabbing her iPhone and finding Corbin's contact information. *I have to cancel,* she thought.

There is no way I can go through with this. What excuse can I come up with that will sound plausible? Tossing her phone on the counter, she snatched a cold Miller Lite to settle her nerves. She rummaged around in her walk-in closet for the perfect casual, yet sexy, yet like-she-hadn't-planned-it-to-be-sexy outfit. She knew she would not cancel. She couldn't.

Her bedroom was covered in rejected outfit options. Almost in tears, Peyton slumped onto her Tempur-pedic mattress and cried, "I have nothing to wear, Molly!" Sensing her stress, Molly purred and rubbed against her thigh. Pulling Molly into her lap, Peyton stroked her soft fur and allowed herself to be calmed by the steady purring.

"Okay, I can do this. He said casual, so let's go casual."

Gently placing Molly on the mountain of fluffy pillows, Peyton grabbed a pair of her favorite faded skinny jeans, with a couple of tears and rips by the knees, threw on a black, boat neck top that slid to one side to expose one white shoulder, and finished it off with her favorite black suede mules with a moderate stacked heel she could sport for miles without discomfort. Finishing the last of her Miller Lite, she brushed her teeth, dabbed on a bit of clear lip gloss, and did a final preview in her full-length mirror.

"Good to go," she told herself, and then took a deep breath. Surveying her bedroom, she laughed at the mess she had created. Instead of hanging all her clothes back up on the white plastic hangers, she simply scooped them up in one big pile and threw them on the floor of the walk-in closet, before shutting the door to hide the mess.

"I'll deal with that another day," she said, laughing, as she heard the doorbell ring. Spinning to look at her digital clock, she was surprised. The display read 7:02. "Hmm, late."

Flipping the dead bolt and unlocking her front door, Peyton smiled as she saw Corbin waiting happily on the other side. He looked at her warmly and said, "Hey, you look perfect."

Smiling and blushing slightly, Peyton said, "Well, thanks. You said casual, so is this okay?"

"Perfect," Corbin replied. "Are you ready to go? You are going to love this pizza. I promise."

"Sure," Peyton said. "Let me grab my purse. Come on in while I get it. The place is still kind of a mess. I've been so busy at work I haven't had a chance to make it my own yet."

"Oh, no worries," Corbin replied. "You should see my dive. I like your place; it suits you."

"Well, thanks," Peyton said, returning to the living room. "Ready?"

Corbin opened the door for her as they headed to their casual, yet electrically charged, pizza encounter.

They made pleasant small talk about work and living in Atlanta on the short commute to Piero's Pizza. As Corbin efficiently wove his way in and out of Atlanta traffic, Peyton was surprised that she never once felt nervous or concerned about his driving skills. She typically chose to drive, even though she hated it, because she never felt safe with someone else behind the wheel.

When they arrived at Piero's, Corbin flipped off the ignition, flashed a smile at Peyton, and said, "Don't move."

Her hand on the door handle, Peyton said, "What?" but Corbin had already gotten out and slammed the driver's side door. Confused, Peyton watched Corbin walk around the front of his Nissan Maxima. Then he whipped open the passenger door and said, "You should always treat a lady with respect," while holding out his hand to assist Peyton from the black leather interior.

Peyton looked at him and his outstretched hand awkwardly, before placing her small white hand into his big, strong, outreached one. Much to her surprise, he continued to hold her hand as he shut the Maxima's door and turned toward Piero's. Sensing her discomfort, she assumed, he dropped her hand as they approached the front door in the guise of it being necessary to facilitate the opening of the front door. Once seated at their secluded table near the back, Corbin smiled at Peyton and said, "Up for a pitcher?"

"You bet. I'm thirsty."

The rest of the night was somewhat of a blur to Peyton. A pitcher of beer arrived, crunchy bruschetta with fresh mozzarella and juicy red tomatoes followed, and then best of all, the Chicago-style pizza, filled with pepperoni, sausage, green peppers, mushrooms, onion, and tons of cheese.

"Oh, my God, Corbin," Peyton said through a mouthful of delicious pizza. "You are right. This is the most amazing thing I've ever eaten! Thank you for introducing me to this place. I've probably gained twenty pounds tonight." She laughed.

"I'm pretty sure you have a good handle on that weight, Miss Alexander. It all looks great from where I'm sitting," he replied.

"Oh, stop! Anyone can look good with the right clothes on."

"Not everyone," Corbin said. "That Lois woman certainly never looked attractive to me at all!"

Conversation flowed so easily that Peyton actually forgot about the complications of Corbin being a coworker. When the bill was brought, Corbin refused to let Peyton contribute a penny. "No, no, this is my treat. Remember, it's your long overdue welcome to Blast gift," he said while pulling his green American Express from his leather wallet.

"Well, thank you, Corbin," Peyton said. "But remember, you already gave me the welcome to Blast gift. Let me."

"Oh, no, ma'am," he replied. "That's what they say here, ma'am. But regardless, let me get this. I know it's weird and old fashioned, but I feel like women should be cherished and spoiled."

"Okay, if you insist. Go on and take me home then," Peyton said. "I mean, my home, take me back to my home, not meaning, uh…."

Laughing loudly, Corbin stood up and held out his hand. "But of course, Madam HR; where else would I return the good lady other than to her humble abode?"

Peyton's pulse raced with desire as Corbin continued to hold her hand while leading her out of Piero's and until he opened the Maxima's door to tuck her safely inside. *What the hell am I doing?* she wondered, knowing this was only the beginning, and there was nothing she could do to stop it. The attraction was too strong for her to resist, no matter the consequences. And regardless of his missing thumb.

Office romance happens all the time, she told herself. *It will have to work out somehow.*

Shifting her focus back to the moment at hand, she placed her left arm on the center console and was excited when Corbin removed his right hand from the wheel and gently covered hers on the leather console. They continued their easy conversation.

In the Southern Towers parking lot, Corbin slid into an open spot and switched off the ignition. "Oh, you can just drop me here," Peyton said, his hand still covering hers. "I'll be fine walking in myself."

"Oh, no chance in hell I'm not walking you up," Corbin replied. "Nowhere in Atlanta is safe this late at night. I'm not being chauvinistic because I know you can take care of yourself, but let me be a bit chivalrous."

Smiling, for more reasons than the sudden memory of her childhood imaginary dragon, Baby, Peyton complied. *Maybe I won't let Baby torch this prince,* she thought as Corbin escorted her to her welcoming apartment on the sixth floor. *At least not right away.*

27

CORBIN

Jessica looked at me with complete fear and surprise in her eyes, gurgling behind the silver duct tape that securely kept any audible sounds from escaping her deceitful lips.

"Oh, Mother," I said. "Are you surprised? You have been the world's worst person to me. I have been a good kid, and I'm smart. Never once did you love me. How could you expect me to love you? But this is a sweet moment for me. No longer shall you control me…at all." As I finished, her panicked eyes grasped the extent of what would happen next.

"But don't worry, my dear mother," I said as the lie filled the room—she had everything to worry about. "I have no desire to make this quick or painless for you. And I want every pain to account for something you did to me. Now where shall we begin?"

Jessica struggled against the duct tape and attempted screams that only came out as unalarming grunts.

"Now, now, Mother, calm down," I said. "I'm going to be much more compassionate than you've ever thought about being to me. And trust me, I will explain the reason for each bit of torture that is about to happen to you. So relax and enjoy." I laughed as my mother now stared with hatred and rage. God, I hated that woman.

Rolling Sam's red Craftsman toolbox from his small office into the brightly lit kitchen, I started opening the various drawers to see what implements I had to deal with. I did not forget the entire kitchen supply of tools ready for my use, remembering my mother's preference for kitchen utensils when abusing me.

First grabbing the bolt cutters from the top left drawer, I placed them over Mother's left thumb and pressed down slightly, enough for her to feel the tension on her exposed digit. I sensed the alarm in her face at the anticipated pain, and I laughed as I quickly snapped through the thumb, easily and swiftly, like my little toddler thumb had been robbed of me. After watching with delight as the gushing blood and severed thumb cascaded to the white tile floor, I grabbed the little nub and reached for the Bic lighter. "I'm sorry, Mother," I again lied because I felt no remorse whatsoever. "I don't have an electric stove handy. So, I'm going to have to use this lighter to stop the bleeding. I'm not ready to let you go yet."

As the red lighter flickered and sizzled against the blood-spewing stump, I was quickly reminded of the smell of burning flesh. Unable to let that and all the ensuing abuse go, I held the lighter closer and harder to her thumb, wishing it was more powerful. Mother passed out at one point, and I let her rest. This needed to last a long time. I was sixteen. I needed to make up for sixteen years of neglect and blatant abuse. This was my moment.

When she regained consciousness, I lovingly stroked her cheek and gazed into her eyes. Over the years, I had learned this action must remind her of my father. Once I knew this, I often used the technique to get a reaction from her. It was so easy. Her pupils dilated and her face softened. "Really, Mother?" I said. "After all of this, you are still smitten? Why? He's never been there for us. He never loved you." She stared at me with hatred.

"Let's see. What shall we avenge next?" I asked. "Which of the abuses shall I forgive next?"

"Let's talk about Earl." I was excited that Jessica's eyes quickly became agitated. "Oh, yes, so you allowed Earl to rape your nine-year-old son, and you did nothing. I'm not going to rape you, Mother, or even violate you like that. I'm rising above, and you disgust me. But you need to know that was the worst and most painful moment of my life. I would have gladly given all ten fingers and ten toes to have never experienced that. And to know that you knew and let it happen."

I selected the boning knife Sam used to cut open the bullheads we caught on Standing Bear Lake (on the rare occasions we kept them) and remove their transparent bones before we battered and fried them. I again approached Mother, who now appeared to be unconscious. Tapping lightly on her forehead seemed to revive her. "Hey, Mother, it's me, Corbin. You know, your baby boy whom you love? Ha ha ha ha." Drawing the boning knife toward her left eye, I drew a deep and severe cut in her flesh from the corner of her watering eye, down her cheek, and then circled back to connect her mouth. "Oh, look; I made a C."

I could never truly avenge all the wrongs Jessica had committed against me. I tried, but there was not enough satisfaction, no matter what I attempted. As she lay on the stainless-steel island, my need for love flooded over me. I let all the torture implements drop, throwing some of them across the room. Screaming at her, I pleaded, "Please, Mother, tell me you love me and that I wasn't the biggest fuckup of your life. Tell me right now, please? All I ever wanted was your love."

Sadly, I watched Jessica's eyes turn black. I recognized, with horror, the same reaction I had when pushed to the limit. Once the eyes go black, there is no feeling, no thoughts, no concerns. It's black and evil and quiet.

Seeing her staring at me, her black eyes drilling into my soul, I knew. I would never have what I needed. With quiet resolve, I drew the boning knife quickly across her white, throbbing throat, feeling no emotion whatsoever. Grabbing her severed thumb from the tile floor, I dropped it in a glass from the Quick Pick and covered it with iodized salt. Defeated and alone, I retired upstairs and slept for more than fourteen hours while Jessica bled out. It was the deepest, most restful sleep of my life. I had gotten revenge. No more abusing Corbin, ever.

The afternoon sun spilling in through the small cracked window of my bedroom above the Quick Pick Diner woke me gently. Refreshed and unburdened, I stretched my arms and legs, feeling the lean muscles sigh with relaxation. Today was the first day of a new life for me. Smiling, I stood, carefully folded the old quilt, and placed it back on the bed. Walking down the rickety stairs and pushing through the back door of the Quick Pick, the strong smell of blood surrounded me and my tongue tasted like old pennies. *Better get to this*, I thought.

First, I dealt with Sam. Rummaging through his pants pockets, I retrieved his black leather wallet and his bulky key ring populated with more than fifteen keys in various metals and sizes. Stripping him naked and stuffing all his other belongings in a black plastic trash bag, I then pulled him by the back door and left him lying there.

Entering the kitchen, I smiled at the bloody scene with dead Jessica lying in the middle of it. Revenge is so sweet. After removing Jessica's pink waitress uniform and other articles of clothing, and placing them in the same black trash bag with Sam's belongings, I picked the red Sawzall and plugged it into a nearby outlet. I had promised Hamilton that I would take care of him, and I had no intentions of lying to that poor, unfortunate old fellow. Cutting Jessica's dead body into manageable portions and cleanup proved to be more time-consuming than I had anticipated, and the Nebraska sun was starting to tip its tired face into the darkening horizon by the time I was finished.

My mother lay neatly stacked on the four glass shelves in the Quick Pick commercial refrigerator. The once bloody kitchen had been returned to its pristine and organized state, the smell of bleach and glass cleaner hung in the air, and her severed thumb cured slowly in the iodized salt on the counter.

Grabbing the keys to the navy-blue rusted Ford Pinto, I walked across the pea gravel-covered parking lot and hopped into the driver's seat. After backing the car close to the back door, I popped open the trunk. I hefted Sam into the trunk, along with the black trash bag containing their clothes and the trash bag containing Jessica's bloody head, the large C now crusted on her face.

I pulled out of the Quick Pick parking lot and drove across town, depositing one of the trash bags into a dumpster outside of Eddie's Taxidermy. I didn't feel a bag of bloody clothes would cause much attention coming from a taxidermist, if it was even ever detected. Heading out west of town, I hoped Farmer Sharp's pig farm was still operating and that Farmer Sharp still retired to bed early. Both proved to be accurate, and I relished the pigs' squeals of delight as they consumed the fresh body and Jessica's head. As I headed back to the Quick Pick, I whistled as the Nebraska wind blew through the Pinto's open windows and tousled my thick, black hair.

Grabbing several servings of Jessica, I opened the back, metal door of the Quick Pick and whistled for the pack, who quickly appeared, led by Hamilton. "Told ya, boy." I tossed some of Jessica's thighs out the door. "Tonight, you guys eat well."

While the dog pack had grown from the original five, it still took several days for them to completely consume the hefty meal. I always made sure Hamilton received the prime pieces. I wonder if that's when I became fascinated with eating humans. Watching Hamilton drooling in anticipation of a luscious piece of liver, his spittle hanging long from his black lips before cascading into a shallow pool on the recently cleared pea gravel near the green metal dumpster, I somehow longed to understand how satisfying that taste might be.

Regardless, the extra few days gave me time to organize the next steps in my master plan. Looking through Sam's wallet, I found his Nebraska State Driver's License, which listed his home address. I thought it slightly odd that I had never been to Sam's house, but I suppose there had never been a reason for me to go there. Sam also had a couple of hundred dollars in cash and a credit card, which I cut into tiny pieces and threw in the trash. Emptying out the cash register at the Quick Pick provided a few hundred more.

I jumped into Sam's old truck and rattled it the few blocks to the address listed on his driver's license, 801 N. Candlestick Drive. Sam didn't have any close family, but I still drove past the house a couple of times to make sure it was vacant before pulling into the driveway. Fiddling with the keys and trying several before finding the match, I pushed open the door and yelled, "Hello? Anyone home?"

When there was no answer, I started looking around. Sam was old fashioned and had a general distrust and hatred for commercial banking. He also lived modestly, so I was certain there had to be a good deal of money some place.

It took me several hours to find Sam's stashes. He was clever and didn't hide all his cash in any one spot. He had some under his mattress. "Oh, Sam, how cliché." I chuckled when I found it. A cigar box full of hundreds was tucked in the freezer next to a bag of frozen broccoli. Opening Sam's closet, I saw a brand-new pair of cowboy boots, shiny brown with deep-green stitching, sitting on the top shelf. Hoping they were my size, I grabbed them only to find both boots stuffed full of cash. While the boots were not my size, I didn't hesitate to empty them, before placing them back in their original spot.

Before I left Sam's house, I threw his keys on the small white kitchen table. I had no more use for them since I still had Jessica's key to the Quick Pick. Making sure all was in order the way it had been when I arrived, I locked the front door and pulled it closed behind me.

Walking back to the Quick Pick with my gym bag full of cash, for the first time in my life, I felt good about my future.

28

SPENCER

Spencer slid his chair back from his cubicle surface in frustration over his deteriorating relationship with Corbin. He simply had to come up with a plan to get his best friend back. He felt Peyton was the problem, so he had recently installed malware on her computer, like he had on Lois'. He had never felt bad about ruining Lois. She had completely deserved it. When the last Information Systems Manager had retired, Spencer had approached Lois in her office, while she shuffled endless papers from one side of her cluttered desk to the other. Spencer always thought the stacks of junk on her desk were how she compensated for having nothing to do.

"Lois." Spencer's eyes were darting from side to side. "I want to throw my hat in the ring for the Information Systems Manager position." Spencer felt like he was going to vomit and looked quickly for a plant or nearby trash can, finding neither.

"Sure, Spencer," Lois had replied while picking up a manila folder and examining its contents, "but Paul and I have decided not to fill the position. We don't think it's necessary. You guys all know what you need to do, and well, we don't think any of you are ready for a senior role. If we do eventually fill the position, it will likely be from the outside."

Shocked at her callous approach, Spencer had stood awkwardly in front of her for a moment, feeling his blood pressure soar and resisting the urge to smash her face into the plate-glass window overlooking Peachtree Street.

"Hmm," he had finally said. "So, why can't I be considered?"

Laughing a little before realizing he was serious, Lois had composed herself and said, "Oh, Spencer, you have so much potential and are so valuable to Blast. We couldn't exist without you in your current role. In fact, we don't have anyone currently in IT whom we could lose or promote without causing a deficit for the organization. You are vital to our success! Thank you so much, and please keep up the good work!"

Spencer had hated her even more for that condescending, empty closure. Turning away in disappointment, he had slumped out of her office and returned to his purple cubicle. He would ruin that woman. He was calmed by the realization.

Brought back to the present, Spencer noted Corbin walking by, glancing at Peyton's office. *Oh, God,* Spencer thought. *What am I going to do about him? I took care of Lois, but damn, I hate to take out my friend. He's just embarrassing right now.*

Spencer wasn't an idiot. He could see how close and affectionate Corbin and Peyton had become. He wasn't sure how far things had gone yet, but he had noted the increased coincidental encounters they seemed to have in the breakroom. He had also observed Corbin talking on his work phone, his smile so broad that Spencer could envy his perfect white teeth. He suspected Corbin was talking to Peyton, and considering the glass office fronts, it didn't take a rocket scientist to note that Peyton was on the phone at the same time with similar expressions. This had to come to an end.

Clicking and tapping away at his Dell laptop, Spencer launched the malware program that provided a mirror image of everything

Peyton stored and created on her matching laptop, set up to ensure easy accessibility to any information he wanted. The IT Director, Tony, was a hands-off manager providing little support or interest in his team's projects. He would never detect the malware on Peyton's computer. Chuckling to himself, Spencer thought, *That's why I should be promoted, you fools.*

As Spencer poured over emails and documents from Peyton's laptop, he smiled as he thought about ruining Lois. It was shortly after she blew him off for the promotion that he had started monitoring her activity. Finding an email from Lois to her sister, Eloise, Spencer had read in shock and excitement.

Hey, Sis,

You are not going to believe what is going on around here. Paul is having an affair! I'm not sure with whom yet, but I caught him in his office with lipstick on his face. It was hilarious. He was so flustered! I wonder if she was hiding in his private bathroom or maybe under his desk. LOL. You know I'm good friends with his wife; we had drinks the other night. She was telling me that they are distant with one another. I think she is getting suspicious. I might have to help her out. He's such a horrid pig—all men are. Remember when Albert broke my heart? Oh, my Gawd, how can men be so awful? At any rate, I'm going to get to the bottom of this, and I'm going to help that poor woman out if I can. Girl Power!

Spencer could barely contain his excitement after reading that email. All he had to do was get it in the hands of Paul Sanderson's wife and Lois would be toast. No one messes with Spencer Davis!

Spencer's revenge plan worked like a charm. Old school as it was, all he had to do was slip a plain white envelope under the massive two-door entrance of the Sanderson estate when Paul was out of town. He had left the "To" and "From" on the email before he printed it for the beautiful, intriguing Mrs. Sanderson to read in her silk pajamas the next morning after approaching the front door to gather the morning paper. Lois had been fired within days.

Spencer smiled broadly, knowing Peyton, who had stolen his best friend from him and turned him into a gooey weakling, was going to pay a similar price.

Then, Spencer felt his heartbeat increase rapidly against his rib cage as a new message from Peyton to Corbin popped up on his screen.

Hey, it's Friday. Piero's is calling my name. Up for it? My place at 7?

Seriously, HR lady? Spencer thought. *How is this appropriate work behavior? This has got to end, and I'm the one to take care of it. No worries, my friend; Spencer will save you.*

29

PEYTON

Peyton's pulse throbbed and her face flushed as she clicked "send" on the email to Corbin. It was a little bold, but she was ready. After that first date at Piero's—yes, she could categorize it as a date now—to all the dinners since, the chance meetings in the breakroom, and all the phone calls back and forth, heavy with innuendos and flirting, she was ready.

She remembered that night he'd first taken her to Piero's, and especially, the perfect ending. Well, actually it was all perfect. After escorting her to her apartment door, he had ended the evening with no pressure whatsoever, which also increased Peyton's desire. Sure, it was wrong to have an office romance; ugh, dare she say romance? Maybe fling was more appropriate. Regardless, she was intrigued, and she wanted more.

Who will ever even know? she thought. *It's not like we're fucking on the counter in the breakroom.* Then she smiled as the visual popped into her head. But Spencer was quite aware, as Peyton would eventually find out.

Peyton giggled when she saw Corbin's reply email that simply said, "I'll be there. 7."

Excited, Peyton did not reply with anything other than, "K," but inwardly, she was about to explode. Anticipating leaving the office by five, Peyton was devastated when Paul called her into his office for a conference call at 4:50. Rushing from the office at six, Peyton navigated through traffic quickly and thankfully arrived home at six-thirty.

"Well, not much time to prepare," she gasped. "Jesus, this is not how I had planned this."

Quickly tidying her apartment, she stuffed random obstructions into the hall closet before she realized she was still wearing her incredibly boring office attire. Quickly stripping and throwing her tailored suit onto the beige carpet of the walk-in closet, Peyton pulled on a T-shirt and a pair of men's boxers. Grabbing a cold Miller Lite from the fridge, she smiled confidently and thought, *You know what. If he doesn't like me like this, then he's not for me.*

Peyton paced around her apartment, absentmindedly picking up random objects, just to set them down in a different place, glancing at the clock that never seemed to change. At 6:54, she rushed into her spotless master bath and brushed her teeth. Had she already done that once tonight? She couldn't remember, but a fresh mouth was important. A cloud of doubt filled the room and encased her. *Wait, we haven't even kissed. Oh, my God, what if I have this all wrong? I'm going to make a fool of myself. He's expecting me to be ready to go out. Oh, shit! What is wrong with me?*

Snatching open the closet door and desperately searching for a quick solution, she heard the doorbell's gentle notification that someone had arrived. Too late to alter her plan.

Wait, I can say I got held up at work and was about to change.

Walking to the front door, she opened it quickly, still in her T-shirt and boxers. "Hey." She smiled, trying to contain her excitement and hide her nerves.

"Hey." Corbin grinned at her while holding a Piero's pizza box. "I thought maybe we could eat in tonight. Is that okay?"

Holy crap, Peyton thought. *Maybe I wasn't wrong. How is it possible this man was perceptive enough to bring pizza? Shit, I'm in trouble.*

When she didn't answer, Corbin awkwardly added, "I hope you don't think it too presumptuous of me, but it is Piero's and it's seven, but if you want to go out...."

"Oh, no! Corbin, this is perfect. As you can tell, I'm not dressed yet to go out, so now I won't have to worry about what to wear." Then she added, "I was going to get dressed more appropriately, but Paul kept me at the office late, and I didn't have time. So, anyway, come in."

"Peyton…" Corbin's voice shook, making Peyton's heart drop as she wondered what horrid news he was about to deliver. "Peyton, wow, you look amazing," he finally got out.

Peyton giggled inwardly because she had never seen his confidence shaken before.

Laughing, while placing a hand on his arm, Peyton replied, "What? I'm wearing an old shirt and boxers!"

"Oh, I know. You look delicious. Good enough to eat." He smiled while looking her up and down.

"Oh, stop it." Peyton laughed and grabbed the pizza box from him. "Let me grab some plates. I'll serve. Thank you, Corbin, for wanting to eat in tonight. It's the perfect plan."

Corbin carefully watched Peyton as she took the pizza and walked confidently into the ceramic-tiled kitchen, her muscled thighs peeking out from the plaid boxers, the over-sized T-shirt making her appear vulnerable, yet sexy.

Pulling paper plates from the cabinet above the stove, she called out, "Hope you don't mind paper!" She opened the pizza box and pulled out a piece of Chicago-style pizza, the mozzarella stringing from the slice. Tilting her lovely head, Peyton stuffed the tip of the pizza slice into her mouth. "I'm sorry. I love that first bite. I should have waited for you."

"Yes, the first bite is the best." Corbin enjoyed watching her from the kitchen door; an expression was on his face that Peyton had not noticed before. He seemed content, yet excited, and his green eyes hid behind a darker hue. He seemed a bit distant. She was confused, yet deeply aroused.

"Hey, would you mind grabbing us a couple of beers from the fridge?" Peyton asked while picking up the two paper plates laden with steaming pizza. "Meet me in the dining room?" Peyton turned away from Corbin.

Quickly dropping the plates back onto the counter, Peyton gasped as she felt Corbin's warm, strong arms encircling her from behind. She thought she might pass out when she felt the tentative, soft kisses on her tender, white neck as he gently moved her hair to one side.

Between the kisses, he whispered, "Peyton, I'm sorry if this is wrong, but I can't help myself. You look so amazing tonight. You always do, but I love when you are casual and *you*."

Turning and gently wrenching from his grip to face him, Peyton softly touched his face and replied, "Corbin. You know this is a bad idea. And inappropriate. And puts both our jobs in jeopardy. When I first met you, I could tell you were different." She paused and retracted. "Well, I hope you are different and that karma isn't fucking with me right now." Then pulling away, she added, "So, anyway, slice of pizza?"

"No, ma'am," Corbin replied. "I don't think pizza is what is required right now." He gently pulled her close again, his body exploding in emotion, anticipation, and hunger. He had waited so long.

As Peyton relaxed into his chest, he was again reminded that she was different. She was strong but caring, loyal but decisive, needy but independent. All of these traits confused Corbin. He had only experienced the Jessica-type woman in his life. Even hateful Marcella was similar to Jessica, leaving her babies alone for the hope of a good fuck. But Peyton—there was something different about her.

A warm rush of comfort swept over Peyton as she felt Corbin meld with her. It was the strangest experience she had ever encountered, yet the most reassuring. It felt as if, at some level, they simply were soulmates who had finally found one another. Peyton was reminded of "Ode on a Grecian Urn," one of her favorite poems in college; she felt this moment was what the two lovers would have experienced if ever the male had fulfilled his pursuit, and well, without the sacrifice part.

Corbin was gentle and tentative while softly kissing her neck, moving slowly down her arms, and lifting her T-shirt above her head, her arms complacently lifted toward the stucco ceiling, the uneaten pizza cooling on the counter.

As passions flared and clothes were removed, Corbin and Peyton made their way to the Tempur-pedic bed in Peyton's sanctuary. Slowly reclining into the fluff of pillows, Peyton sighed and welcomed Corbin to join her, only to be confused by his suddenly dark, practically black, eyes.

"Hey," Peyton asked, sitting up quickly, "what's wrong?" She reached for him, but he pulled away.

"No. No, no, no, no. This isn't right," Corbin said. He backed away until his bare back collided with the corner farthest from Peyton. "I can't be like her. This isn't right; this isn't okay."

Peyton slowly approached him, and stood naked in front of him. Reaching out, she took his left hand and pressed it gently against her heart. "Corbin, I don't know what is happening right now, but I promise you, I am here for you. Please don't shut me out."

Peyton gazed into his troubled eyes and continued to stare deeply and softly. *What has happened to this poor man?* she wondered.

After what seemed like hours, Corbin finally took a deep breath, his left hand still held by Peyton, and said, "Peyton; I'm sorry. This isn't about you. I'm kind of a mess, emotionally.... My mother, well, I have a lot of baggage. I should probably go. You're right. I don't want to put your job in danger."

Pulling his hand from Peyton, Corbin stomped out of the room, picking up items of clothing along the way. Peyton felt her eyes well up with tears, but she would not admit defeat. Following Corbin into the kitchen while pulling her shirt back over her head, she watched him fumbling to get dressed. Advancing quickly, she grabbed his hands.

"Please stop," she said. "Corbin, I don't know what's going on right now, but we both want this. We get along great, and we'll figure things out as we go. But, right now, I'd like you to stay. Will you?"

Corbin froze, staring at her, searching her face for answers to questions he hadn't, nor ever would, ask. Finally, he suggested, "Maybe let's just eat some pizza."

Peyton nodded slowly, noticing his eyes were black, and he stood perfectly still. She couldn't even detect his breathing.

"Sure; let's eat pizza and watch a movie. If you want to talk about something, we can. If you don't want to, there's no pressure from me. Look; we all have fucked-up pasts. But you and I are here, now. And what is happening is wonderful and different."

"Okay; give me a minute. You find something to watch, and I'll warm the pizza and come in," he said.

Peyton complied and walked quietly into the living room, feeling a little like she had looked into a rampaging tiger's fierce eyes and been allowed to escape. As she picked up the remote, she listened carefully, but she heard no sound coming from the kitchen. Finally, she heard the water in the sink running, and then more silence. She waited.

I don't know what's going on, but I feel sorry for the guy, she thought as she started flipping through movie options.

30

CORBIN

Oh, that Peyton Alexander. She has definitely gotten into my head. I thought I could handle her, but as I gazed upon her beautiful ivory body, lying naked and welcoming, all I could think about was Mother and how she willingly gave herself to any man who showed her interest. My plan for that evening was to arrive with pizza in tow, and then later dine on a lovely morsel of Miss Peyton's still-warm liver, but things don't always work according to plan.

When she opened the front door, wearing that old T-shirt and boxers, my plan was in jeopardy. Peyton was different. *But is she different?* I thought as I followed her into the kitchen, mesmerized by her swaying hips. *You thought Sam was different, too, you fucking moron.*

I was greatly embarrassed by the events in the bedroom, but I wasn't even sure what was happening. I was starving but wanted to make love to her instead. Well, we saw how that turned out. As she stood before me in the kitchen, I think we made some small talk, but I can't be certain. I was gripping the granite countertop so tightly my knuckles turned white. My heart was pounding in my head, and I wanted to end the confusion. I waited until Peyton had left the room before letting out a huge breath of air I'd been holding for who knows how long. Taking a few deep breaths, I tentatively moved my hands from the counter, noticing they were shaking almost uncontrollably. Taking the few short steps to the sink, I turned on the cold water and let it run over my hands and wrists before cupping the icy water in my hands to douse my face. I felt my pulse returning to a normal rate, my breathing becoming more regular. And that's when I saw the knives.

"Oh, Corbin, we're right here," they seemed to call to me. "It's not too late for your original plan. We know you are hungry."

I grabbed the bright-blue terrycloth towel draped over Peyton's stove handle. While wiping my face, I stared at the knife block. The glinting stainless steel shown against the harsh fluorescent lighting that all kitchens seem to have. Slowly, I reached for my specialty, the sleek boning knife. It wasn't my boning knife, which was readily handy in my inside jacket pocket, tucked safely into its leather sheath, should I need it. But this one would do quite nicely.

Slowly pulling it from the wooden block, it made a small zing as it blossomed into the kitchen light. I carefully inspected the blade, noting it was exceptionally sharp, and turned it over and over in my hands. I lost all sense of time and the world closed in around me. All that existed at that moment was me and the boning knife—well, and my devastating hunger. Slowly and unexplained, a welcoming comfort and warmth swept over my body.

Gripping the boning knife tightly, I lifted it into a strike position, stabbed it directly into the Piero's pizza box, and pulled it out before throwing it in the sink. Grabbing the plates of pizza Peyton had prepared earlier, I headed into the living room.

Settling onto the burgundy couch, plates full of pizza and cold beers handy, we sat beside one another. Peyton found a campy horror movie about some inbred hillbillies who trapped people and later consumed them. Oddly ironic. The plot was horrible, the acting worse, and we laughed and laughed into the evening.

At some point, Peyton pulled a soft velour blanket from the couch back and asked me to turn lengthwise on the couch, which I did. Peyton snuggled her warm body between my legs, resting the back of her head on my chest. Relaxing into the pose, I was starting to put the horrible earlier experience out of my head. Well, no one can erase that embarrassment, but I was trying.

The campy horror movie was wrapping up. Peyton snuggled close when I said something that shocked even me. Who was this person speaking? "Peyton," I heard myself say, "I do need to talk to you."

She rolled her head back slightly and kissed my chin. "Only if you want to. I'm perfectly content and happy as we are."

"Were you being honest earlier? About truly caring for me?" I instantly regretted it because it sounded so lame.

"Absolutely," was all that came from her lovely lips.

"Well, if I told you something horrible, something really horrible, would that change how you thought of me?"

Peyton turned so she could look me in the eyes, thankfully green again, and said, "Well, that would depend on what it was, but I can't imagine a wonderful soul like yours ever doing anything that would cause me to change how I think of you. Unless, you tell me that you abuse animals and children. Those are about my only two hot buttons. Don't hurt the innocents. Oh, and don't ever lie to me. That's about it."

Unable to stop myself, I gently lifted her chin and kissed her invitingly warm mouth for several minutes before letting go.

"Well," she said, smiling and sinking back onto my chest. "That was lovely. I guess I got the answer right?"

"Yes, yes, you did," I said with more emotion than I expected. "But I do want to tell you some things." Holding up my left hand, I said, "For starters, can I tell you what happened to my poor thumb?"

"Oh, my God, Corbin. Please? I've been so conflicted about how to ask. It's obvious, but one of those things a person doesn't ask about."

"Does it bother you?"

"No, no, but I do want to know." It seemed she was trying to hide that my physical deficiency was a concern for her. Was it the lack of the thumb, though, or the lack of the reason for its absence? That would be a critical discovery for me. I decided, however, to share the truth with Peyton because I hoped she was truly different and knew what that could mean for my future.

Over the course of the next several hours, I recounted numerous stories about my horrible childhood with Jessica and a make-believe version of how I escaped it all. I omitted certain parts, like what happened to Jessica; no mention of Marcella, nor my desire for raw liver, ever entered the conversation. Peyton did not learn of my preserved thumb, only the story of how I had lost it, and no mention of my collection.

When I told her how Earl had raped me, she surprised me by jumping off the couch. "What the fuck was wrong with your damn mother? Who allows that?"

Then, just as quickly, she reclaimed her seat beside me. "I'm sorry, Corbin; please go on."

It was after three in the morning before we retired once again to Peyton's soothing bedroom. Lying naked next to one another, Peyton whispered, "Corbin, can I ask you one thing?"

"Ha, after all I shared tonight? Of course, you can. What?"

"Well, it doesn't make a difference one way or the other, but I want to know," Peyton said. "Um, well, have you ever, you know, had sex with a woman?"

Pulling her close to me, I kissed the lovely Peyton Alexander's forehead. "No, ma'am, but I'm about to."

31

SPENCER

The malware was working great for Spencer. He saw everything Peyton sent, received, and viewed online. He also learned how much money she made, the bitch, and was devastated to learn that Corbin's salary was close to his. *He's just a customer service guy*, he thought. *It's because he's good looking. And he's fucking the HR lady, so that has to help his salary, too.*

Spencer was copied on her emails, and continued to read more and more alarming, yet perfectly exciting, exchanges between Corbin and her.

"This weekend was amazing," one email read. "I can't believe how perfect it was. Thank you for spending it with me."

Corbin's reply was, "Oh, whatever the lady wants, the lady shall have. I had a great time, too. I hated to leave Sunday morning. This is just the beginning."

Spencer thought he might vomit. So disgusting and deceitful. Since that bitch's arrival at Blast, Corbin had been ignoring Spencer. He tried to remember the last time they had hung out and couldn't place a time in the last three months. They had hardly spoken since Corbin brought those tempting donuts, like that was supposed to make up for everything. Now that he knew Corbin and Peyton were fucking, he had to start taking action. He needed his friend back.

Spencer admired Corbin, his arrogant attitude, and how he never dated a woman twice. But now, Corbin had fallen into the same woman trap as all men. It was Spencer's duty to save him. Corbin didn't realize he needed saving, but Spencer knew. Women were horrid and evil, all of them.

Rolling his chair back and pushing it into the aisle, he said to Corbin, "Hey, man, what's up? We haven't talked in a while. How's life?"

Corbin slid back and turned to face Spencer. "It's all good, man. You?"

"All good."

"Okay, then, anything up?" Corbin asked.

"Naw, was wondering if there was anything new going on with you? Seeing anyone or anything?"

"Nope, just work, and you know, my free time is spent trying to get that damn basement finished. Old houses are not all they are cracked up to be."

"I see," Spencer said, seething inwardly at Corbin's lies. Then, he heard Corbin's extension buzz.

Corbin glanced at the phone, a smile unconsciously glowing across his face, and said, "Hey, man, gotta get this." He rolled back and picked up, saying, "Thank you for calling Blast. This is Corbin. How may I help you?"

Spencer noticed as he rolled back into his cube that the bitch, Peyton, was also on the phone, smiling.

Uh-huh, Spencer thought. *He's a goner. I need to save him.*

Picking up his receiver, he entered 763. He was pleased when Mr. Sanderson answered. "Yes, Spencer; what is it?"

"I need to talk with you. When you have a moment. At your convenience, of course."

"Sure, sure. I'm about to get on a call, but how about coming to my office at eleven?"

"Great; see you then," Spencer replied into an already-dead receiver. *Not one person respects me.* He sighed.

32

CORBIN

When I left Omaha, I slowly made my way through Nebraska, up into the Badlands of South Dakota. I took the time to visit Custer State Park, driving on the Needles Highway along the twisty pavement leading me through the dark tunnels, to visit Mount Rushmore, before heading down past Hill City to view the famous Crazy Horse Monument, still under construction. I worked for a short time in Custer as a server at the Bison Café. I still had the majority of Sam's money, but I wanted to save it. I think a little of me also wanted to prove to myself that I could make it on my own. Jessica never instilled much self-confidence in me, after all, so I needed to do it myself.

My obsession with raw meat continued to grow and fill my thoughts. My behavior was not socially accepted. You can't forget the trauma of losing a thumb as a child because of it, but I couldn't contain it. I often volunteered to do late night cleanup at the Bison Cafe so I could grab a few raw steaks and sneak them back to my car to rip apart with my bare hands, teeth gnashing while enjoying the cool bloody texture. I sometimes laughed when I caught a glimpse of myself in the rearview mirror, eyes black and wild. Some days, I let out a deep, throaty growl while consuming my steak. But even that never seemed to satisfy me.

Jack Duffy, our lame restaurant manager, whom I'm pretty sure was hired for his lamb-like qualities that allowed the restaurant owner to use the café as a front to launder drug money, approached me one day, and said, "Corbin, we need to talk. Come to my office?"

"Sure," I replied, following him to his tiny 5" x 6" office, which always smelled like body odor and musty paperwork, located next to the greasy kitchen. From his office, he could keep an eagle eye on the time clock to make sure no employee cheated him out of five minutes of work. I'm sure Jack had been the nerdy kid in class who always volunteered to be hall monitor.

"What's up?" I asked, even though I didn't give a shit what was up. This was a temporary gig and a free source of raw meat. I wasn't stressing.

He stammered and fidgeted, his youth accentuated by a bulging whitehead, full of puss, poking out on his fuzzy chin. "Well, it seems we have quite a few steaks that have been, uh, well, unaccounted for."

"So," I asked, "what are you implying?"

"Oh, no, no, no." He pushed his black plastic frames back up his greasy nose. "I'm not implying anything. I was wondering if you knew what may have happened to them."

I noticed small drops of sweat had popped up across his pimply forehead. *Better watch that stress, Jack,* I thought. *Not good for the complexion.*

"Well, Jack," I grinned widely and gave him a two-thumbs-up, "I'll be sure to keep my eyes peeled for a steak thief here at the Bison Café. If I find the culprit, we'll have a hanging, Pilgrim," I said, mimicking the great John Wayne.

Spinning quickly, I exited the tiny office and resumed my regular duties. That night when left to clean up and close, I grabbed a case of beautiful Ribeye steaks, threw them into the trunk of Jessica's old Pinto, remarkably still running, and left the Bison Café. I smiled, knowing how anxious Jack would be when he arrived in the morning to find the floors not mopped, the trash cans still brimming with garbage, and nothing prepped for the breakfast crew.

I'm not sure what prompted me to head west into Wyoming before turning north toward Great Falls, Montana. Not surprisingly, I never had received a response to my letter to Franklin, even though I had remained in Omaha a few months and checked the Quick Pick's battered mailbox frequently to make sure. Without a response, I figured I wouldn't hear from him. I guess it didn't matter. I was designed by the universe to be alone and take care of myself. No one ever cared for me or ever would. Did I expect him to swoop in and take me under his wing? Hell, I didn't even want that. Or did I? No matter.

After driving through the night, I pulled into Great Falls. My first stop was our crappy old trailer where I had lived the first few years of my life; oh, and let's not forget, where I lost my little thumb. I had to drive around a bit before finding it since I was only six when we left for Omaha. But when I drove into the Shady Hills Trailer Park, I felt my heart race with anxiety at the sight of the dilapidated trailer, now more rusted than I remembered, with unkempt bushes reaching tall toward the sky. Oddly, my eyes watered up as all the memories of that horrid place raced through my mind. The soiled diapers, locked in my room alone for hours, the beatings, the neglect, and the thumb removal. It's unbelievable that I could still remember so many details. My face pouring with sweat, tears streaming down my cheeks, I sat until the sun was sliding quietly behind the horizon before returning to reality.

A couple of days later, I found a little basement apartment to rent on a month-by-month basis. Two hundred dollars a month, all utilities included. It was on East Elm Street, underneath a shabby little abode that was so distressed I was never even curious about its inhabitants. As I handed Luis the $50 deposit that he snatched greedily from my hand, I asked, "So, can I get the key?"

"Oh, no key, man," he replied with a thick Mexican accent. "Screwdriver above the door; jam it in the crack in the door. Release dead bolt."

Laughing, I said, "You got it, man. Thanks for the place to crash." Luis shook my hand quickly before darting into his S10 pickup, which had been lowered and painted sunflower yellow with red flames consuming both sides.

Walking down the dark steps to the basement, I felt for the screwdriver above the door, which I easily found. Sliding it gently into the one-inch crack to disengage the deadbolt, I noted that Luis was correct. I pushed open the creaking door to reveal my new digs. It was a small cinder-block apartment, but it had an adjoining kitchen to the small bedroom that also served as a living room. In the back was a bathroom with a stand-up corner shower and a rusted, stained toilet near the sink sticking out of the wall with no cabinet.

Flipping on the lights and opening the refrigerator to feel the welcoming cold on my face, I placed the remaining ribeye steaks in the cool interior. "All I need," I said as I retired to the twin bed tucked in the corner.

Considering my growing experience in the restaurant industry, I was excited by the "Help Wanted" poster in the window of the Waffle Castle out near the interstate. Upon entering the diner, I approached the counter and asked to speak to the manager.

Allison, according to her nametag, said, "Uh, is there a problem? I don't even recognize you, but we've been so busy, let me know what the problem is before we go to Bob. Please? I need this job."

"Whoa, chill, Allison," I said. "I just wanted to apply for a job."

Laughing and relieved, she rolled her head back and then twisted it from side to side while stretching her arms outward. "Oh, I'm so sorry. It's been super-stressful today. Sure; I'll get him."

Immediately impressed with my experience, Bob hired me on the spot. "When can you start? I desperately need a fry cook, and I'm lucky you happened by today. I can't believe your experience. At your age, you ran the kitchen at the Quick Pick Diner?"

Knowing there was no one left to disagree with that information, I replied, "Yes, yes, I did. I have had a fortunate upbringing and a strong mentor in my life." Man, how I had learned to play with words.

"Great!" Bob said. "Start tomorrow?"

"Sure. What time shall I arrive?"

"We open at six; can you be here then?"

"Yep. See you tomorrow, Bob."

I distinctly remember the morning I saw my father. I was flipping hash browns and eggs on the sizzling grill of the Waffle Castle when he pushed through the double-paned glass doors, his intimidating presence dominating the restaurant. Shocked that he looked so much like me, I quickly diverted my attention to the sizzling patty melt popping on the grill, regretting that the beautiful red meat was turning a disgusting grayish-brown.

33

PEYTON

Peyton was working on her talent-mapping spreadsheet when her phone buzzed. Seeing Paul's extension on the display, she picked up and said, "Hello, Paul; how can I help you?"

"Have a minute to come here?" he asked.

"Sure; uh, do I need to bring anything?"

"Nope." The line went silent.

Grabbing her pad and pen to be prepared, Peyton walked briskly down the hall to his extravagant walnut office. As she advanced toward his desk, Paul said, "Please close the door."

Closing the door, Peyton noted his dark mood and her heart raced. Sitting carefully in the taupe leather side chair on top of that creepy bearskin rug, Peyton smiled and said, "So, what's going on?"

Paul glowered at her and said, "Well, I don't know, Peyton; you tell me! I'm so sick of all this drama and bullshit. I thought you were an upgrade from Lois, but you have greatly disappointed me."

"I—I—I don't know what you are talking about, sir! What's going on?"

"Really? Well," he huffed while shoving a piece of paper across the desk at her, which cascaded violently to her feet, "explain that."

Somehow, Peyton already knew the secret that paper held. She had been inappropriate. She had been sloppy. She had been wrong, but she didn't regret a thing. Picking the paper up slowly, she read the email exchange between Corbin and her about their beautiful weekend together.

"Where did you get this?"

"Is that the question, Peyton? It doesn't matter where I got it. I can't believe you're involved with a customer service rep. But here's the situation. Corbin is ready to file a sexual harassment suit against you for your inappropriate behavior. You are our human resources professional. You cannot be associating with the employees."

"I have to associate with them," Peyton said. "I'm Human Resources."

"Don't get smart with me. You know what I mean," Paul replied. "I can't have a lawsuit right now. Not after all the mess Lois caused. God knows I'm still doing damage control from that. Not to mention the sale. We can't have things like this escalated to WFS. Anyway, Corbin isn't at fault; you are. You took advantage of him, and he was scared to tell you no because of your position. Peyton, you could have had him fired if you wanted!"

"But it wasn't like that."

"It's over between you and Corbin. If there are no more advances on him, I'm assured he won't sue us. Can you do that? Because if you can't, I will fire you, immediately."

"Yes, sir," Peyton replied. "I will do the right thing. I will have no interactions with Corbin other than those needed professionally. I promise."

"Good," Paul said while spinning his chair to face his computer, effectively dismissing Peyton, who stood up slowly, her world shaken, wondering how things had suddenly turned bad.

Peyton walked down the hallway to her office, closed the glass door, and slumped into her chair. *How could Corbin betray me like this?* she wondered. She thought he was different, but apparently, he was out for himself like every other loser she'd ever met or dated. The blood rising in her cheeks, she looked up to see both Corbin and Spencer peeking over their cubes looking at her. Aggravated and humiliated, she rose from her desk, walked to the windows, and quickly snapped the blinds tightly closed. Returning to the safety of her desk, she felt so used and misunderstood. She'd had only the best intentions with Corbin. Their relationship wasn't work related. How could he think his job would be in jeopardy if he didn't fuck her? Plus, there was that beautiful weekend together where he shared so much of his past. Nothing added up, but despite her logical thoughts, she realized Corbin had betrayed her.

Moments later, her computer dinged the alert for a new message. Opening the message from Corbin, she read, "Hey. You okay? You looked white as a ghost walking down the hall."

Peyton took a deep breath and let the refreshing air pour from her mouth. Moving her mouse to highlight the message, she swiftly clicked "delete" and returned to her talent mapping.

For the rest of the day, she received message after message from Corbin, all of which she deleted.

She intentionally stayed in her office until everyone had headed home. Gathering her things, she finally left her office around seven and headed for the elevators. As she stepped off on the lobby level and walked onto the sidewalk, she was alarmed when her arm was suddenly grasped from behind. Spinning wildly, she saw Corbin, his face tight with tension.

"What the fuck is going on?" he asked. "I've been trying to talk to you all day with no answer. What's the matter?"

"It's over. Paul told me about your potential lawsuit. I can't even believe you'd do this. What the hell, Corbin…. I didn't force you!"

"Peyton, I don't understand. What are you talking about?"

"Oh, you know exactly what I'm talking about. I can't believe you would do this to me. Why, Corbin?" Her beautiful eyes crinkled, close to tears.

"Peyton, I don't know what's going on. Talk to me," Corbin said.

Chuckling and biting her lip, while looking away so hopefully he wouldn't see her tears, she replied, "Oh, screw you, Corbin. You know exactly what's going on. We are done. I can't even believe this is happening and that you did this to me. I never want to see or hear from you again. End of story. Now, kindly let go of my arm."

Corbin dropped her arm, and Peyton swiftly walked away, her beige heels clicking on the pavement. Corbin, noticing her lovely baby blue sheath dress and how it hugged her body perfectly, let out a sigh of longing.

Spencer, standing undetected on the sidewalk, smiled contentedly as he witnessed the exchange.

34

FRANKLIN

Franklin rolled his roaring diesel truck into one-and-a-half parking spots in front of the Waffle Castle, not caring that half of it blocked the handicapped parking spot. Stepping out into the brisk Montana morning, he slammed the door and pushed through the front doors. He headed toward his regular group of morning cronies, already seated at their cluttered round table in the back corner near the door, which supported the two worn and battered swinging saloon doors that concealed the restrooms.

Pulling up a mildly ripped, brown vinyl chair, Franklin waved at Maureen, their server, and said, "Coffee, black, Maureen. Thanks."

Then, to the group, he said, "Morning, boys. How's everyone?"

Chatter began about the upcoming winter, and the forecast that it would be one of the coldest and windiest in Montana history. "I expect we'll have to bring the herd in earlier than usual from the leased land," Hernando, Franklin's ranch foreman, said. "Would hate to have any of them freeze to death."

Over the years, Hernando and Franklin had become close. Hernando's father, an illegal immigrant, had worked for Franklin's father for as long as Franklin could remember. Almost the same age, Franklin and Hernando had been best pals growing up, playing cowboy and Indian in the forest around the ranch, climbing rocks, and swimming in the Sun River. After both Hernando and Franklin's fathers had passed, Franklin immediately promoted Hernando to ranch foreman.

Surprisingly, they continued their friendship into adulthood. Franklin shared more information and valued Hernando's opinion more than anyone else in his life, his wife Emily running a close second.

"Well, you got it different from us little guys," Alvin said. "Ol' Franklin here could lose his whole herd and still have more money than the rest of us combined." He pointed his thumb toward Franklin and rolled his eyes.

"Oh, come on now, Alvin; no need to get ugly about things," Franklin replied. "You know I care more about the cattle than that goddamn oil. I wish Father hadn't let those vultures in."

"Cut the crap, Franklin. You wish you weren't one of the richest men in Montana? That's the bullshit you're going to throw at us this morning?"

Franklin's cheeks flushed with anger and embarrassment. He hated being called out about his wealth, and he loathed the oil men, the massive mansion passed down from his father that his family lived in, and all the politics of being rich. He much preferred riding around on his red dun mare, Blaze, and surveying his ranch while sitting high on a hill watching the grazing cattle sprinkle the valley below. But, also bull-headed and aggressive, he would not tolerate disrespect.

"All right, that's enough of that talk," he said. And because the group knew well the power Franklin Eastman had in Great Falls and beyond, they simply let it go and resumed talking about the weather and each one's personal ailments as most recently diagnosed by Dr. Morrison.

"Anyway, I got the gout," said someone at the table, but Franklin had stopped paying attention to who was saying what. His eyes were focused on the fry cook behind the counter. He had first noticed the tall, black-haired young man when he turned to put a plate of steaming bacon and eggs onto the low counter separating the griddle from the serving area, intentionally designed so patrons could view the entire food preparation and cooking process, not that anyone paid the least attention. He noticed the young man's green eyes as he called "Order up" to Maureen, who blushed and giggled.

Franklin continued to stare at the young man until he looked toward Franklin and their eyes met briefly. The young man held the gaze for a few seconds before quickly turning back to the griddle. Franklin continued to bore holes with his eyes into the back of his blue cotton work uniform as if that would reveal the young man's true identity. Feeling Hernando's eyes upon him broke the trance Franklin had fallen into. As Franklin looked at Hernando, his eyes asked the silent question, which was answered with a soft, almost undetectable, nod of Hernando's weathered and sun-wrinkled face, his eyebrows lifted slightly in confirmation.

Quickly grabbing his phone that had not made a sound, Franklin rose from the table. "Boys, I gotta go. Work emergency. Breakfast is on me," he said, throwing a hundred-dollar bill on the table and quickly rushing from the Waffle Castle. Franklin did not look toward the fry cook, who had mustered the courage to watch him leave. The cook's beautiful green eyes now appeared a deep, empty black.

Franklin slammed the door of his diesel truck and turned it on, comforted by the engine's powerful roar. Quickly speeding from the parking lot, he took a moment to breathe before grabbing his phone and calling Rod. When Rod finally picked up on the fourth ring,

Franklin said. "What the fuck, man? I thought you said I didn't have anything to worry about!"

"Hey, wait; what are you talking about?" Rod asked. "I cover up so much shit for you, you gotta give me more information than that."

"Just left my usual breakfast crowd, and guess who is the fucking fry cook at the Waffle Castle? That fucking little shit bastard you said I didn't need to worry about." Franklin was practically blind with fury.

"Hey, hey, hey, calm down," Rob said. "How do you know it was him? Did he approach you? Ask you for money or anything?"

"No, the little bastard barely looked at me, but it was him. My God, I showed you the picture. He looks just like me."

"Well, maybe you are...." Rod paused because he needed to tread lightly. "You know, maybe taking this more seriously than his intent? If he hasn't approached you or asked for anything, what has he done wrong?"

"What the fuck is he doing in Great Falls? He was in Omaha; why the fuck would he come here if not to mess with me?"

"All right, all right. Let me do some poking around. Don't worry. Trust me."

"Fine. I will expect some better news tomorrow."

"Sure thing, boss. You truly don't have anything to worry about," Rob replied, even though he had no idea whether Franklin had anything to be concerned about or not.

Ending the call, Franklin sped quickly toward the Lucky Draw, his sanctuary when the world became too complicated. Pulling into the horse barn parking lot, he turned off the truck and quickly exited, walking swiftly toward the barn.

Young Joseph, the barn boy, greeted him politely and said, "Hello, sir. Can I help you with something?"

Pushing Joseph aside, Franklin said, "I don't need your help."

Opening Blaze's stall, Franklin was instantly comforted by the horse's soft nose, which quickly nuzzled his arm for a fresh carrot or apple. Rubbing her face and neck, Franklin felt himself calming down. He gently grabbed her halter. "Come on, girl. Let's go for a ride."

Franklin brushed her gently before putting the red-and-black-checkered pad on her well-muscled back, making sure to position it perfectly on her withers to protect her from his custom-made roping saddle that was placed next. Leading her from the barn, Franklin smoothly swung up into the saddle and clicked Blaze into a trot. Upon reaching the grassy field, he slackened the reins and let her run, not caring where she took him. Allowing Blaze to set the pace and slowing when her well-conditioned body started to feel burdened, Franklin found himself in a grassy field and detected Hernando in the distance mending a barbwire fence. Slowing Blaze to a walk, Franklin approached Hernando.

"How's the fence coming?" Franklin asked.

"All right."

"'Bout done?"

"Yep."

Franklin sat calmly on Blaze's back, his hands relaxing over the horn, while he watched Hernando finish up and tuck the tools into the chocolate-brown saddle bags, stained with sweat from years of hard work. As Hernando pulled himself onto the back of his sorrel gelding, he looked at Franklin and said, "So, need to talk?"

"Yep."

They rode in silence to their favorite overlook on the bluff, high above the valley.

Watching the cattle below, Hernando knew to wait for Franklin's lead. They sat for about half an hour before Franklin said, "So, you saw him?"

"I did," Hernando replied.

"No denying it, is there?"

"None that I could see."

"Why do you suppose he's here? They lived in Omaha."

"Well, you told me the mom was dead. Reckon he might just want to get a peek at his dad?"

"Hmm." Franklin sighed.

Hernando waited a few moments. Then he spoke more boldly than he ever had. "Franklin, you are my best friend, and I respect you and your position. I know what's at stake for you. And I will be by your side forever regardless of how you handle this. But you and Emily have no kids. He's done nothing wrong. In our culture, family is the most important thing we have. It doesn't matter if planned or not. Family is family. I think sometimes you have to look in the mirror to know what the right thing is." Then, he quickly pulled the leather reins to the left and nudged the sorrel gelding into a soft lope as he left Franklin alone with his thoughts.

35

CORBIN

I stood mortified on the streets of Atlanta as the beautiful Peyton Alexander stormed off in anger. Burning hot in my memory were the months we had shared following our perfect weekend at her apartment after I delivered Piero's pizza and shared so much about my past. I didn't understand why she had betrayed me, but a recognized voice reminded me, *Oh, silly Corbin, you can trust no one. Remember Sam? He betrayed you, and so will everyone else.*

Feeling my green eyes turn black, I made my way through the crowded street and headed to the closest bar. Tonight, I needed to eat.

Pushing through the door to the newest trendy techno-crap place in Buckhead, the Effervescent, I was immediately annoyed and hated my decision, but man, I was so hungry, my anxiety about Peyton magnifying the desire. Greeted by an attractive young woman wearing barely more than a tube top covering both her boobs and ass, I wanted to vomit, but I continued my ploy.

"Hey," I said, my stomach growling, "How are you tonight?" I could feel my eyes deceptively turning back to sparkling green.

"Hey," came her Southern drawl as she placed her delicate hand on my shoulder before running it seductively down my arm. The giant diamond ring on her index finger indicated she was from a wealthy family.

Oh, such a baby and an amateur, I thought, acknowledging the ease with which I could trap women. Then I remembered my last encounter with Peyton.

"So, want a shot?" I asked while casting my eyes downward and looking innocently through my long, dark eyelashes. "My treat."

"Hell, yeah! Oh, but, I'm with friends, so I probably shouldn't."

"Well, what is your name?" I asked.

"Samantha."

"Well, Samantha," I said, reaching for her hand, "I'm all about friendship, so let me buy all your friends a shot. How many are there?"

The evening progressed with Samantha and her three girl-friends taking shot after shot as they vied for my attention. Having a difficult time deciding who was the most likely candidate to sat-isfy my hunger, the decision was made for me when Samantha pulled me aside and said, "Hey, I'm drunk. Could you take me outta here, please?"

So, I accommodated. My intent for her was confirmed as she quickly went for my zipper the moment she was snug in the pas-senger seat. *Another slutty whore.* I sighed, remembering how I had thought Peyton was so different.

After feeding on Samantha's warm, bloody liver and snipping off her left thumb to add to my collection, I disposed the sloppy remains in a dumpster outside the Home Best store. Realizing I was getting a bit rogue in my cleanup, I scolded myself. *Need to be more careful about this.* I felt less hungry, but still bothered and confused by the earlier Peyton encounter.

As I drove home, my mind wandered and relived the last few months with Peyton. That first weekend with her was completely perfect, well, other than my desire to eat her liver. It was without question the best weekend of my life. I remembered the complete melding of souls as we had sex for the first time. That night, I felt all the wrong in my life vanish only to be replaced with sweet, comforting understanding and acceptance. I forgot about Sam, my horrible mother, the abuse, the neglect, my missing thumb that I still carried, preserved, in my right front pocket. My world became Peyton.

In the following months, that comfort and attraction only magnified. Peyton Alexander was the most beautiful, wonderful, perfect person I had ever encountered. She looked at people without judgment, assessing their true qualities, not the desirable qualities dictated by society. She didn't reject people for their looks, age, or size. She looked through them and found their hearts and souls. I noticed she had made some bold hires at Blast, breaking the traditional stereotypical hiring patterns prevalent in the South. Sweet Peyton was not corrupted by corporate America, and she truly wanted to give people an opportunity.

My mind drifted to a particularly fond moment—the weekend the circus came to town. I was at Peyton's apartment after work, changing out a leaky faucet, when she burst through the front door holding a cheesy flyer with trapeze artists and elephants wearing elaborate head décor. "Oh, my *God*, Corbin! It's the circus! *This* weekend. Please, please, please, will you go with me?"

Laughing genuinely, I replied, "Peyton, what are you—six? The circus?"

Sobering immediately, she said, "Well, Corbin, if you don't go to the circus with me, I shall need you to leave and never return!" She stuck her nose in the air and dramatically turned her back to me. Smiling, I leaped and grabbed the flyer from her hand.

"Oh, my…" I feigned surprise. "You didn't tell me the bearded lady and the tiniest man in the world were going to be there, too. That's a completely different story." I watched with total enjoyment as Peyton looked at me like a little child ready to open her Christmas presents.

"Are you kidding me?" she asked, reaching for the flyer I easily kept from her grasp. "I didn't see that! Now we have to go!"

Doubling over in laughter, I couldn't control myself.

Realization clouded her face. "Oh, Corbin Callahan! You're such a jerk! I love the circus. Seriously."

I composed myself long enough to pull her close to my chest, and after kissing the top of her head, said, "If you want to go to the circus, we will definitely go." Then, lowering my voice to a whisper, "If we're lucky, the three-headed dog will be there, too!" before quickly bolting from the kitchen as Peyton chased me about the apartment, both of us laughing. That evening ended as sweetly and comfortably as every other night I'd shared with Peyton.

I loved her—a love I had never felt before. I let her see the real me, well, almost the real me. I never introduced her to the basement where I carefully kept my treasured thumb dolls, changing the scenes periodically, depending on my mood and stress level. But I had never shared so much with anyone in my life. I trusted Peyton, and I thought she was different, but she wasn't. I suppose that's what I get for believing in people and letting down my walls. Had I learned nothing from Sam? Peyton had turned on me. I had to accept that.

36

PEYTON

Peyton rushed into her apartment and threw off her heels. "What the hell happened today?" she asked. "How could Corbin do this? A lawsuit? A freaking lawsuit?"

Feeling the most betrayed of her life, she grabbed a bottle of Merlot from her bar and poured a full glass. "So, what was the purpose of all this? Was he playing me so he'd have leverage? None of it makes sense."

Quickly swapping her baby blue sheath dress for her T-shirt and boxers, Peyton pulled a long swig from her blue-tinted wine glass before taking a deep breath. *Nothing I can do at this point,* she thought, *other than, move on with my fucking life. Fuck him.*

Trying to rationalize her feelings, she called for Molly and snuggled into the burgundy couch, pulling the soft gray throw over her legs. Gently cuddling Molly and soothed by her purring, Peyton allowed her mind to wander.

The start of this relationship was scary and disturbing, but she thought Corbin was a good person. She was scared when he rejected her in the bedroom, but when he finally conceded, it was the most memorable sex she had ever had. But whatever—that was gone, and it was all a big lie and plot to ruin her. This was the second time she had let a work relationship develop into more. Seems like she would learn, but she truly wanted to trust people. Why did they have to be so evil? She felt she was a good person and treated others kindly, so why did people want to ruin her. But, bigger than that, why did she continue to trust people?

Grabbing her mobile phone, she deleted all of Corbin's texts and emails without responding or reading them. "After all of this, no, I'm done, so done," she said. "You're a freaking nasty human for doing this to me! What did I ever do to you, other than care about you? Fuck!" She screamed loud enough to make Molly jump and stare at her.

"I'm sorry, baby," Peyton said. "Mommy's had a difficult day and I'm so confused. Never trust anyone. Ever." Peyton finished the last of her wine before grabbing the remote, hoping to find a diversion that wouldn't come.

Almost a month after her meeting with Paul, Peyton walked into her office and saw the white, letter-sized paper sitting upside down on her office chair. Flipping it over expecting to see some budget requirements or new policy, Peyton was surprised to read:

Ms. Alexander,

I hereby tender my resignation from Blast. I have found alternate employment, and my last day will be two weeks from today. I have enjoyed my tenure at Blast and only wish the company and my valuable mentors the best in the future. I will do whatever is necessary to train my replacement during my remaining time at Blast to ensure a smooth transition. Please let me know how I can be helpful in this process.

Thank you for all you have done as an outstanding HR professional at Blast.

Sincerely,
Corbin Callahan

Peyton felt her heart skip a beat. While she had been ignoring him at work, as dictated by Paul and because she was crushed, she still took every opportunity to watch him from her glass-fronted office. She enjoyed seeing him laugh with the other teammates. His confident stride. His fashion sense. Occasionally, her mind wandered to what could have been if he'd not done this to her. Sometimes when she saw him laugh at something Spencer had told him, she wondered if that was how he had laughed about her the day after he'd fucked her for the first time, and later, the day he'd fucked her over with Paul. His resignation was the best scenario and she felt relieved that she would never have to see him again. But still, it hurt that he'd done this to her.

Grabbing the resignation letter and heading to Paul's office, Peyton noticed Corbin staring at her, his beautiful green eyes dark and foreboding. *Whatever,* she thought. *I've done nothing wrong. He resigned.*

Marching into Paul's office and placing Corbin's resignation letter on his giant desk, Peyton stated, "Thought you might want to see this."

Barely glancing at the document, Paul smirked. "Well, got you outta hot water, didn't it? Hope you've learned your lesson. This better not happen again."

Flustered beyond words, Peyton felt her face turn bright red as she replied, "Already told you—nothing to worry about."

"Sure," Paul said. "Make sure it doesn't happen again, with anyone." He returned to reading the newspaper.

Who still gets a newspaper? Peyton thought before grabbing the letter and exiting Paul's ridiculously oversized office. *Pompous ass.*

37

FRANKLIN

Franklin had no idea how long he sat upon that Montana bluff and surveyed the sprinkling of Black Angus cattle below. Watching a couple of bulls tussle about, he was reminded of the joke his dad had always recounted when they had sat together on this hill.

"Son," he would start—Franklin had heard the joke at least a thousand times, but he continued to pretend it was brand new up until his father's death several years ago—"so, there was a young bull and an old bull looking down from this bluff at a herd of heifers. The young bull, eager and excited, shouted to the old bull, 'Come on! Let's run down there and screw a heifer.' The old bull just smiled and said, 'Why don't we walk down and screw them all?'"

While Franklin was never sure of the intended life lesson from that story, he personally thought the moral was to "screw them all." He'd done that pretty much his whole life. He was privileged and could get away with things other people couldn't. It wasn't that he was unaware, but he didn't care. It wasn't his fault he was richer than many. It wasn't his fault others were poorer. It was the cards that had been dealt. There was no emotion assigned to that life designation.

Taking a deep breath, Franklin let his mind wander back to Jessica. She had been a beautiful woman. He supposed now, reflecting back so many years, she actually had been good to him. She was always accommodating and took care of him, placing his needs before hers. She paid attention to whether or not he needed another beer and would retrieve a cold one without being asked. Deep in his heart, he knew she hadn't been lying about the baby being his—not that he'd admit that to anyone, not even Hernando. He had been young, like her, and it wasn't something he could deal with, so he pulled out the Eastman intimidation and got away from her. He couldn't be associated with someone like Jessica. She came from a poor family, only able to go to college because of a scholarship. She was rough, lacked manners, and certainly had lived a sheltered life. He'd done the right thing, he concluded, even though that tiny inner voice whispered, *Or, were you too afraid to tell your dad you knocked up a college girl?*

When he'd first gotten the letter from Corbin, Franklin had sent Rod to Omaha to investigate. After tens of thousands of dollars in fees paid to Rod, all Franklin received were some pictures of the kid going to school and walking into some shitty little diner called the Quick Pick. He had received only that one letter. Unlike Jessica, that kid did not send him letter after letter only for them to be returned unanswered. It had been several years between the letter and Corbin's appearance in Great Falls. Maybe Hernando was right; he usually was, after all. If Corbin wanted to cause trouble for Franklin, he could have already done so many times. An easy and extremely alarming act would have been simply to knock on Franklin's front door and announce to Emily that he was the long-lost illegitimate son. All he had done was write one letter and take a job as a fry cook in Great Falls.

Hell, he was born here, Franklin thought. *It's not necessarily me that has brought him back.*

Acknowledging the urge as it flowed through his body, Franklin spun Blaze toward home and urged her gently into a strong gallop. Tonight, he needed to feed.

As Franklin stepped from the granite-covered walk-in shower and grabbed the plush, light-gray towel to dry himself, he remembered the first time his father had taken him deer hunting. He had only been about eight years old on that first male bonding outing to kill an animal. Getting up in the dark and quickly dressing in warm clothes and snow boots, they had grabbed fried egg sandwiches the maid had prepared and headed toward the four wheelers, Franklin's rifle slung across his small back. Sitting high in the camo deer stand, Franklin's eight-year-old mind soon became restless, and he whined to his father, "Come on, Father; how long do we have to sit out here? It's freezing, and we haven't seen a single deer."

"Patience, son; patience," his father had replied. "And keep your voice down or we will never see one."

"But, Father!"

"Shh." His father averted his eyes to the clearing below. A beautiful tan doe was slowly making her way into the clearing. Seeing the deer, Franklin grabbed his rifle and took his stance. His father quickly grabbed his arm and shook his head to indicate the action was premature; his brows furrowed in annoyance at young Franklin's eagerness. "I'll tell you when," he whispered.

Franklin waited for what seemed hours, constantly looking at his father for confirmation. Finally, when the deer was in the optimal position, his father put his hand on Franklin's back and gave him the acknowledging nod. Franklin perfected his pose, lined up the sights on the doe, and slowly squeezed the trigger, exactly as his father had taught him in their hours of shooting lessons at the range.

Franklin saw the deer jump and then fall instantly. His first kill! Spinning toward his father, he beamed with pride. "I got it! I got it!"

His father let out a hearty belly roar—one of the few times Franklin ever saw his father laugh—and said, "Yes, son, you did it perfectly! Now let's go get it."

Climbing down the tree stand's metal ladder, Franklin couldn't wait to take his trophy home. Approaching the deer, he detected a unique smell of copper and felt an animalistic urge he didn't understand as he watched her blood oozing slowly onto the frozen Montana ground. It was, oh, so beautifully red. Franklin felt an urge to wrench out her insides and cover his face with her warm, bloody organs. He didn't understand the desire, but he was overcome, nonetheless.

Sensing the inherent gene had successfully been passed down from generation to generation, Franklin's father stepped in slowly, handing him the Bowie knife made from a deer antler, and said, "It's okay, Franklin. It's what we do."

Grabbing the Bowie knife quickly and losing all control of himself, Franklin slit the deer and watched as her beautiful welcoming intestines and organs flowed in front of him like a holiday feast. Feeling the heat rising from the still palpitating organs, Franklin quickly grabbed the liver and pushed it solidly into his watering mouth. The exhilarating euphoria poured over him as he gobbled and chewed, trying to satisfy his hunger.

38

SPENCER

Spencer sat in his purple cubicle working on an internet usage report requested by an insignificant line manager wanting to fire an equally insignificant human. He was annoyed that the apparent breakup of Peyton and Corbin had not resulted in his renewed friendship with Corbin. Corbin came to work, sat in his cubicle, and rarely ventured forth. Spencer had tried on many occasions to get back into his good graces, but he was shot down each time. He didn't understand what he had done to cause this riff in their relationship. He had noticed that Peyton kept to herself more as well, but that was what an HR leader should do. He was always annoyed by her prancing around the office in her snug dresses and high heels, acting as though she were better than everyone else.

Peyton had been at Blast for several months before Spencer realized his anger toward her was based on a completely different emotion. One evening, sitting in his parents' basement where he lived after his failed marriage to Olivia, Spencer slammed another Mountain Dew, noting it was his twelfth of the day, and said, "Man, that bitch is hot." At that moment, Spencer understood his anger toward Peyton and his desire for her failure. She rarely gave him the time of day at work, focusing only on the handsome Corbin. "Yeah,

yeah, yeah, we all know Corbin is the shit. He's funny, and he helps find homes for dumb dogs no one wants, and he overdresses at work, and we get it; we're all about Corbin. But what about Spencer? Why won't anyone give me a chance?"

His cheeks flushed as he recalled the Olivia disaster. His second marriage had ended worse, if that were even possible. He had met Donna at a local bookstore where she worked and devoted her Saturdays to reading books to annoying and loud, unappreciative children. Spencer never cared much for children, which was probably good since he'd likely never procreate. But Donna had caught his eye as he sat in the store, searching porn sites on his tablet because the store had free Wi-Fi. Her face wasn't all that attractive, with her broad forehead and mousey brown hair pulled into a high ponytail on top of her head, and her mouth was unusually large, extending well beyond the ending of her eyebrows if you were to draw a vertical line, but wow, her boobs were huge! The day he first saw her, she was wearing a thin-strapped, linen summer dress, and he instantly felt his crotch twitch as he gazed upon her. When she bent over to place Dr. Seuss' *The Cat in the Hat* on a lower shelf, he had to look away to control himself.

He began the acquisition of Donna slowly and patiently. He wasn't a great catch, but she wasn't either. Perhaps this was the perfect match. His first move was to ask her for help finding books about network connectivity, communication, operations, and management of an enterprise network because he was researching a project for work. He wasn't, but he thought it sounded impressive. He laughed inwardly at his request because he could find whatever he needed on the internet, but it was a great first step.

He continued to seek Donna's assistance daily. Finally mustering the courage to reveal his true intent, he stammered as he tried to look into her ugly face rather than at her beautiful breasts. "Hey, so, um." He felt his eyes starting to dart back and forth quickly, a reflex he could not control when nervous or angry. "I was wondering if maybe, well, would you consider getting a coffee, or dinner, or something with me one day? I'll pay."

Donna looked up from her computer, where she had been focused on locating a certain title for another customer. Opening her gaping slit of a mouth to smile, she revealed a crooked line of shark teeth, some white, some brown, some an odd color of yellow, and replied, "Well, sure, honey. I was wondering when you would finally get up the courage to ask! When and where?"

Spencer was elated. His eyes immediately stopped twitching and he said, "Well, when do you get off?"

Giggling loudly and inappropriately, she replied, "Whenever I want to," insinuating another meaning that made her snort. "But my work ends at 4:30 today."

They were married less than a month later, a decision Spencer made after the first time he penetrated her. Although he would never admit it to anyone, especially not Corbin, he rarely had sex, and as expected, he finished too abruptly.

"Oh, don't worry about it." Donna rolled over and fell asleep quickly, confirmed by her throaty snores.

Spencer lay on his back and smiled at the spackled ceiling of her cheap apartment near Euclid Avenue in the trendy and Gothic part of Atlanta.

Things were finally looking up—well, until a couple of months into their marriage when Donna was fired. Spencer was concerned, but she reassured him she would get another job. Justifying her position, she said, "Well, my manager made a move on me and I told him to go to hell; that's why I was fired."

Soothing her, Spencer held her close and said, "Oh, don't worry. I make enough money to support us. I won't tolerate anyone abusing you."

Donna grinned into his chest because she had fucked her manager, which had resulted in her termination. She quickly worked Spencer to obtain access to his checking and savings accounts. After draining both accounts dry, she left him a handwritten note, scrawled on the back of a receipt from the local Walmart. "Thanks for the short ride. I'm out. Found a biker who loves me. See ya. Divorce papers will soon follow."

And they did. Spencer, crushed and taken advantage of yet again, signed them quickly and without much thought. *Why can't I get this right?* he wondered.

Breaking Spencer's train of thought, Corbin appeared in his cubicle. "Hey, man," Corbin said, "just wanted to let you know I've resigned."

Spencer snapped abruptly around. "What? Why?"

"Ah, gotta go," Corbin replied. "You know, things have been tense around here." He nodded toward Peyton's office.

"Well, yeah, I knew that wouldn't end well for you," Spencer replied. "But you wouldn't listen to me."

"I know," Corbin said, "but I needed to give it a shot. But whatever; I'm not worried about it. Fuck her. I'll find a better job somewhere other than Blast. Well, anyway, you're a solid dude. You were a good friend to me. So, thanks."

"Oh, sure, man; no problem," Spencer replied, his eyes darting. "Glad to have known you. Let's stay in touch," he said, knowing his words fell on deaf ears.

As Corbin exited his cubicle, Spencer allowed his face to break into a wide grin. Finally, Corbin was out of the way, and Peyton was fair game. Maybe, for the first time in his life, he'd caught a break. Again, his crotch twitched in anticipation.

39

PEYTON

As Peyton clamped the two-hole punch into the top of Corbin's resignation letter before sliding it gently onto the two metal clasps at the top of his personnel file, she smiled with unemotional finality. He would no longer be a problem in her life. She had corporate aspirations and did not need a silly lawsuit destroying her professional career. She had made an error of fire-able magnitude, so she was lucky to still have her job. Corbin's resignation closed the file on that matter. Quickly slamming the gray folder shut, she flipped around in her black leather office chair to enter his termination of employment into the system.

Fuck him, kept resonating through her mind. *Let someone ask me for a recommendation. Burn those bridges, baby; burn them all.* She laughed.

The real emotion she felt was betrayal and remorse that his relationship with her was based only on his desire to ruin her career, but she quickly pushed those emotions down deep and relied on anger. Raised Catholic in a family that never talked about feelings, she had perfected the craft of deeply burying her emotions. "Better to hide it than to cause problems for others," her mother had told her repeatedly.

Suddenly finding herself reliving a vivid childhood memory, Peyton felt the shame of the event. She had been in the car with Stella, her mother, on the way to the Wash It Here Laundry Mat because their washer and dryer at home were temporarily inoperable while the laundry room's plumbing was being reworked. They were driving down the dirt road to town, past the mud hole where the battered old minivan frequently got stuck.

Peyton had her little purse shaped like a cat's head with her. It bore googly eyes on top of its furry pink exterior. Pulling out a tiny pad of paper and a three-inch pencil with no eraser, Peyton scribbled "I love you," and presented it proudly to her mother.

Snatching the note quickly and crumpling it upon reading, her mother threw the note out the open car window. "You have to stop this shit!" she said. "People are going to get the wrong idea if they hear you tell me you love me."

Peyton never understood what was so wrong with telling her mother she loved her. She had gathered that it was shameful for some reason to love another female, but she hadn't known your mother was included. Apparently, emotions of any kind were simply unacceptable. From that moment, Peyton knew she could never allow her emotions to get the best of her. But then she had let it all slide for Corbin. How could she have been so naïve? The worst part was her realization that he was using her. She had been made a fool for caring about another person.

Slamming Corbin's file into the large, beige, metal filing cabinet, Peyton cursed silently. *Jesus, can't we upgrade to cloud storage?* She secretly hoped the closing of the cabinet would close her feelings for Corbin.

I have to move on, she told herself. *I can't trust anyone, and this is proof. Fuck him.*

She glanced up to notice Spencer smiling into her glass-fronted office, his weird eyes darting quickly back and forth. She softly raised her delicate right arm and delivered the queen's cupped wave. He darted below his purple cubicle wall, clearly embarrassed that she had caught him looking.

Giggling, Peyton returned to her tidy desk and began replying to ridiculous emails about the upcoming open enrollment period for employee benefits for Blast colleagues.

Later, at home with a bottle of cabernet sauvignon and Molly curled peacefully in her lap, she allowed her busy mind to let go and consider all the events that had occurred. Yes, she had been betrayed. It was wrong on her part. She also needed to take action, in a discreet manner, to avenge the situation. Could flirting with Spencer be a conduit to such rectification? She remembered the first day she had caught him peering at her from his cubicle. Maybe this was the right course of action. And she wouldn't even have to sleep with him to get the revenge her heart desired. Letting him believe it was possible would be enough.

Grabbing her phone, she scrolled through her contacts. She had saved Spencer's number when he had given it to her in case she needed technical support setting up her VPN access at home. After a couple of searches, she successfully found his number saved as *IT Guy from Blast*.

Smiling, either from the idea or the wine, she sent Spencer a text, her left eyebrow twitching upward, holding a high arch, a skill she had taught herself at fifteen when she realized it was interpreted as intimidating and condescending. "Hey, it's Peyton. Sorry things at work have been so crazy."

Spencer's quick reply reassured her she was making the right decision. *Wow, this is going to be so easy.* She chuckled as she replied to Spencer's eager text with, "Sure, let's get coffee sometime. Maybe we can talk about what's going on at work."

Smiling at his eagerness, Peyton knew Spencer would brag, and probably embellish, to Corbin. This was going to be perfect.

She met Spencer after work the following Thursday at The Coffee Bean, not far from Blast. She strolled confidently through the front door, a little bell strapped to the door jingling to announce her entrance. She spotted Spencer sitting in the far corner, coffee already in hand, little beads of nervous perspiration popping out on his bare forehead that seemed to get larger every time she saw him as his thinning hairline receded farther and farther toward the top of his head. Peyton approached the small table and said, "Oh, I'm going to order. Can I get you anything?"

"No, I'm good," he replied, his eyes moving faster than she had ever imagined possible.

Returning to the table with an ice-cold diet soda—she couldn't tolerate coffee after 10 a.m.—Peyton sat down, crossed her lovely legs, and asked, "So, how was your day?"

The next thirty minutes were quite possibly the most painful moments of her life. As Spencer babbled on and on about his "accomplishments," Peyton decided she felt a little sorry for the guy. *The guy builds toy trains and thinks it's cool, but maybe no one has given him a chance.*

Sucking the last of her drink from the cup, she stood up and excused herself. "Hey, I'm sorry, but I need to do some reports for Paul tonight. I better get going, but thanks. Have a great evening."

Walking back toward the office, she wondered, *Can I do this? It would be sweet revenge, but man, this is going to be difficult.*

40

FRANKLIN

After wiping his bloody mouth boldly across his white dress shirt sleeve, Franklin looked up from devouring the insides of an unsuspecting patron of the Lone Ranger Bar in Helena, Montana. She had been such an easy pick up, robbing Franklin of the thrill of the hunt, but he was so hungry he didn't care. He acknowledged becoming reckless, but he was comforted because he was protected in so many counties, including Lewis and Clark County. He could leverage his father's success at any given moment. Without it, he would have been in prison years ago. He figured his luck would eventually run out, but he could not help himself. He was doing better, after all. He hadn't fed on human organs in more than five years, relying on deer or antelope from the ranch to keep him somewhat satisfied. While he did enjoy the warm bloody liver of a freshly shot doe, it was nothing compared to the real thing. One slip up here and there couldn't be helped; plus, he had Hernando to clean up and take care of things.

Franklin fondly remembered his first, Anna Beth, whom he had met well before he was married. She was a beautiful, charming young lady whom Franklin had actually courted for a few months before she trusted him enough for him to act. He would never forget her.

She tasted better than anything he'd ever had, and all that followed paled in comparison to her sweet, warm taste.

After he was done eating Anna Beth, he'd loaded her remains in the back of his old ranch truck. After knocking on the bunk-house door where Hernando lived, he announced to the bleary-eyed Mexican who opened the door, "Hey, I need you to take care of something."

"Sure, boss," was the quick reply. "Let me get dressed. Be right out."

Two minutes later, approaching the truck bed, Hernando was expecting a sick calf or anything other than the beautiful Anna Beth bleeding from the stomach. Leaping back in surprise and shock, Hernando turned to Franklin. "What the *fuck*!" Hernando never cussed.

Overcome by the situation's uniqueness, Franklin started laughing uncontrollably. Infuriated, Hernando's emotions continued to escalate. "Fuck, man, this isn't funny!"

"I know, I know," said Franklin, giggling. "I know it's not funny, but God damn, your reaction was priceless." Gasping for air, Franklin added, "Hey, look; I'm sorry."

"What? Are you telling me this isn't a joke? Is that girl dead? What the hell happened to her?"

Controlling his hysteria, Franklin answered, "Well, it's kind of complicated…but I need you to take care of this. Now."

"How…wha…Franklin? This is a dead girl. Did you do this?"

"Hey, let's don't get caught up in the details. It needs to go away. You got this, right?"

Hernando pulled his fingers through his sleek black hair in frus-tration before saying, "Yeah, boss. That's how things work around here. I'll do my best, but I can't make any promises."

Franklin felt his chest expand like a proud peacock as he allowed his body to reach full stature, towering over Hernando. "No, this isn't a request. Make it so."

Hernando pursed his lips into a tight, fake grin and replied, "Yes, boss," before throwing up his hands and walking slightly away. He stopped to place his hand on his left hip, waiting for Franklin to leave.

"Good deal, man," said Franklin. "I appreciate it, and I'm gonna need to borrow your truck. Cool?"

"Sure."

That had been his first, and now Franklin had another one for Hernando to take care of. Franklin never knew what Hernando did, nor did he care. He was glad that no police or detectives came calling; that's all that mattered to him. Over the years, the frequency declined; only in extremely stressful situations did he feel the overwhelming desire to feed. But Hernando was always an efficient cleanup man.

As the headlights reflected against the bunkhouse windows, Hernando appeared without Franklin even knocking. As Franklin exited the truck, Hernando said, "Come on, man? Again?"

"What?" was the quick reply. "It's been years."

"You are getting sloppy. I can only do so much. Did you wear your rich person mask at least?"

Franklin chuckled. It annoyed Hernando that he'd had a Hollywood designer create a realistic Playtex mask that completely altered his appearance. When Franklin put it on and added the heavy makeup to cover the lines, he felt invisible. "I did. You don't need to worry."

"You need to worry," Hernando replied. "Not because of me, but there are still so many risks! Your truck, your credit card, your reputation. Think about it."

"Oh, don't worry," Franklin said. "I'm gonna grab a shower inside, and then I'll need to borrow your truck."

Hernando sighed as he watched Franklin disappear into the bunkhouse. Shaking his head in disgust, Hernando walked toward the barn to get the shovel.

As Franklin headed home in Hernando's truck, he remembered he had not called Emily earlier to let her know he would be home late. He pulled up to the house and was relieved all the lights were off. Hopeful Emily was asleep, he quietly opened the front door and stepped in. Pausing for a moment for his eyes to adjust to the darkness, he made his way toward the stairs. Light flooded the room and Emily said, "Where have you been?"

Spinning quickly around to face her, Franklin said, "Oh, hi. I thought you would be asleep."

"Where have you been, Franklin?"

"I'm sorry, Emily. I forgot to call you, but I had some things I needed to take care of tonight after I left the office. It was a tough day."

"I don't care. I asked where you have been, and I'd like an answer please."

"Hernando and I went hunting coyotes. It's a release for me when I've had a particularly bad day."

"I see. When you go hunting and kill a coyote, do you gather the carcasses?"

"No. Why would I do that?"

"Just curious. Trying to figure out the routine of my husband when he is so stressed that he can't even let his wife know what he's up to."

"Emily, l said I was sorry. Can we let this go?"

"No, Franklin. You can answer my questions. So you don't gather the carcasses. Do you touch them? Do you shoot them or kill them with your bare hands? A knife perhaps?"

Not sure where this line of questioning was going, Franklin knew he had to answer. "We shoot them with our rifles."

"So you don't touch them? Ever?"

"No, Emily. Where is this going?"

"Well, dear Franklin, I'm trying to figure out how you got blood on your shirt if you never touched them."

Franklin looked down at the smear of blood on his shirt-sleeve. Damn, he hadn't noticed it before and felt embarrassed for over-looking such a detail. Laughing in an attempt to lighten the mood, he said, "That isn't blood. We grilled some burgers, and I spilled a bottle of ketchup on my shirt. Damn it, Emily, quit being so paranoid. I forgot to call you; that's it. Nothing you need to worry about. Now, I'm going to bed."

Franklin made it to the fourth step before he heard the familiar sound a shotgun makes when a shell is racked into the chamber. Turning slowly, he stared at Emily as she confidently aimed a 20-gauge shotgun directly at his chest. "You aren't going to bed yet. You are going to tell me the truth or I will shoot you. Oh, I won't kill you, but I'll hurt you. Then I'll call the cops and tell them I accidently shot you because I thought you were an intruder. It is four in the morning, after all."

"Emily, please. This is ridiculous. Put the gun down and let's go to bed."

"Franklin, your time is running out. I was out looking for you and saw headlights at the bunkhouse. I saw what was in your truck when you went inside. Now, you can grab a drink if you like, but this shotgun will be aimed at you until you tell me what is going on. All of it."

41

CORBIN

I stalked the beautiful Peyton Alexander. While she had betrayed me, I was obsessed with her and her liver. If Peyton were like all the others—and she was proving that to be the case—at least I could enjoy that delicious liver.

Every morning, I woke early, donning my running clothes, including a hooded sweatshirt. It was impossible for me to run from my house to her apartment and then to Blast. I compromised and parked in a deserted lot a few blocks from the Blast parking garage. I waited anxiously on the corner until Peyton's gray 4Runner appeared in the stop-and-go traffic. She never saw me, and I was comforted because I knew she was answering emails when traffic came to a halt.

"Peyton," I had told her as we cuddled on the couch one night as she replied to email after email. "Baby, you need time for you. Work is for work. Sometimes, you have to let go."

"Oh, Corbin, you don't understand," Peyton had replied. "Paul expects me to answer emails within two hours. I know he's a dick, but that's what I'm under. You don't understand what my role entails."

"Well," I had said, slightly annoyed by the condescending explanation because I clearly knew she could stand up for herself, "why do you give a shit what Paul wants? You are the most remarkable person I have ever met. Fuck Paul. You could go anywhere and do anything. You don't have to put up with this shit, Peyton."

Smiling the smile that meant "Stop talking," she replied, "It's what I have to do, Corbin. It is what it is—you don't understand."

Now I was happy about her email addiction; it allowed me to follow her without being noticed. Later that afternoon, I watched in horror as she entered the Coffee Bean to meet Spencer.

Spencer? My mind reeled. *Seriously, she is meeting Spencer?* I felt the betrayal wash over me and knew my eyes were black, not understanding what was happening before me. My beautiful Peyton couldn't stoop as low as Spencer. That was worse than her unexplained behavior at Blast.

As I stood across the street, gazing through the glass front of a tiny shop, I recognized Peyton's power stride as she approached the table where Spencer sat almost quivering in her wake. As she moved to the counter, swaying her beautiful hips from side to side—a practiced movement she only performed when seeking attention—it felt as though a knife had sliced through my heart. An even more crushing blow was noticing Spencer's excited gaze as he watched her walk away. *Oh, my God, is he going to cum on himself?* Thankfully, he was able to control himself, but I was still bothered by the power stride. What was she trying to do? Hadn't she hurt me enough?

To have a better view, I left the shop and tucked myself into an abandoned brick doorway. From this new vantage point, I could see everything happening in the Coffee Bean. Peyton returned from the counter holding a cup that contained Diet Coke since she never drank coffee after 10:00 a.m. Sliding the chair out herself, because Spencer lacked the social politeness to stand and slide it out for her, Peyton sipped her soda and smiled at Spencer, who was sweating profusely and staring at the napkin dispenser instead of making eye contact.

My blood pressure surged through my temples, and my heartbeat sounded like an African drum calling the hunters in from the safari after a day of tiger hunting. Boom, boom, boom—the sound seemed to resonate off the dirty brick entrance covered with old chewed gum stuck in the stained mortar. Peyton tossed her head gently back and let out a hearty laugh; I could hear her melodic laughter above the drums beating, even though a busy Atlanta street separated us. *What could Spencer have said to evoke a moment of true laughter from Peyton?* I wondered, becoming more and more irate.

When I witnessed Peyton reaching her hand out to lightly touch Spencer on the arm, I couldn't take it anymore. I pushed violently from the abandoned doorway, almost crashing into a busy gentleman in an Armani suit speaking dramatically into his Blue Tooth. Accepting the aggressive finger he thrust at me, I pulled my hood tightly down around my face and bolted toward my car. I had to get out of here. I had to release. I couldn't take her being with another man—especially the man who used to be my best friend. I had to get her back, no matter the cost. She had to be mine…and she would be, I resolved, while slamming into the hood of my parked car. Panting and sweating, I circled my Maxima a few times before sliding behind the wheel and starting the ignition. I needed to retreat to my basement to devise my plan.

42

SPENCER

Spencer watched as Peyton exited the coffee shop. He wasn't sure if it had gone well or badly. His raging hard-on hadn't been pleasant to deal with, but he couldn't help himself. He was embarrassed that he couldn't even stand, but he couldn't let her see that. Maybe he'd text her later and see what might happen. He wasn't as nice-looking as Corbin, but he was a decent guy. Well, at least that's what he tried to tell himself.

Stop thinking like that, Spencer! he reprimanded himself. *Old hag Lois Hutchinson deserved to be fired. You did the company a favor.*

He had realized early in the conversation that Peyton wanted information. He told her all the right stuff—that Corbin had been uncomfortable with their relationship and hadn't known know how to end it since she was an executive. He'd gone to Paul for help, and Paul had assured him he would handle it, but it was so uncomfortable around the office that he had to resign. "We're lucky he didn't sue us for sexual harassment or a hostile work environment," Spencer had said. "He could have won both the way you two were carrying on."

It was all lies, but Peyton had no idea. Spencer had wanted to ruin their relationship mostly because Corbin deserved better than her, but also because he wouldn't mind having a shot at her. Now that he had facilitated the breakup, there was no way he would give her any information to the contrary. He did regret that Corbin's friendship had not been renewed since his departure from Blast, but he was confident that time would heal that wound.

Pushing away from the table, he headed home. He needed to do some digging on Peyton and see if he could find anything useful. Plus, he needed to text her tonight. *Oh, why wait? I'll do it now*, he reconsidered.

Stopping midstream on the sidewalk, he texted Peyton. "Hey, I had a great time. Can we do it again soon?"

He waited a few minutes for a reply before continuing his journey to his parents' basement, fondly referred to by him as his pad.

By 8:45 p.m., he had still not received a reply from Peyton. Growing angrier and angrier at her delay even to send him a polite reply, he resumed his search of her emails since his Google searches had returned nothing worthwhile.

Ignoring her work-related emails, Spencer's eye's landed on one from Stella8675309@gmail.com. Clicking open the email exchange, Spencer's attention piqued.

Stella: Hi, Peyton. I just ran into that handsome Mark Masters in the Red Owl yesterday. You remember him? Cecelia's older brother. He was always such a nice young man. He told me he recently finished dental school and is starting his own practice. You should have never ended things with him.

Peyton: Oh, Mother. Of course, I remember him. And it wasn't me who ended it. Remember, he did after all the stuff that happened with Cecelia.

Stella: Peyton, why do you have to be so dramatic? That was a difficult time for everyone, not just you. Anyway, do you want me to try to get his number for you?

Peyton: No, I don't. I don't even live there. And, honestly, I don't even like thinking about that anymore.

Stella: Okay, I'll tell him that you said hi and regret that things didn't work out between you two. I have to go now. It's Bunko night, and I'm hosting. Bye.

There was no reply from Peyton. Spencer's beady eyes gleamed. Even though he had no idea what had transpired with Cecelia, it was certainly worth investigating. Starting with a simple Google search of her name, Spencer launched his investigation. Peyton was a total bitch. She couldn't even text him back a polite reply. He would search high and low, and he would find some dirt on Peyton Alexander.

It had taken several weeks, but Spencer was diligent. He learned from Cecelia's social media page that she had once worked at Protect Your Home, a telemarketing firm that provided home warranties and maintenance services to homeowners. But there had been no tie to Peyton. Tonight, he had finally found Peyton's resume. He had searched all the HR records from Blast to no avail. After searching through Paul's files, he had found it. Peyton had also worked at Protect Your Home before coming to Blast.

I wonder if something happened there? He had called directory assistance for Mitchell, South Dakota, but there was no listing for Cecelia Masters or Mark Masters. That wasn't odd to Spencer, though, because few people still had land lines. Reviewing the "Contact us" tab of the Protect Your Home website, Spencer found a task for the following day.

Arriving early for work, then annoyed because of the time difference between Georgia and South Dakota, Spencer busied himself with mundane work until, finally, it was 9:00 a.m. in Mitchell. Grabbing a pen and paper, Spencer went into the conference room and shut the door. Quickly dialing the number to Protect Your Home, Spencer was pleased the call was answered on the third ring, "Protect Your Home. How can I help you?"

"I need to speak to someone in Human Resources, please," Spencer said.

"Well, we are a small company. We don't really have a Human Resources Department," came the reply.

Sighing at their ignorance, Spencer asked, "What about the office manager? Someone who could tell me about a former employee?"

"Oh, sure; that'd be Dale. Hold, please." Typical elevator music followed.

Spencer noticed his hands were shaking with excitement. This was going to be a great day. Peyton had never replied to his text. This was definitely the best move for him to make.

"It's Dale," finally resounded in Spencer's ear.

"Yes, sir; thank you for taking my call. This is Investigator Tomley with the Internal Revenue Service. I'm hoping you can help me. I'm trying to track down one, uh, hold on, where did I put that file? Oh, here it is, Cecelia Masters. Our records indicate she worked for you for a time. Is that true?"

"Yeah, she worked here a while back. What's this about?"

"Well, it has to do with a tax situation. I can't go into much detail. I'm sure you understand. Privacy laws. At any rate, would you be able to share with me her last known contact information?"

"Hang on; let me see where her file is," Dale replied, then said, "Susan" before the music filled Spencer's ear.

After a long pause, Dale picked back up. "Okay, looks like I have her phone number and her email address from her resume before she was hired. I don't know if either are still good, but I'll give them to you."

"That would be wonderful. I and the IRS appreciate your assistance," Spencer said before jotting down the information provided.

"Yes!" Spencer screamed after completing the call. "This has got to be something good!"

Dialing the phone number resulted in, "I'm sorry; that number could not be completed as dialed. Please check the number and dial again."

Damn, Spencer thought. *My only hope is the email address.*

Leaving the conference room and returning to his purple cubicle, he typed, "Hi, Cecelia. You don't know me, but I mean you no harm. I want to talk to you about Peyton Alexander. Please reply. It's important."

After pressing send, Spencer stared at his screen, hoping for an immediate reply that did not come.

43

CORBIN

After resigning from Blast, I'm not going to lie, I took some time for me. Well, it wasn't by choice. Heavy depression and anger caused me to take to the hermit lifestyle for a couple of weeks. I think it was the eleventh day I caught a glimpse of myself in the mirror. It was quite shocking—that fuzzy, dirty, bleary-eyed man who looked back at me. Vowing at that moment to change things, I hopped in the shower to cleanse my body of the dirty film, some of it resembling Cheetos residue, that covered my body.

After a shower and a nice shave, I decided to go out for breakfast. Oh, wait; I guess it was lunch, and work on my resume. I still had a lot of Sam's money. I was frugal with it, and tried to use it only for emergencies. I had been unemployed for a while now, so getting out of the house was an emergency.

Heading to a nearby coffee shop with free Wi-Fi, I nabbed a quiet corner table and opened my email to see if anything important had happened during my stay in my hermitage. Disappointed, I started the daunting task of updating my resume. Going from my resume to job boards, I spent several hours and was about to leave when a guy I knew from Fit Bodies, Vince Hilton, walked in and approached the counter. While waiting for his caramel macchiato, he noticed me in the corner.

"Hey, man," he said. "How's it going? Haven't seen you in a while."

"Yeah, I haven't been to the gym lately. You know how those things go."

"What you doing at the coffee shop in the middle of the day? Get fired?" Vince laughed.

"Well, not fired, but I did resign," I said, noting Vince's surprise and slight embarrassment.

"Oh, man, I'm sorry; you know I was kidding around."

"Hey, it's cool. Just here working on my resume. Had to get out of the house or I'd get sucked into Netflix and not do anything." I laughed.

"I hear ya," Vince said. "So, you have any leads on a job?"

"No, not a single one. I just started looking today, though. I don't know what I'm looking for. All I know is I do not want to be a telephonic customer service rep."

"What about sales?" Vince asked. "You ever think about a career in sales?"

"Hadn't thought about it," I said. "But isn't that pretty risky as far as income goes?"

"Most places, yes, but not at my dealership. We cover your salary until you know what you're doing. By the time you go on commission, you're already killing it in sales."

"Really? Dealership?"

"Now, don't laugh. I know it's not something you're going to think is a great opportunity, but it is. You have unlimited income potential. I was making over six figures after just two years in sales. Now, I own Hilton Mercedes."

"You want me to be a car salesman?" I asked incredulously.

"Ha, ha…no, not a car salesman. A seller of dreams. Brand new, overpriced Mercedes dreams." Pulling his business card from his coat pocket, he handed it to me. "Give it some thought. If you're interested in talking more, let me know. I gotta run. Hope to hear from you. I think you'd be great at it."

"Hey, thanks, man. I'll probably give you a call."

Sitting back down at my table, I looked up Hilton Mercedes Benz. Damn nice vehicles.

44

SPENCER

It had been days since Spencer had emailed Cecelia. The anticipation of her reply was overwhelming for him. He couldn't focus on work. Thankfully, his boss knew absolutely nothing about what he was supposed to be doing, so he could skirt by as much as necessary. He couldn't focus. Cecelia held the key to ruining Peyton's life. He wasn't sure why or what, but he had that feeling.

He'd returned from the breakroom eating a chocolate éclair. Last thing he needed, but whatever. It looked delicious and did not disappoint. Wiping some cream filling from his upper lip with his sausage-like finger, Spencer almost choked to see an email from CeceliaJM18@hotmail.com, the email address Dale had given so willingly to Inspector Tomley.

Shoving the remaining bit of éclair into his mouth, Spencer eagerly clicked on the email to read, "Who are you and what do you want with me?"

Typing quickly, Spencer replied, "I'm a friend to you. I only want to talk about what happened with you and Peyton Alexander at Protect Your Home. Please, I mean you no harm." He was going out on a limb by his assumptions, but it was the only shot he had.

Almost immediately, the reply came, much to Spencer's delight, "She's a bitch and I hate her. What else do you need to know? She fucking ruined my life."

Spencer was giddy with excitement. He still didn't know what had happened, but this was going to be fun. Replying, he typed, "I hate her, too. Can we talk?"

"Sure. Why not?" And she provided her number.

Dashing into the conference room, Spencer called the number. After a few rings, he heard "Hello."

"Well, hello, Cecelia," he said. "I'm so excited to talk to you."

45

PEYTON

Things at work had been fine for Peyton. She kept long hours, which helped ease her mind from Corbin. She had been promoted to Vice President of Human Resources, but the title felt empty and meaningless with no change in salary. Paul kept promising the salary would match the title once fourth quarter goals were met. She hoped he was telling her the truth.

Taking a deep breath, Peyton clicked open her calendar. Another long day with a lot of conference calls. She had a team meeting at ten, which she dreaded, but was more than prepared for. Starting to work on her data analytics report for Paul, her phone chirped the arrival of a new text message. Picking up her phone, she noted an unknown number before reading, "I found Cecelia."

Peyton's blood ran cold and yet she started to sweat. With shaking hands, she managed to reply, "Who is this?"

Her heart throbbed and her mind raced. *Who could know my connection to Cecelia? Who would also know my mobile phone number?* Then she remembered Corbin had gotten her mobile number with ease. After an uncomfortable delay, her phone finally dinged again. "Oh, Peyton. Cecelia likes to share."

Peyton dropped her phone and pushed violently away from her desk. *How is this possible? How can this be coming back to haunt me again?*

About that time, her mobile dinged again. "Oh, I know, you are trying to figure out how I know. It doesn't matter. I know and soon everyone else will, too."

She felt the bile building in her stomach. Her hands were shaking, and she felt clammy. Her office walls closed in around her and she felt the panic surge through her veins. Her heart raced as she considered her situation. In full fight-or-flight mode, she picked up the phone and dialed Paul's extension.

"Paul? Hey, I need to go for the day. Personal stuff. I need to go. Sorry."

"Peyton, you okay?" he asked. "I don't need to know what's going on, but can you handle it? We have that meeting tomorrow, and I can't be embarrassed by your presentation."

Peyton rolled her eyes because she had never let Paul down and, of course, she was prepared for the meeting tomorrow. "Paul, I'm sorry, but I gotta go. I'm ready for tomorrow and it will be fine."

Peyton arrived at home and kicked her heels into the corner of the living room. Molly squeaked and ran toward the bedroom. Peyton didn't care. She was furious, worried, and didn't know what to do. She opened the refrigerator and grabbed a cold Miller Lite, popping the top and allowing the cold beverage to wash through her mouth. She needed to think. She needed to deal with this problem.

Why would Cecelia be bothering her again? Who could have found her? It seemed so long ago, and she had thought it was over. But now this?

As she changed into a pair of sweats and a T-shirt, she wanted to call Corbin. She wrestled with the idea before grabbing her phone and entering Corbin's number, which she had memorized long ago.

"Hi. Can we talk?" was her simple text request.

More minutes passed than Peyton liked before the reply came. "Are you going to yell at me again?"

Peyton replied, "No. Just need to talk, please?"

After a few moments, her phone rang. "Hey" was all he said and just what she needed.

"Hi," she replied. "I know I shouldn't have contacted you, but I'm in a bad place and wanted to talk. If that makes you uncomfortable or whatever, hang up."

"Peyton, what are you talking about? I have been devastated about what happened."

"Then why did you tell Paul you were going to sue Blast for sexual harassment, which by the way, you can no longer do because you are not an employee."

"What the hell are you talking about?" Corbin replied. "I never had a conversation with Paul about us. I enjoyed what we had. Why would I mess that up for a dead-end job at Blast?"

"So…so, you didn't? I thought I would lose my job. He said all these things…. Corbin, I'm so confused."

"Peyton. I promise. I lo…, I mean, I really like you. I didn't take any action against you there. I know what we were doing was against the rules, per se, but I didn't care."

"Wow. I'm not sure how to feel about this," Peyton replied.

"It killed me that day on the street when you wouldn't even listen to me," Corbin said. "It was like I went from being lover to enemy, and I had no idea why."

"Well, because Paul told me you were going to file a sexual harassment suit," Peyton replied.

"That's bullshit. Peyton. I am not your enemy. I would never do anything to intentionally hurt you, and I would take care of anyone who was trying to hurt you."

"I don't know what to say, Corbin."

"What do you want to say?"

"I want someone on my side. I got these creepy texts about something that happened years ago and it will ruin me at Blast. Paul is such a dick. If this gets out after the lawsuit thing, I'm done. And I didn't even do anything wrong, but she will spin it to ruin me. I don't know what to do, and I don't know anyone here. I'm not a bad person."

"You know me, Peyton. Can I come over? Just to talk, please? We need to figure out what is going on."

Peyton woke the next morning curled next to Corbin. Realizing the sun was beaming through the window, she bolted out of bed and grabbed her phone to see the time.

"Oh, holy hell! I'm late and the meeting is today!"

Peyton flew around the apartment getting ready, while Corbin lay smiling in bed watching her.

"Really?" she said. "You are enjoying this?"

"Naw, just enjoying you."

She stopped for a moment and kissed his forehead. "Thanks. Thanks for coming over. I'm glad we talked. Oh, and I'm glad you didn't want to sue Blast for my inappropriate behavior."

Corbin smacked her on the butt and said, "What inappropriate behavior? Get to work, woman!"

Peyton bounded out of the apartment, late, but knowing she would still make the meeting on time. Corbin stretched. He needed to find and deal with whomever had the Cecelia connection.

I wonder what a Cecelia may taste like, he considered as he stepped into the shower.

46

FRANKLIN

Franklin's hands shook as he lifted the bottle of bourbon to his lips, the shotgun now aimed at his back. No need for a glass in times like these. His thoughts raced: *So, Emily knew. She saw me, caught in the act, well, not in the act, but in a compromising position. Could I blame it on anyone else? Maybe one of the farm hands? That's it—one of the hands did it, and I was cleaning it up. No, she would never go for that; I would never be the clean-up guy.*

"Franklin, it's time to start talking," Emily reminded him. "I can see the wheels spinning in your head, but the truth is the only thing I will accept."

"But, baby, it's complicated."

"I don't care," she said. "If I am to be your partner for life, I have to know the truth. Our future depends on this moment, so think about that as you decide how you want to play this."

Defeated, Franklin sunk into a leather wing-back chair. He had to come clean. Emily could always tell when he was lying. Worst-case scenario was he'd go to jail. He'd plead insanity or something, and with his money and the Eastman reputation, he'd have it easy.

"I…I have this thing inside me that I can't control. I know that sounds weird, but please hear me out. When I get pushed too far or feel backed into a corner, there is something inside that needs to be fed. I don't like it, I'm not proud of it, but I can't control it. My father had it, too. My first hunting trip, I killed a deer and I ate its liver. Father encouraged me to. He knew that's what I needed. I can still taste that delicious warm, bloody organ."

Franklin smiled as he recalled that moment. Then, he focused on Emily. She stood frozen, the gun still pointed at his chest, her face white as a ghost.

"Emily, I'm so sorry. I love you. I try to keep it under control, and most of the time, a deer or an antelope will do, but sometimes, it gets the best of me. It's the monkey on my back that is always there, knocking, taunting. I face it every day, and somedays, well, it wins."

"And who are these women? How many have you eaten? Is it… sexual?" She swallowed hard.

"No, no, no. Nothing like that. Baby, I promise. It's not an emotional or control thing. It's not about the person. It's this obsession I have with fresh liver. The women aren't anyone, usually prostitutes." This was a lie; his first had been the furthest thing from a prostitute, but he felt confident that a few white lies wouldn't matter now.

"Franklin, they are still someone. How many? Tell me how many women."

"There have only been two. I hate myself after I do it, but I'm only human, so sometimes I slip." Another lie, but what's in a number anyway?

"Are they always strangers? Would you hurt…?" She couldn't finish the question.

"Never. Emily, you are my soul mate. I love you completely, and I would never hurt you. They are strangers. They aren't human to me. They're like a…a…a commodity. I know it is so wrong; believe me, I know. I'm a weak, horrible person." Franklin put his face in his hands and seemed to shrink into the large wingback.

He heard Emily put the gun on the coffee table and her soft steps as she walked toward the stairs, then the familiar creak from the last floor board before the first step. Then, silence. He looked up and saw her standing vulnerably on the step. Her face looked hollow as the pre-dawn light surrounded her, casting dark shadows behind her small image. He stood and started toward her, but he stopped when she raised her hand.

"Franklin, I'm going to bed. It's been a hell of a night. I'm tired. You can sleep in the spare room."

But Franklin could not sleep. Wrought with worry about what Emily might do, he poured bourbon into a glass and sat again in the wing-back chair. *What would I do if she left me? Emily is the best thing that ever happened to me. She's my rock.*

He reflected back to when they had been dating. It had taken several months before Emily had agreed to go to dinner with him, but Franklin's persistence had finally paid off. On their first date, they went to Joe's Chop House, an upscale restaurant in Great Falls. Emily had worn a simple black, sleeveless dress with a string of pearls around her neck. Her hair was swept into an elegant up-do held with a diamond clasp. Franklin had thought she was the most spectacular woman he had ever seen.

Franklin had believed the evening was progressing nicely. He had been impressive when he demanded the best table, critical of the wine choice the waiter recommended, and sent back the crab leg appetizer because his woman deserved the best. Emily hadn't commented on the exchanges with the staff, until the last one. After the server had left, she said, "Franklin, I am not your woman. And I will never be your woman if you continue to treat people this way in my presence. I understand you're a big, rich, tough guy who thinks you're supposed to act that way, but you won't be like that around me. I simply will not tolerate it ."

"But I'm an Eastman. We deserve respect and the best," he had replied.

"Well, then you can take your Eastman ego and go on. I'll have none of it."

Franklin had never been put in his place like that before, and especially not by a woman. He wasn't sure how he felt about it, but he said, "So you think you are better than me?"

"No, not at all. I simply demand respect and will not be in a relationship without it. How you treat people when you are away from me is up to you, but when you are with me, you will treat others and me as equals. If you can't agree to that, you can just take me home now. I'm not impressed with your money or your ego."

Franklin had sulked a few minutes before changing the subject and complying with Emily's demands. He had surprised himself with the difference it had made in their evening. He listened to, and enjoyed, her stories about breaking into the construction business. It was somehow freeing to let the pretense go and just be himself. He treated the servers respectfully and was encouraged by her warm smiles. Maybe, just maybe, this was the one woman who could tame Franklin Eastman.

Over the next few months, he realized he had developed a deep respect for Emily and found her to be smart, capable, and strong, one of the strongest women he'd ever known. She continued to be unimpressed by his money or the ranch or his reputation—the things that made all the other girls swoon. She truly didn't give a shit about that stuff and frequently put him in his place. She never once asked how big the ranch was, what it was worth, or how he'd become so powerful in Montana. He had found a gem and she liked him, regardless of the money or power. It was new and different for Franklin, but he was hooked. A year later, she became his wife.

Franklin woke the next morning on the couch. He was still wearing the bloody shirt from the night before and his neck was stiff. He wondered how the morning would go. Would Emily call the cops? Would she ask him for a divorce? He threw the shirt in the laundry before tromping up the stairs to take a shower. He smelled bacon cooking.

Walking into the kitchen, he saw his Emily preparing breakfast as usual.

"Good morning, love," he said.

Much to his surprise and delight, she replied, "Hey, baby. How'd you sleep?"

The morning progressed as normal. They never spoke of his addiction or that night again. Franklin wasn't sure how Emily was able to internalize it, but she gradually returned to her normal self, or at least appeared to be her normal self. She laughed, socialized with her friends, and treated Franklin as lovingly as ever.

If Franklin stayed out late or disappeared, she never said a word, but she would insist they have fried chicken livers for dinner the next night. He thought it was her way of saying, "I know what you did last night." She would smile and put the plate in front of him. "I prepared your favorite dish: liver." He would laugh. He deserved it.

47

CORBIN

Several weeks passed since the night the beautiful Peyton Alexander called me. I was so excited to have made amends with her. We had something special and I needed to take care of her. I actually knew in my heart that I would do anything, literally anything, to keep her safe and happy. I didn't understand what was going on with the whole Cecelia thing or who was trying to leverage it against Peyton now. Peyton was also vague in what had transpired between her and Cecelia, stating only that Cecelia had been fired and blamed her. Neither Peyton nor I knew the phone number sending the texts, which continued to be sent regularly, but it could be anyone with a burner phone. It could even be Cecelia herself trying to throw Peyton off-track. The one thing I was 100 percent positive about was that I would figure it out and take care of it.

Now that Peyton was back in my life, I was her protector and would not harm her. No matter my desire, I could never hurt Peyton. She wasn't like Jessica. She made me happy and complete, and wasn't mean or condescending. She almost made me feel, dare I say, almost normal. Oh, sure, you laugh at that, but I did say *almost* normal. Probably more people than you realize have a desire for human organs.

But today, I couldn't worry about figuring out the Peyton dilemma. I had promised Pam I would swing by the shelter and help get the animals ready for the big pet adoption drive taking place tomorrow. No way could I let Pam down. In some ways, she was more like the pitiful animals craving a safe, happy home than she was human. If she could take a PTO day, I could certainly spend some time helping her out. If we were able to save only one pet, it would be worth it.

Arriving at Furry Friends Animal Rescue Shelter, I greeted my fellow volunteers and set about my standard task of bathing the dogs. That always seemed to be my chore, which I didn't mind. It was better than cleaning out the puppy pens, for sure. Plus, it allowed me the opportunity to work with the shyer dogs to increase their socialization skills.

Pushing open the kennel door, I greeted my favorite dog, Jackson, a now three-legged pit bull who had been dumped at the shelter in the middle of the night. His left back leg had been practically shredded with the bone exposed in most places. Several other smaller wounds had been scattered across his filthy body, covered with feces, dirt, and loads of fleas. He was barely breathing, but he was alive and whimpered when I softly stroked his head. Lamar, the rescue director, wanted to put him down, but I argued, almost begged, and offered to pay for the veterinary bill no matter the cost. Lamar agreed, but he grumbled that Jackson would probably never find a home anyway. Lamar could be a little too grumpy and cold for the line of work he'd chosen.

I left Jackson with the emergency veterinarian down on Blackmar Street and hadn't even made it back to Furry Friends when the office called. "There is no way to save this leg," said Dr. Kincade. "He'll be lucky if he lives at all, but this leg has to go."

"Take the leg and please save his life," I choked into the phone. I didn't understand why that dog was so important to me—why the existence of that one in particular was so critical—but he was.

"Okay, we'll try," was all I heard before he ended the call.

Jackson pulled through surgery with flying colors, and after a lot of rest with much needed blood and fluids, he was returned to the shelter…and to me. I slipped him extra food and worked with him daily, swinging by on my lunch hour during the week. He quickly gained back his weight, his wounds healed, and he adapted to his tripod status with ease. He was a beautiful tan and white dog with a sleek, soft coat lightly concealing his permanent scars and lean muscles. His great personality was displayed to potential adoptees as he wagged his tail and smiled, but a four-year-old pit bull rescue is a hard dog to place.

Pam walked up with the next pooch to be bathed, Spice, a goofy, fluffy yellow dog of an unknown mixture of breeds. Waiting for me to finish rinsing off Jackson, Pam inquired, "So, have you found another job yet, or you are going to retire?"

"Ha, ha. Oh, I wish I could retire, but no can do. I have a job offer from Hilton Mercedes to sell cars. I have to let them know in a couple of days."

"Oh, you'd be great in sales, Corbin," Pam said. "With your outgoing personality and charm, you'd be selling fancy cars to all the ladies."

"You flatter me, Pam," I replied, "but I don't know. I have to think about it. How are things at Blast?"

"Well, it's not the same since you left and since we've been sold, for sure. I don't know what's going on now, but the atmosphere is heavy and serious. Lots of closed-door meetings with Paul and Peyton. Oh, and poor Peyton, ever since you left, she's been a wreck. Stays in her office with the door closed, only coming out if neces-sary. I'm worried about her. The poor dear doesn't look well."

Knowing Peyton didn't want anyone at Blast to know about us, I said, "Well, that's unfortunate. She seemed like a nice person who wanted to do well for the company. Do you have any idea what is going on? I'm not prying, just curious."

"No, I'm not sure what's going on. I'm stuck in Accounting, you know—not privy to any corporate goings on. I can tell you that Spencer has been oddly happy lately. After you left, he acted like he'd lost his best friend. For the last few weeks, though, he's almost been dancing around the office. Do you still hang out with him?"

"No, it's hard to keep a friendship going when you don't see someone all the time. I wonder what's made him so happy." Those tiny hairs of intuition raised on the back of my neck.

"Well, you know I don't like to gossip, but since you don't work there anymore, I guess it's fine." Pam lowered her voice as she delivered that lie; gossiping was one of her favorite things. "Rob and he were talking the other day, and then later Rob told Sally that Spencer had got the goods on Peyton. I don't know what that means, but Sally said Rob said Spencer was all excited when he said it."

"Hmm, well, I'm sure I don't know," I replied with as much disinterest as I could muster. "But I better get busy bathing these dogs. We have a lot more to do. Take Jackson back for me?"

"Sure thing, Corbin." She smiled and took his leash. "I'm so proud of you for continuing to volunteer here."

"I love these guys," I said, ruffling Spice's fluffy ears.

When all the dogs were bathed and ready for the adoption day tomorrow, I jumped in my car, and before pulling out of the parking lot, I dialed a number I no longer enjoyed dialing. Sooner than I appreciated, Spencer picked up. "Hey, man, what's up?"

"Not much," I replied. "Wanted to see what you're up to. Now that the Peyton thing is over, you want to hang out?"

"Yes. That would be great."

48

SPENCER

Spencer loved how clever he had become. His goal was to ruin Peyton, like he had gotten rid of the old cow Lois Hutchinson. Spencer had known Lois was evil from the moment he had started working at Blast. He had thought he was victorious when he brought her down by hacking into her computer after she laughed at his promotion opportunities, but this Peyton was a much bigger chip to reckon with. Paul seemed to trust her opinions about the company and support her when she presented new ideas in the team meetings. Spencer didn't understand why, but with the help of his new friend, Cecelia, he was confident he could ruin Peyton, too.

As an added bonus, Corbin had called and wanted to hang out. Peyton was always the problem; Corbin couldn't see it. Spencer saved his friend and was pleased Corbin wanted to renew the friendship. But even with his friend back, Spencer was committed to hurting Peyton. Plus, he hated how she strutted around the office—well, until recently anyway. No, he took that back. She still strutted around when she came out of her office, her head held high as if nothing were happening, but she rarely came out of her office. Spencer chuckled, certain he was the cause of it all.

Oh, you wait, Peyton, Spencer thought. *Wait until Paul calls you into his office to fire your ass over what Cecelia has given me. You won't have a pot to piss in, you bitch. I'm tired of people underestimating me.*

Corbin arrived at Spencer's basement apartment a little after six-thirty with a six pack of beer, for Corbin, and a Piero's pizza.

"Hey, thought this would bring back the good old days," Corbin said while handing the pizza box to Spencer, who snatched it eagerly.

"Yeah, man, this is great," Spencer replied. "I hadn't even thought about food. I do have all the trains and props ready, though. I missed this. Thank you for calling."

"Sure thing." Corbin grabbed a beer. "So, what's the project for tonight? It feels like I haven't worked on this train scene in years."

"We need to finish the logging area. I've been having trouble with the loader missing the train car."

As they worked on constructing the elaborate model train display, Spencer asked, "So, what happened with you and Peyton? You ever talk to her anymore?"

"Naw, man," Corbin replied. "That bitch went crazy on me. I don't even know what happened, but all of a sudden, she wouldn't even talk to me. Acted like I was the worst person ever. Never understood it, but whatever. Who cares? I moved on."

"Well, she could have thought you were a threat to her."

"Why? What did I do?" Corbin asked.

"You were sleeping with her, man! She's management, and you were a customer service guy. That's wrong."

"She told you this? She seemed fine with us doing what we were doing."

"Well, she didn't say that exactly, but you know, she confided in me," Spencer said.

"Yeah? Well, I wish you would have told me. Damn bitch."

"I tried, but you were too sucked into her. You had googly love eyes when she walked near you. You weren't yourself, and you shut out your best friend because of it."

"Hey, I wasn't that bad, but come on, she was a good fuck," Corbin replied.

"Well, I'm taking care of that whole situation for the good of Blast," Spencer said. "I have dirt on her that she will never live it down with Paul. Unless she's fucking him, too. And if that's the case, I'll publicize it more. I'm not scared."

"Yeah? What are you talking about?"

"Oh, I found some dirt in her past that she won't want public. But Paul will soon know."

"Wow, you hate her, don't you?" Corbin said. "I didn't realize she was on your radar so much. Hell, I don't care. Good for you, man!"

Accepting the offered fist bump, Spencer replied, "Good to have you back, man."

49

FRANKLIN

Franklin looked into the bathroom mirror and noticed the increasing amount of gray that filled his whiskers and hair. He felt he was still a nice-looking man, but hell, he was fifty-six now and had lived in this Montana weather his entire life. His face showed signs of the brutal winters, with the accompanying valleys and rivers on the landscape of his face. Still, he lived a comfortable lifestyle—had more money than he could ever spend.

He also had Emily, the best thing that had ever happened to Franklin. He had never cheated on her; he didn't consider feeding to be cheating. She understood him…all of him, and she was the only person besides Hernando whom he had trusted with his darkest secret. So why had he kept the secret of Corbin from her for all these years?

Considering that question for a moment, Franklin recalled that back then they had both been going through a rough time. It had been Emily's third pregnancy and her third miscarriage. It was hard on both of them. They had wanted a big family. When they were first married, they had talked of a huge family and how they would teach the kids to ride, fish, and play in the creeks. In the winter, they

planned to go sledding behind one of the brood mares that pulled
the handmade sled his grandfather had built for his family to enjoy.

None of that had happened, and it had taken a toll on Emily
especially. He simply could not have burdened her with the news of
his bastard son. It was probably the wrong decision, but one he had
made, and now it was too late to correct.

He wasn't quite sure what had been bugging him the last few
months. It was a little tapping in the back of his brain that was
more of an annoyance than anything else. Maybe that was what
old men felt? He was far too past midlife to be having a midlife
crisis. He had become settled and calm the last several years. His
angry alter-ego had been dormant for some time. He treated
people nicer than he had in, well, his entire life. But something
in the back of his mind wanted to be heard; it just hadn't made it
through to his consciousness.

"Hell, I can't worry about such shit today," he told himself in the
mirror. "Big board meeting. Focus."

He finished dressing and headed to his office at Eastman Cattle
Company.

After the board meeting, which was a complete waste of time
and made him question why he had established a board, Franklin
returned to his office and started going through his mail. Janet called
a few minutes later and said, "Mr. Eastman, Rod is on line one."

"Thank you, Janet," he replied and answered line one.

"Hey, Rod, what's up?"

"Hey. Time for your annual update. Nothing alarming. It seems
Corbin is doing well and staying out of trouble in Atlanta. He left
Blast and has secured employment at Hilton Mercedes Benz," re-
ported Rod.

"He's a fucking car salesman?" Franklin was appalled at such
a career.

Rod laughed. "Well, yes he is, but that's a high-end dealership. He seems to be doing well. Last month he was awarded top salesman for the month. Sold over twenty cars."

"Hmm. So, anything else?"

"Nope," Rod replied. "Franklin, you know I'm happy to keep taking your money year after year to follow this kid—hell, he's a grown man now—but are you seriously worried about him? He sent you one letter, showed up briefly in Great Falls without any attempt to contact you, and it's been what fifteen, sixteen years with nothing?"

"Why do you care why I want this information? Do I fucking pay you to care?" Franklin asked, his alter ego coming out for the first time in years.

"Of course not, Franklin. It just seems that he's not a threat to you or your dynasty in any way whatsoever."

"Well, that's why I pay you, Rod—to make sure he doesn't become a threat. Do you want me to stop?"

"No, sir," said Rod. "That was not my intent at all. I simply mean I do not perceive him to be a threat to you. Nor do I think he will become a threat, well, ever."

"Fine. What about his personal life?"

Rod ran his hand through his thinning hair and thought, *Why do you care?* But he replied, "Seems like he's doing well. Dating an attractive executive woman."

"Any improprieties?"

Confused, Rod asked, "Like hookers or strippers and whatnot?"

Knowing he couldn't reveal more than that, Franklin replied, "Yes."

"No, I have found no improprieties."

"Okay, we done?" Franklin was tired of this conversation, and that pecking in the back of his brain was more prevalent than of late.

"If you are, sir."

"Thanks. Oh, and Rod?"

"Yes?"

"Fuck you." Franklin slammed down the phone.

Maybe he hadn't mellowed over the years. Storming out of his office, he said, "Janet, I'm gone for the day."

Janet smiled politely and said, "Okay, Mr. Eastman; have a great rest of your day," while thinking, *My God, he's such a prick. How can anyone with so much money be that angry?*

50
PEYTON

The texts from the unknown number were becoming increasingly aggressive. Peyton typically received one a day, each text more threatening than the last. She had stopped replying to them early on, but each new message sent her into a tailspin of worry. She had started carrying her phone with her whenever possible, even into meetings with Paul. Today, he was droning on about the state of the nation when her phone buzzed in her lap. Quietly, she moved the papers so she could see the content.

"Peyton," the text threatened, "I'm getting tired of you ignoring me. You better reply within the next two hours or Paul will receive some interesting information. You don't want to fuck around with me."

All the blood rushed from Peyton's face as she stared at the phone. Corbin had advised her not to reply, but she couldn't have information leaked to Paul. She needed her job. Staring wide-eyed at her phone, she finally heard Paul saying, "Peyton, Peyton, hey, are you okay? You look like you've seen a ghost."

Peeling her eyes from her screen, she replied, "Oh, yes, sir. Everything is fine. Are we done here?" Without waiting for his reply, she started gathering her reports and stood up.

"Yeah, sure; we're good. But you're sure you're okay? You've been acting weird lately."

"I'm so sorry, Paul. It's family stuff, and I'm sorry it follows me to the office. My dad's health isn't so great right now. I'll do better to keep it from affecting my job."

"Okay. That'd be great," Paul said.

"Thanks, Paul," said Peyton, managing to pull off fake sincerity. "I appreciate all the opportunities you've given me."

"Well, you wouldn't be where you are without me. So, I'm glad you recognize that."

Peyton returned to her office, pissed at this fucking texting maniac who was out to get her for no reason. Slamming her office door, she snatched up her phone and typed, "Fine, you fucker. What do you want? I'm tired of this shit and your threats."

"Oh," came the quick reply, "I see I've finally gotten a rise out of you. Thank you, Peyton. That's enough satisfaction for me today."

Peyton threw her phone on the desk in disgust. "Fuck!" she screamed into the air.

Watching Peyton from his cubicle, Spencer chuckled quietly.

51

CORBIN

I had gathered enough intel from Spencer to know what my next step had to be. While he wouldn't give me any concrete details about what he had on Peyton, he revealed he had found an old acquaintance of hers who still lived in Mitchell who had provided the dirt on Ms. Alexander. I couldn't push him too far or he would become suspicious, the last thing I wanted. I settled for Cecelia's name, and later, while Spencer took one of his many lengthy bathroom breaks, I obtained her contact information from his phone, including her address.

Pounding on the bathroom door, I called out to Spencer, "Hey, man; I gotta get going. Let's plan something for the weekend maybe?"

"Sure; sounds good," came the muffled reply. "Probably a good call. This duty may take me a while."

"You're gross. Text me later." I laughed and left.

To find out the exact threat to Peyton, I needed to pay a little visit to Cecelia. I felt certain I could make her talk. And if I couldn't, at least I could feed on another deserving candidate. Peyton was out of town for an HR seminar, so I wouldn't even have to lie to her or make up some excuse not to see her.

The next morning, I walked into Vince's office at Hilton Mercedes. "Hey, man, let me ask you something."

"Sure; what's up?" Vince stopped looking at the latest inventory and turned toward me.

"I need a couple of days to take care of a personal issue with family back home. Is that a problem? I don't want to jeopardize this job, but I have to take care of this."

"Hell, the way you've been selling cars, it's not a problem for anyone other than the commission you'll lose. Someone else might be able to sell something if you're gone for a couple of days."

"Great," I said, "but you guys are far better than me. I've been lucky."

"Yeah, sure. When do you need to go?"

"If it's okay, I'd like to go up there tomorrow, and then I should be back on Friday," I said, adding, "So, only two days for you guys to make your commission."

"That's a quick trip. You sure you can do what you need to? You can come back Monday if you want. Spend some time with your family."

I wanted to laugh in his face at the absurdity, but instead replied, "What—and let you losers get the Saturday commissions? No way!"

The day wore on. A middle-aged advertising executive in a cheap worn suit insisted on purchasing an entry-level C class Mercedes. He couldn't afford even that lower-end model, but he was hell-bent on having a Mercedes. I assumed he thought his failing career would be saved by driving the same brand of car as his boss based on his comments about his boss' car. His credit was decent enough to lease for seventy-two months, but he'd get killed on the interest and mileage. Sadly, there is only so much a salesman can say. As the man happily drove away, I imagined what his wife might say upon his arrival at their suburban, construction-grade, ranch home in a subdivision of identical homes only differentiated by the numbers on the mailboxes.

I slid out of the dealership a little after 3 p.m., but Vince was understanding. Rushing home, I threw some essentials into a duffle bag before changing into jeans and a hooded sweatshirt. I needed to look average for this trip. Grabbing cash from the Sam stash, I hopped in my car and started my eighteen-hour drive to Mitchell.

Around Kansas City, I felt the effects of the energy drinks wearing off, so I pulled into a dirty rest area filled with sleeping truckers and a few prostitutes hoping to get a quick gig. Pulling into an empty space below an overhead light, I made sure the doors were locked before laying the seat back and catching a cat nap.

I woke about an hour later to a scary-looking woman wearing heavy theatrical makeup and a skimpy outfit of sequins and leopard print—or was that fur?—knocking on my window. Uncertain and not caring, I turned the ignition, glided gently from my parking spot, and continued my journey.

I arrived in Mitchell around noon on Thursday. Pulling into a little diner called "Ralph's Place," I had enough energy to think, *I wonder if Ralph owns this place*, and chuckled at my wit. Walking into the restaurant, I was reminded a bit of Sam's Quick Pick, but mostly of Sam. I hated that he'd betrayed me. Pushing that thought from my head, I chose a stool at the counter.

"Oh, my," the waitress with "Beatrice" pinned to her uniform said, "you look like death warmed over. What can I get you, sweetie?"

"Well, thank you for the compliment," I said, trying to be lighthearted. "I've been driving most of the night. Right now, I need a very caffeinated soda and a bacon cheeseburger, rare."

"Rare? Well, you know you ain't supposed to eat hamburger rare, right? I think it can kill you."

"Well, Beatrice," I lowered my voice and pulled out the charm, "I'm prepared for the consequences. I promise." I wanted to laugh considering all the things I have consumed that the FDA, well, and the FBI, would not have recommended.

"Okay, sweetie; fries with that?"

"Absolutely, and thank you, Beatrice." I smiled appreciatively at her, watching in amusement as the thought crossed Beatrice's mind that maybe she still was hot. She was not, but it never hurt to flatter people, especially when you are hungry and tired.

Tossing twenty bucks on the counter, I called out, "Thank you, Beatrice. That meal was perfect, and you keep the change."

"Oh…." She blushed. "Well, thank you. You know, my daughter is single if you're interested. She's a real good woman."

"I'm sure she's almost as charming as you," I replied; why not make someone's day? "But I'm just passing through. If I were staying, I'd probably have to pick you over your daughter."

"Well, aren't you the charmer? You be careful out there, okay?"

"I will." I smiled and left Ralph's Place feeling good about making someone else happy that day because what was about to happen would only make me happy. It's all a balance with karma, right?

Entering 1721 S. Main into my GPS and seeing I was only five minutes from meeting Cecelia, my adrenaline surged. Soon, the grueling drive here would be worth it all. I would know what power Cecelia had over Peyton, and I would be able to solve this problem. I had asked Peyton as many questions as I could without revealing the amount of knowledge I had already gathered, but she had instantly become agitated over the topic and shut down. I knew the look. It was futile to try any further. I had to find a different source, and that's where Cecelia came into play.

Nearing the address, the GPS guided me to Happy Homes Trailer Park. Looking at the state of some of the residents' trailers and the cars parked (or on blocks) in the driveways, I guessed few had a happy home. Looking for number twenty-one, I rounded the corner, and much to my surprise, saw a street covered with police, news media, and onlookers wanting a good story to share over dinner that night.

Pulling to the side of the road behind a WGKL News van, I walked toward the crowd and stood in the back, trying to figure out what was going on. Police tape blocked the entrance to 1721. News cameras flashed and reporters called out to the police officers guarding the taped off area.

"What's going on?" a smartly dressed woman with a press badge and a cameraman lurking over her shoulder called out. "We heard they're all dead. Is this true?"

The tired police officer rolled his eyes and said, "I told you; the chief will make an announcement."

"I heard they even killed the dog," came a voice from the crowd.

"No comment," replied the police officer, but his face told me that what had happened inside 1721 was far worse than the killing of a dog.

I worked my way into the crowd, looking for someone near the front who might have some information. Sliding near one of the more vocal bystanders, I asked, "What's going on? Any idea?"

"They're all dead! This doesn't happen here. Who could have done this and why?"

"All of them?" I asked. "Who were all of them?"

"Cecelia, her son, and even the dog," replied the citizen. "All killed."

"What? That's horrible. How old was her son?"

"He was only eight," the man stated, sadness overtaking his excitement. "I can't imagine. My boy is only six. What if this isn't a one-time thing? We need to get this guy."

"I'm sure the police are on it," I said. "Looks like they have things under con—" I stopped midsentence as the coroner pushed out a cart covered with a black body bag, followed by another cart pushed by a police officer, the body inside only filling a small portion of the otherwise flat, black bag.

The reporters went wild, screaming questions at the police, who remained silent and at post. The crowd quieted momentarily as the bodies were whisked away and the police chief emerged from the trailer. Holding his hands high to quiet the crowd, he approached the police tape barrier.

As cameras flashed and reporters demanded answers, the police chief yelled to the crowd, "Okay, okay, everyone; settle down!"

After the crowd hushed, he continued, "Inside this trailer was a gruesome scene. All I am prepared to state at this moment is Cecelia Masters and her eight-year-old son were found dead at the scene, as well as the family dog. It is being investigated as a murder at this time. I will hold a press conference later today outside my office. That is all for now." He vanished back inside the trailer, even though the crowd screamed for answers.

52

PEYTON

"Peyton, oh, Peyton," the text started. "Cecelia has been forthcoming. Don't forget our arrangement. You talk to me; I don't turn over this evidence to Paul."

Even though Peyton had promised Corbin that she would not respond to these threats, she had to. Paul could not find out about this or she would be fired. She could not survive being fired at this stage of her career. Blast, especially after the sale, was her way into the corporate world, and she couldn't let anything get in her way. Picking up her phone, she typed, "Right. What do you want?"

"Well, that will be revealed in time," came the reply. "Let's just say vindication is in order."

"Who are you?"

"LOL. Like I will share that. Rest assured, though, justice will be served."

Peyton tossed her phone on the desk. "Damn it!" she said to her empty office.

The Cecelia thing seemed so long ago to Peyton. They had become friends quickly after being hired at Protect Your Home. They were both hired as administrative assistants and had worked for this insecure, manipulating woman, Nancy, the office manager.

On Peyton's first day at Protect Your Home, Nancy went over her basic rules and then introduced Peyton around the office. After each introduction and upon walking away, Nancy would express her opinion about the person last introduced.

"Clint is a womanizing bastard," she told Peyton. "If I see you talking to him, you are going to have to answer to me."

And the directives continued. Peyton was uncomfortable with the instructions, but Nancy was her boss, so there was not much she could do. After being introduced to Cecelia, who answered the phones and directed calls all day, Peyton was informed by Nancy that Cecelia was a trusted person whom she was encouraged to associate with. Taking that lead, Peyton and Cecelia would occasionally go for drinks after work, and they developed a friendship that extended beyond the work environment.

As the months passed, it became obvious that Nancy and Dale, the owner of Protect Your Home, were sleeping together. Caught in many awkward situations, they laughed off the relationship and Peyton looked the other way. Neither Dale nor Nancy were married, so it wasn't scandalous, but it created a weird work environment. She also ignored the rules Nancy had set and secretly built relationships with people at work if Peyton felt they provided professional value.

Sitting in her cubicle one day, Peyton received a call from Nancy. "Come in my office *now*."

Peyton sighed and walked the six feet to Nancy's door. "Yes, Nancy? How can I assist you?"

"Get in here and shut the door."

Accommodating the request, Peyton took a seat in one of the gray fabric and silver-framed, but uncomfortable guest chairs.

"I saw you talking to Andrea," Nancy said.

"Yes," Peyton replied.

"Well, she's not someone you should talk to. What did she want?" Nancy asked.

"She was simply telling me about her grandson and his T-ball game."

"Hmm." Nancy rolled her eyes. "It's not good for you to be seen talking to her. Don't let it happen again."

Because Nancy was her boss, Peyton nodded to confirm her fake compliance.

A few days later, Peyton was working on calculating time sheets for the Protect Your Home employees when Nancy called her. "Hey, Cecelia and I are going for drinks after work. You're coming, right?"

Because it had been delivered as a directive and not a question, Peyton replied, "Sure; sounds fun. When and where?"

They met at a local pub called Delaney's and started the evening. Nancy ordered shots of vodka, followed by shots of tequila, followed by shots of things Peyton couldn't even remember. Peyton woke the next morning in a strange motel room next to a naked Cecelia with little recollection of what had happened. And that's when things started to get ugly.

53

FRANKLIN

Getting off the plane at the Delta B2 terminal in Atlanta, Franklin gathered his suitcase at Baggage Claim 3 and made his way to the train that would take him to the Rental Car Center. Settling into the overpriced, rented SUV, he entered Hilton Mercedes into the GPS. Upon arrival, he was greeted by a greedy salesman. "How can I help you today? Interested in one of these great vehicles?"

"Yes, I'm interested in an S65 AMG Cabriolet," Franklin stated. He was instantly amused by the reaction of the salesman who thought he could actually sell one of these $250,000 vehicles.

"Oh, oh, yes, sir," came the salivating response. "Let me help you with that."

"No," Franklin said. "I will only buy from this guy named Corbin."

Crushed by his response, the salesman replied, "Well, Corbin isn't here right now, but I can certainly help you."

"Are you an imbecile? I will only buy from Corbin. When will he be back? Is he at lunch?"

"Well, no, he took a couple of days off," said the flustered salesman.

"Hmm, figures," stated Franklin. Pulling a business card from his suitcoat pocket, he said, "Give him this, and tell him I am in town until Tuesday. After that, I'll find somewhere else to buy this car."

Taking the card, the salesman replied, "Sure thing. He's supposed to be back on Saturday."

"Well, I don't wait," Franklin said before leaving Hilton Mercedes.

Sliding into the rented SUV, Franklin pondered whether this had been an error in judgment. He wasn't sure why he was so obsessed with Corbin lately, but he couldn't deny it. Maybe age had something to do with it, or the realization that he was getting older with no heir to the Eastman Cattle Company. Hernando would be the best choice to run the place, but he lacked the business sense to run it with the Eastman bravado. But a bastard son might not be the right choice either. Or was he simply curious whether that unique gene had been passed along to the next generation of Eastmans?

Returning to the Ritz-Carlton in Buckhead, Franklin changed from his business suit into a pair of jeans and a pink golf shirt before heading to the bar to unwind.

54

CORBIN

I hung around Mitchell so I could hear the press conference later that afternoon outside the police chief's office. I checked into the Rocket Travel Lodge and took the opportunity to grab a few hours of much needed sleep. Waking at 3 p.m., I took a quick shower before heading downtown to the Mitchell Police Station.

A lively crowd, large for Mitchell, had already gathered in the street by the time I arrived. This was apparently a serious and unusual event for an area filled with dedicated farmers and wholesome, hardworking Americans. News crews swarmed and weaved their way through the crowd, which gave way so they could secure the front. Handsome women with worried faces held their babies close or firmly gripped the hands of their toddlers as if the killer would suck them away into the black abyss.

The crowd hushed without command when the police chief opened the front door and walked toward the podium. Cameras flashed, but not even the reporters spoke. Looking even more tired than earlier, the chief stated, "At this time, we do not have a lot of news to report. The death of Ms. Masters and her eight-year-old son, Justin, has been declared a homicide. There were signs of a struggle, and the family dog also fell victim. The coroner placed the time of death as late afternoon this past Tuesday. You have my promise that the Mitchell Police Department will dedicate as many resources as possible to finding and bringing this perpetrator to justice. The FBI Field Office in Sioux Falls will be assisting with the investigation. If anyone has any information or has witnessed anything that may be helpful, please contact my office. Thank you."

Ignoring the questions pelted at his back, the chief continued toward his office and disappeared.

Not yet tired, but also not ready to face another eighteen hours of driving, I decided to spend the night and leave early in the morning. Peyton had been gone all week for her seminar. We had already discussed that her return flight from Dallas wouldn't get her home until about eleven Friday night, so I had my pass until Saturday night.

Driving around Mitchell, I decided to stop at the sports bar, creatively named The Sports Bar. "Well, I guess there's no doubt what the place is," I said, chuckling to myself as I walked inside the dimly lit bar and found an open barstool made from an old metal tractor seat. The stool was next to a couple of pot-bellied locals who looked more like part of the furniture than patrons.

Ordering a draft Miller Lite from the red-headed Stephanie, I nodded to the locals who nodded back, but I didn't engage in conversation. I watched the giant television behind the bar that was airing the press conference from earlier. As the chief disappeared from the screen, Stephanie switched it to some college basketball game. Turning to the locals, she said, "I can't believe she's gone!" Tears formed in her eyes.

"Now, now, Steph," said the man next to me. "Try to keep things under control."

"But it's hard not to think about. Right here in our nice town!" She seemed on the verge of hysteria, either real or feigned for attention. Either way, Farmer Joe here was taking this opportunity to show his sympathetic side. I was certain of his ulterior motive.

"Well, I'm sure they will catch whoever did this. Try not to think about it," he said before taking a long drag from his beer mug.

"You know I was home Tuesday afternoon, right?" Stephanie replied. "She lived a couple of trailers down from me. I was there right when poor, dear Cece was getting God-knows-what done to her!" Tears started rolling down her cheeks.

Farmer Joe offered to buy her a shot of her choice, which she quickly accepted. "Hell," Joe said, "let's all have one in memory of Cece."

To my surprise, Stephanie placed four shot glasses on the counter, filled them to the brim with Patrón, and placed one in front of each of us. Picking up our glasses, Farmer Joe toasted, "To Cece and Justin, and the little dog; may they rest in peace."

Clicking our glasses and simultaneously saying, "Here, here," we slammed the tasty shot and bit into the provided lime slices.

"Thank you for the shot," I said to Joe. "It's horrible what I heard on the news. Sounds like you guys knew them?"

"Knew them?" said Stephanie. "Cece was my best friend! Well, we used to be; I still loved her like a sister, but you know, people grow apart. Anyway, yes, I knew them, and I'm scared. Shit like this doesn't happen around here."

"Well, Steph," said Farmer Joe, "you know I'd be glad to stay over tonight and protect you."

"Oh, you stop. You never give up, do you?" Stephanie laughed as she patted his arm.

"Well, it never hurts to keep offering. One day, you might take me up on it," Joe replied.

As the evening wore on, Stephanie accepted more and more sympathy shots and her tales of the beloved Cece became more and more theatrical.

It was around eleven when the long drive, lack of sleep, and alcohol caught up with me. I hadn't gathered any useful information—wasn't even sure what I was hoping to find—but it was time to sleep. Paying my tab, I wished them all a safe evening and headed back to the Rocket Travel Lodge. Falling into a deep sleep, I slept soundly until my alarm blared at 6 a.m. Time to get back to Georgia.

55

PEYTON

As Peyton sat in the Sioux Falls Regional Airport waiting for the plane that would deliver her to Minneapolis for her three-hour lay-over, before another flight to get her back to Atlanta, she considered how wise this trip had actually been. She had made the trip to see her dad in the hospital, but she felt guilty about lying to Corbin. He would have wanted to come if she had told him the truth. She wasn't ready to introduce him to her dad. He also wanted to know what had happened between her and Cecelia, but she just wanted to put it behind her. He had been respectful when they had talked about this texter who continued to badger her, but she could tell by his expressions that he wanted to know everything.

That's probably logical, she thought. *He shared all his horrible past with me. Why shouldn't I do the same? But I don't want to. At least not yet.*

Upon her arrival in Mitchell on Monday, Peyton checked into the American Lodge. Sitting in the outdated room, she called Corbin, who answered after the fourth ring.

"Hey," she said. "What are you doing?"

"Not much; just got home from work and was going to grab a bite to eat somewhere," Corbin replied. "How was your flight?"

"Oh, it was fine. Nothing special. Just checked in here in Dallas," Peyton lied. "My hotel is right downtown, so I have tons of fun restaurants to experience while I'm here."

"Aren't you going to have to hang out with your HR counterparts from around the world and talk about harassment and policies and junk?" Corbin teased.

"Oh, shut up," Peyton said, giggling. "You know I don't hang out with those people. Once the seminar is over for the day, I'm out!" A twinge of guilt crept into her stomach at the lie and how easily it had been delivered.

"I know." Corbin laughed. "I'm picking on you. Glad you made it to Dallas safely, and enjoy your time there. I miss you already."

"I miss you, too. Hey, remember, I'm not going to be back in Atlanta until late Friday, so can I see you on Saturday night?"

"Yes, we already talked about that," Corbin replied. "I'm all yours on Saturday. I'll come straight there from the dealership."

They ended the call. Peyton ventured forth to her favorite fast food restaurant in Mitchell: Taco King. The franchise didn't extend to Georgia, so she missed the tasty cheap tacos she had grown up enjoying. Ordering two tacos and a burrito, she slid into the red plastic booth and filled her mouth with a huge bite of crispy goodness.

"What the fuck are you doing here?" someone asked.

Looking up, her mouth full of beef taco and a bit of taco sauce on her lip, Peyton gazed into the face of none other than Cecelia Masters. Chewing rapidly and trying not to choke, Peyton was finally able to say, "Oh, hi, Cecelia."

"Oh, hi, Cecelia?" she replied. "How about answering my question: What the fuck are you doing here?"

Feeling anger flush her face, Peyton replied, "Oh, I'm sorry; is this your fucking Taco King? Did some miracle happen that pulled you out of the trailer park and now you're the queen of fucking Taco King?"

Peyton could tell the comment hit home with Cecelia, and she momentarily felt a bit of remorse, but that quickly evaporated when Cecelia replied, "I thought you left to be some successful Atlanta bitch with a whole new crowd of people to fuck over to get ahead."

"Cecelia," Peyton said, "that's not how it happened, and you know it. You stopped doing your job, and the threats…."

"And the threats. That's a classic Peyton move. 'Oh, I am a pitiful little victim.' Well, who got fired?"

"You stopped working. You were fucking Simon from service and got caught in the garage. I didn't do that," Peyton replied. "I'm sorry things turned out the way they did."

"Oh, you're sorry that I got fired? Somehow, I find that hard to believe."

"No, I'm sorry that you stopped doing your job. Firing you was the only option Dale had, but you did that to yourself, not me. So, basically, you fired yourself."

"That's some bullshit. You came out all rosy and I came out fired," Cecelia replied. "So I'm thinking you did something to save your job after the stuff I showed Dale. You suck his dick?"

"No!" Peyton was getting angry. "He backed me because I have always worked hard. I deserved my position. Jesus, Cecelia, you could have kept your job if you had only been performing at the bare minimum!"

"Whatever." Cecelia changed subjects, still sore and feeling wronged. "I loved that job, and you took it from me. Anyway, what's up with this creepy guy calling me for shit on you?"

"What creepy guy?"

"Some guy keeps calling me wanting me to give him dirt on you. Says he wants to ruin you, which you deserve, by the way."

Peyton's pulse raced; maybe she could find out who was doing this to her. "Do you know his name?"

"No, he says he works with you and hates you. Wants to bring you down. Shit like that," Cecelia replied.

"Have you…you know?"

"Given the videos to him?" Cecelia was suddenly enjoying herself. "Ha! Wouldn't that be a special treat for the underdog!"

"Well, have you?"

"Guess you'll have to wait to see what this guy does. Then you'll know." Cecelia stormed out of Taco King, her white paper bag filled with steaming Mexican food gripped firmly in her clenched hand.

"Fuck!" Peyton slammed her hand on the table. "God, I hate that bitch." She had spoken louder than she intended, and she noticed an elderly couple in the next booth looking at her with disgust.

"Sorry, sorry," Peyton said. "Sorry for the language. Never mind. Just sorry." Grabbing her tray, she dumped the rest of her dinner in the trash and left Taco King.

She had only been back in her hotel room a few minutes when her phone dinged. Hoping for a text from Corbin, she grabbed her phone and read a message from her mysterious harasser: "Peyton, it's not a good idea to fuck with Cecelia. It's not part of the game."

"Crap, she started it!" Peyton screamed. Then, feeling the need for release, she let the tears come.

"Now boarding Zone 3 for flight 1483 to Minneapolis at Gate B5," the Delta counter person said over the intercom. Grabbing her stuff, Peyton couldn't wait to get back to Georgia. At least she now knew it was a man at work after her and that Cecelia hadn't changed one bit.

56

CORBIN

I got back to Georgia around 3 a.m. Saturday, thankful that Hilton Mercedes didn't open until ten. I could completely perform with optimum energy on six hours of sleep. I lived fairly close to the dealership, so my commute time was only about thirty minutes, a luxury many Atlanta commuters did not have.

It had been a disappointing trip. I had hoped to learn what Cecelia held over Peyton's head. Instead, I came back with nothing other than knowing Cecelia was dead. But I didn't know if Spencer had already obtained what he needed from her. Frustrated, I crawled into bed and fell into a fitful, dream-filled sleep.

I was transported back to my unfurnished room in our first trailer in Great Falls. I had to have been older than three, because I was playing with my thumb doll, the only toy I had. I was alone in my room when, suddenly, a dark mist started flowing into the room from the heating vents. Accumulating into a massive form, a woman appeared, her neck slit and bleeding, her eyes empty black sockets. Holding her arms out to me, she pleaded, "Corbin, it's Cecelia. Come to me, Corbin." Backing away from her in fear and tucking my thumb doll into my pocket for safekeeping, I tried to scream at her to leave me alone, but my voice wouldn't come. She slowly kept advancing until I was curled into the smallest ball I could form in the corner of my room under the window. "Corbin, oh, Corbin," the dead Cecelia kept chanting, while she came closer and closer.

"No, no, no," I kept trying to scream without success.

"Corbin, Corbin, Corbin, I'm coming for you next," Cecelia threatened. "What if I tell the world your secrets? I'm coming, Corbin."

Mustering my courage, I opened my eyes and looked the dead Cecelia square in her empty eye sockets. "Go to hell," I managed to say.

Cecelia laughed heartily, and as her mouth opened, a little fluffy dog with blood-matted hair and vacant holes for eyes emerged. The dog drew close to my face, opened its mouth, spraying dark bile in my face, and emitting a resounding alarm that exploded in my ears. Clapping my hands over my ears, I shut my eyes and tried to make it stop.

Slow to waken, I realized the noise was my alarm going off, signaling the start of my Saturday. Switching off my alarm, I took a few deep breaths before getting into the shower.

Arriving at the dealership a few minutes before ten, I grabbed a cup of coffee before heading to my tiny office, barely big enough to hold a small desk and two guest chairs. I had just turned on my computer when Vince appeared in my office and worked his large body into one of the small guest chairs.

"So, how was your trip?" Vince asked, smiling like he was up to some shit.

"Fine," I replied.

"Fine? Just fine?"

"Yes," I said. "What's going on with you, man? You look like you're about to explode."

"Would you like to know what happened while you were gone?" Vince could not hide his excitement.

"You win the fucking lottery or something?" I asked.

"No, even better; well, I guess not even better depending on the pot, but still this is amazing."

"What? Tell me."

"Some guy came in here who wants to buy a fucking S65 AMG Cabriolet!" Vince yelled. "A fucking S65 AMG Cabriolet! I can't even fucking believe it!"

"You're so full of shit." I laughed. "If he wants to buy one, why didn't he just buy one? He's yanking your chain."

"No, here's the thing. He said he would only buy it from you."

"What? Who is this guy?" I asked.

"Hell if I know," said Vince, tossing a business card on the desk, "but he asked for you. Seems like a douche, but hell, if we get to sell a fucking S65, who gives a shit?"

"Oh, now it's 'we' selling this car?" I said.

"Well, I didn't have to give you his card," Vince replied, laughing.

"And then he wouldn't have bought a car, so you lose," I said while picking up the card. My expression changed instantly when I read it. Looking seriously at Vince, I asked, "He asked for me? By name?"

"Yeah. Whoa, what's wrong?" Vince caught the change in my mood. "You know this guy?"

"No, I don't." It wasn't a lie because while I knew who Franklin Eastman was, I didn't know him. "But I'll give him a call," I said, turning toward my computer.

Vince stood and looked at me for a moment before saying, "Whatever, dude. I don't know what's going on right now, but sell him that fucking car, okay?"

"Yeah, sure," I replied, "but you don't even have one here."

"We order it. Whatever the man wants," said Vince, mirroring my suddenly ill mood. "Don't fuck this up," he added before leaving.

Coming back, Vince popped his head in and said, "And he said he's only here until Tuesday, so you better call him today. Said he'll find one somewhere else if you miss him. Again, don't fuck this up. This is huge."

"Got it," I replied.

When Vince was finally gone, I picked up Franklin's card again. "What the fuck is he up to? I've left him alone, so why is he bothering me?"

I was angry to be in this position. I would have to contact Franklin or Vince would have my ass. Feeling manipulated, I couldn't call him until I was ready, if I'd ever be ready.

"Fuck him, sweeping in here and delivering ultimatums; who does he think he is?"

I tossed his card into my pencil drawer and tried to put it out of my mind. It was Saturday. I didn't have to call him today. I worked through the day, avoiding Vince as best I could. Right when we were about to close, he confronted me in my office. "You didn't call that guy, did you?"

"Nope; didn't have time today," I lied.

"Fuck, Corbin; don't make me fire you. Call that mother fucker."

"I will; just couldn't do it today. Don't worry. I won't fuck this up for the precious dealership, Vince." I knew I sounded petty.

"Hey, this dealership has treated you well. Don't forget that."

"Oh, I know. I get it. I'll call him on Monday; relax." I had to give Vince something.

"Okay, make sure you do. This is a solid lead; I know it." Vince sounded excited again.

"You got it, boss," I said, smiling insincerely.

When I arrived at Peyton's Southern Towers apartment, I was greeted with open arms. Peyton wrapped herself around me as soon as she opened the door and started crying. I had no idea what was going on, but felt she needed me to hold her, which I did. Finally, when the crying subsided, she said, "I'm sorry. I really missed you."

I knew there was more to it than that, but Peyton shared only what Peyton wanted to share, so I said, "Hey, I missed you, too. You want to order in and hang here?"

"Yes, please," she said. "Can we do Chinese?"

"Anything you want." I smiled at her softly. "Let's grab a beer and call in an order. Then, you can share why you are so upset."

"Maybe," she replied, crinkling up her adorable nose.

Finishing up the last bit of General Tso's chicken from New Beijing Chinese Restaurant, I felt the time was right.

"So, how was your conference?" I asked.

"Good."

"Then what has you so upset?"

"Oh, Corbin, I don't know; I don't want to talk about it."

"God, don't say 'us'," I joked and received a fortune cookie to the forehead in return.

Laughing, I tossed it back on the table and said, "But, Peyton; I want to know what's going on with you, and I want you to share your burdens with me. I am here for you. I freaking love you, okay?"

Looking at her shocked face, I realized I had never said those words to her before. I felt a bit scared as my words hung heavily over the now-empty containers of General Tso chicken and fried rice.

"You do?" she asked, her face searching mine.

Taking her hand, I said, "Yes, I love you. Please tell me what's wrong."

"I love you, too," she barely managed to get out before flying around the table and kissing me long and hard.

Pulling away as her eyes filled with tears again, she said, "No matter what?"

"Jesus, no matter what, Peyton; love is love. Why are you being such a girl right now?" I kidded, knowing I had to get her off her emotional roller coaster.

"Oh, fuck you," she said, kissing me again. "I am bothered by this shit about Cecelia. And my mom called today and said Cecelia and her son were murdered. Oh, and they killed the dog, too."

"What?" I tried to feign surprise. "They were murdered?"

"Yes; the police are saying someone broke into their home and killed them all. Slit their throats. Who could do such a horrible thing?" Peyton asked, but I wasn't sure if the appropriate amount of shock was behind the words.

"Well, that's horrible, but does that at least alleviate your issue with whoever is texting you?" I asked.

"I don't know. I guess we'll see." She paused, then said, "Would you mind if I took a quick shower? I feel icky."

"Sure, no problem; go ahead, and I'll clean up. I'll meet you in bed?" I laughed.

Kissing me again, she whispered, "You bet; be ready."

As she left the dining room, I began gathering empty cartons and clearing the table. Upon finishing, I stripped down and was getting into bed when I noticed Peyton's suitcase on the chest at the end of her bed. Laughing because Peyton hated to unpack a suitcase, I grabbed it to help her out. Sliding the zipper around the top, I noticed the Delta baggage ticket wrapped around the handle. Sioux Falls, final destination Atlanta.

So, Peyton had lied to me. Grabbing her phone, I quickly reviewed her texts and saw one from an unidentified number: "Peyton, it's not a good idea to fuck with Cecelia. It's not part of the game."

What had my Peyton been up to this week? Clearly, she hadn't been in Dallas for an HR conference. Although difficult, I pretended to be asleep when her warm, dewy body slid under the freshly laundered sheets. I needed to understand what was going on. She had lied to me. Was she like everyone else? My eyes were dark as the familiar feelings of betrayal surged through my veins. I tried to sleep, but it was futile.

57

FRANKLIN

It was Monday afternoon, but Franklin had not received the demanded call from Corbin. *This little fucker is going to play games with me?* Franklin thought as he sat in the Presidential Suite of the Ritz-Carlton.

He felt as though this was a wasted trip and a mistake. He picked up his phone and called Hernando.

"Yes, boss?"

"Hey, everything good on the ranch?" Franklin asked.

"Yes," Hernando replied. "Why do you ask? Aren't you on vacation?"

"A man like me can never really be on vacation," Franklin replied.

"Because you only have more money than you could ever spend in twelve lifetimes?" Hernando asked.

"Fuck you," Franklin replied. He was tired of how cocky Hernando had become in the last few years, but he could never fire him. He was too valuable and knew too much.

"Sure, fuck me," Hernando said. "Do you need something, boss? How's the family reunion going?"

"That's not what this is. I just wanted to know if the ranch is fine. Don't you forget who butters your bread, damn you."

"Never do, sir. The ranch is fine. It's calving season, and we've encountered no problems. Lots of young blood running around here."

"Fine, thanks." Franklin disconnected the call, annoyed by the reference to young blood.

In Montana, Hernando laughed. He knew Franklin's level of annoyance. He was tired of kissing his butt. Franklin would be in prison if it weren't for him. But he still lived in the bunkhouse and continued to clean up Franklin's shit.

It was around 4 p.m. when Franklin received the call he was waiting for.

"Hello, Mr. Eastman; this is Corbin from Hilton Mercedes. I'm told you wish to buy a car from us," said his son's voice.

"Yes," was, surprisingly, all Franklin could say.

"Great. I'm also told that you would like an S65 AMG Cabriolet. As you can imagine, they aren't housed in inventory, but we can order one to your exact specifications. What exterior color would you like?"

"Silver," Franklin said. Then added, "Corbin?"

"Yes, I'm Corbin. I believe you asked my supervisor to work with me."

"Yeah, yeah." Franklin had his thoughts back. "Do you suppose we could get a drink later and discuss the features I will need in my new S65?"

"I'm not sure that's a good idea," Corbin said. "We frown on conducting business outside of the dealership."

"Cut the crap, Corbin. Meet me tonight at the bar in the Buckhead Ritz-Carlton."

"Oh, I'm delivering crap? Who showed up on my turf pretending to buy a $250,000 car? You don't give me orders."

"Be there." Franklin disconnected the call.

Not sure what he was feeling, Franklin decided to take a walk around Buckhead and distract his mind until that evening. Annoyed that the only places within walking distance were shopping malls and boutique stores, Franklin walked across the street to Lenox Mall. He wandered around for some time observing people, mostly the beautiful young women who would taste so delicious. While he enjoyed the times he could feed, he regretted that he wasn't normal. Why did he have these desires to eat human organs? It wasn't right. It wasn't normal, but nothing could stop the desire. And for some inexplicable reason, he needed to know if Corbin shared that desire. Maybe it was age or what Emily was going through right now, but he needed to know.

Returning to the hotel, Franklin showered and pulled on his most comfortable faded jeans and a light-blue, button-up shirt, finishing the look by adding his favorite black belt that held his one trophy belt buckle he'd secured many years ago at the Augusta rodeo. It was worn and faded, but it was a burning memory of what he'd always hoped to be.

Riding the elevator to the lobby, Franklin stepped off and headed toward the hotel bar. He secured a corner table and ordered a Tito's with a splash of soda and a lime. He was positioned to observe people coming into or out of the bar. Hours passed before he witnessed a young version of himself walk into the bar and look around. Quickly recognizing him, Corbin approached the table and sat down. The waitress appeared instantly. "Welcome to the Ritz-Carlton, sir; what can I get for you?"

"I'll have a beer," Corbin said. "Miller Lite?"

"It would be my pleasure," was the trained response.

Franklin waited until Corbin faced him before saying, "Thanks for coming."

"Well, you wanted to buy a car. My boss wants me to sell a car. It's not like I had a choice."

Franklin scanned Corbin's face. It was like looking in the mirror twenty-five years ago.

"I don't even know why I'm here," Franklin said and then grabbed his drink.

The waitress chose that moment to return, so Corbin gratefully took a long swig from his beer.

"I don't either," Corbin replied. "I don't want shit from you. I don't need you."

"I know you don't," said Franklin. "I appreciate that you didn't follow in your mother's footsteps and harass the shit out of me."

"I wrote you one letter, and you never replied. I saw you that day in the Waffle Castle. You fucking freaked out."

"Yep," Franklin said before picking up his drink. "Thing is, I need to know something."

"Well, I want to know a lot of things. Like how you could abandon me to a life of mental, physical, and sexual abuse. You knew about me. I know you did. Sure, the letters started coming back unopened, but you still knew. You had to have."

"I didn't—"

"I don't believe you," Corbin said. "You had to have known."

"She told me she was pregnant, but I didn't know it was mine. It's not like your mother and I were together back then. She made all kinds of assumptions."

"Fuck you. Why didn't you open her letters?" Corbin was feeling more emotion than he was comfortable with.

"Like I said, we weren't together. Hell, I only saw her once in a while. I figured she was trying to trick me for the money."

"Whatever; I don't care. I want you to leave me alone." Corbin drained his beer and stood up.

"Wait, please?" Franklin managed a soft, almost gentle tone. "Please sit down. Hear me out. I'll buy the fucking car. I don't give a shit."

Laughing loudly, Corbin replied, "I don't need your goddamn money. I don't need you. Fuck you. Get your ass back to Montana and never, fucking-ever, approach me again."

"But I'm a billionaire," Franklin said. "I want…."

"Yeah? Who the fuck cares what you want?"

Corbin turned to leave, but Franklin grabbed his arm. Making eye contact, Franklin pleaded, "Please, please, let me ask you one question?"

"What's that?"

"Do you have the gene?"

"What are you talking about?" Corbin snapped, pulling his arm free.

"You know, the gene that makes you want certain things," Franklin replied.

"Want certain things? Like to never see you again? Sure, I have that gene," said Corbin, laughing.

"No, this is important. Do you have…it?"

Corbin suddenly realized what Franklin was asking, but he would not give him the satisfaction. Scanning Franklin up and down, Corbin took a deep breath and said, "Get your ass back to Montana. Leave me the fuck alone."

Corbin stormed from the dimly lit bar, leaving behind the soft murmuring of businessmen and woman networking and flirting after a busy day of travel and meetings.

It would have been easy to admit it. And while he didn't understand why it was important to Franklin, withholding the information was the only card he held. He wasn't about to give this guy any satisfaction.

Sitting alone in the Ritz-Carlton bar, Franklin realized he would probably never know, though he suspected.

58

CORBIN

I was annoyed at the people in my life and the emotional games they were all playing with me. What the hell did Franklin want with me after all these years? And, why, oh why would my beautiful Peyton lie to me? My emotions were so conflicted. I could barely stand to kiss Peyton goodbye the next morning after I realized her deceit. What was Peyton's business in South Dakota if not to cause harm to Cecelia? But more importantly, why would she lie to me? With everything I had shared with Peyton, why would she not feel comfortable telling me the truth? What had happened in South Dakota? Why was Spencer harassing her, and why wouldn't she share the information that I could possibly use to help her? Did she not understand that I was now hers and I would do anything, literally anything, to keep her safe and happy?

When I arrived at Hilton Mercedes, I was not in the mood to deal with the overly anxious Vince who greeted me at the door, salivating like a starving dog waiting on a scrap of rotting bologna.

"You close the deal?" Vince asked upon my arrival.

"Nope."

"What? Corbin, what the fuck? That was a done deal. The guy wanted the car. What did you do to fuck it up?"

"It was all a bunch of bullshit, Vince." I headed toward my small, glass-fronted office.

"No, no, it was not," said Vince. "I talked to the guy. He was ready to buy. What the hell did you do?" Vince grabbed my arm and slung me against the wall.

Grabbing him swiftly by the throat, I said, "I told you. He was a lying piece of shit who never intended to buy a fucking car. I tried to tell you that and you wouldn't listen. Now, I'm going to allow you to breathe again and you are kindly going to walk away knowing that I was right."

After I released my grip on Vince's fatty neck, he gasped for air before he barely choked out, "You're fired, mother fucker. Get the fuck out of my dealership."

"No problem. I'm out."

Driving home, I wasn't concerned about my future. I'd been through worse and had no concerns about my ability to secure alternative sources of income. I was charming and sold myself well. I would be fine. Hell, I had bullshitted my way into all the jobs I'd ever held. What I wasn't sure about was my future with Peyton. If she would come clean with me now, there was a chance I could forgive her. Sure, it was a small chance, but that opportunity still existed, although the window was quickly closing.

Annoyed and needing a detoxing distraction, I grabbed my phone and called Spencer.

"Hey, man, what you doing?" I asked.

"Oh, not much. At work. What's up?" Spencer replied.

"I was thinking maybe we blow off work today and go catch the Planet of the Apes marathon at the Cinemax 8. Thoughts?" I laughed, knowing it would be irresistible to Spencer.

Much to my dismay, Spencer replied, "Uh, yeah, I can't today. Sorry; I gotta go."

Staring into a dead phone, I felt exasperated and even more frustrated. Why would Spencer turn on me, too? Spencer of all people? Spencer had no other friend. Now I'm not even good enough for him? Holy shit. *I guess Jessica was right all along,* I thought as I sped down 285 east headed to no particular destination. I needed to get away. I felt the world was closing in, wrapping me in a haze heavy with deceit and betrayal. I felt the familiar pang in the pit of my stomach, signaling my inherent need to feed. Crushing the accelerator to the floor, I weaved and darted through Atlanta traffic. I needed some release, and more importantly, resolution about why Peyton would betray me.

Peyton had lied to me. Peyton was like every other person in my life. Everyone betrayed me. Sam, oh, poor Sam. I had loved him more than anyone, but all he could do was fuck Jessica and abandon me. I sometimes felt bad about Sam, until I remembered his fat, sweaty body thrusting into Jessica's ass. He had gotten what he deserved. Peyton would have to fall victim to a similar fate for her lies. I loved her completely, but why had she lied to me? What was she doing in South Dakota? Why can no one love me or be honest with me?

Racing around Atlanta, I realized I needed to play this game more cleverly. First, I needed to understand what had happened in South Dakota and the role Peyton had played in eliminating Cecelia. Taking a deep breath, I slowed the Maxima and pulled into the right lane. I needed to keep my temper under control. I needed to manipulate the events. Maybe, just maybe, the tables would turn and I could actually enjoy the beautiful Peyton Alexander's warm liver. But I'd need to play my cards carefully. Knowing Peyton was no longer my ally oddly reassured me.

Exiting 285, I pulled into an Arby's parking lot. My heart racing and palms sweating, it was clear what needed to happen. Everyone had betrayed me. Everyone must pay.

59

PEYTON

The next morning, Peyton realized the luggage tag was still on her red suitcase. She quickly pulled the sticky adhesive tape apart, crumpled it up, and tossed it into the trash. The deceitful pit rumbled in her stomach as she wondered whether Corbin had seen it.

I know; I should have been honest, Peyton thought. But truth be told, she would only look guilty in regards to Cecelia's fate. She hadn't had any more interaction with Cecelia after the taco night, but who would believe her? The reason for her visit to South Dakota had been innocent, and she never intended or expected to see Cecelia. Her father had called, asking her to visit due to his recent diagnosis with colon cancer.

She was worried because Corbin acted so distantly. She had known he wasn't asleep when she had slipped into bed. In the morning, he had barely kissed her cheek before leaving, and his eyes had been dark and brooding. Should she come clean? But what if he thought she had something to do with Cecelia's murder? Who could have committed such a horrible act? It wasn't like Cecelia had any money or valuable property. She lived in a shitty trailer and worked as a bartender, hoping to get better tips and being willing to take money in exchange for giving a blow job in the alley on her break.

Peyton was better than that. She was ashamed of that night, but not enough to murder. But what would Corbin believe? She regretted the night she had agreed to go out with Cecelia and Nancy. They had been close friends, or so she had thought at the time. They had all worked together, and she had thought she was in safe company.

Beers had led to shots that led to more shots. Two attractive guys had approached them at the bar, resulting in more shots. Nancy, their boss, was encouraging more drinking and dancing. At some drunken moment, Peyton vaguely recalled Dale showing up. Before Nancy left with him, she had whispered something into Cecelia's ear.

At last call, the men suggested getting a hotel room and more beer to finish off the evening, offering to stop on the way and buy a case. Cecelia and Peyton were both inappropriately drunk, or so Peyton had believed at the time, and when the men suggested some flirtatious kissing between the women, Cecelia quickly complied. One thing led to another, and before Peyton realized it, the guy, who may have been named Larry, was joining them. Too drunk and too naked to care, Peyton gave into the moment. And then things went dark.

Waking the next morning, the men were gone, and she had only a vague recollection of what had happened the night before. Rolling over to see Cecelia's naked body lying next to her, Peyton had tried to console herself by reassuring that nagging little voice pounding loudly against her forehead that Cecelia was a friend. They were close friends; it would be fine. They had been through a lot together, like the night early in her career at Protect Your Home when Cecelia had called Peyton because she had been drugged and gang-raped in a fraternity house. Peyton had been there for her, had picked her up, and had been supportive while listening to the grueling events.

Things would be fine. She trusted Cecelia. Slipping out of bed, Peyton hopped into a hot, steamy shower. After enjoying the hot water washing away all of the disgusting bar's smells and vague memories, she slid the frosty glass door open. Peyton gasped as she saw Cecelia standing near the toilet, watching her closely, a smug smile decorating her freckled face.

"Oh, hi," Peyton said while grabbing a towel. "Did you have fun last night?"

Laughing softly, Cecelia held her phone out, revealing a video of Peyton in a compromising threesome with Larry from the bar and Chris from work. Peyton didn't remember Chris ever being there or having a threesome.

"Yes, Peyton. I had a super-fun night. Maybe you should stop kissing up at work and making me look bad. I'd hate to share this with Dale."

Peyton felt like she had been kicked in the stomach by one of her grandfather's Holstein bulls, but she tried to play it off. "Ha, you're so funny. Work is work; play is play."

"Sure; we'll see about that," Cecelia said before exiting the bathroom.

Monday morning had been interesting and terrifying. Cecelia arrived forty-five minutes late with no text or call to Peyton. When she arrived, Peyton approached her cubicle and said, "Hey, everything okay? I was worried!"

"Sure; it's great," Cecelia replied. Holding out a thumb drive, she said, "Hey, I made this for you, so you will never forget Friday night. I made a few copies for myself, too—you know, insurance."

"What?" Peyton asked. "What are you talking about? We're friends."

"Yeah, sure," Cecelia said. "If we're friends, stop making me look bad at work."

"I'm just doing my job. I'm not trying to make you look bad."

"Whatever. Nancy told me she was leaving, so you better hope I get her job instead of you. You know, unless you want Dale to see the real you."

"Cecelia, you wouldn't. You were there, too. We were just having fun."

"Funny that I'm not in any of the pictures or videos, isn't it?" Cecelia said before turning around and dismissing Peyton.

As Peyton exited her cubicle, she wanted to cry, scream, and vomit, all at the same time. Holding it together, she sat staring into her computer monitor, hoping Dale would not realize something horribly wrong was happening. Hours later, Nancy announced her resignation and Peyton was promoted to office manager. Happy to have a better position and more pay, Peyton was horrified at what Cecelia might do.

From that Monday forward, Cecelia did whatever Cecelia wanted and absolutely nothing more. Discussing her performance, offering words of encouragement, and even expressions of love were all met with deaf ears. Peyton remembered when the matter was escalated to Dale.

Cecelia, who had been away from her cubicle for over an hour, rushed in one afternoon, her lipstick smeared across her cheek and her clothes disheveled; she quickly sat down at her desk and started typing. Peyton wasn't sure what had happened, but a few moments later, Peyton's phone buzzed. It was Dale.

"Come to my office, please," he said. "We have a situation."

When Peyton walked into Dale's office, he was shaking his head. "Peyton, I need you to talk to Cecelia. She was caught having, um, inappropriate relations with Simon from service in the shop. That poor kid, Jared, walked in on them. Tell her she is on probation effective now, and we should fire her. Tell her she doesn't get another pass."

"Sure," Peyton replied. "I'll take care of it."

"Thanks," Dale said. "You're a great employee. I appreciate it."

Peyton's palms were sweating as she approached Cecelia. "Hey, can I talk to you for a minute?"

"Sure; I'm finishing up something. I'll come see you when I'm finished," Cecelia replied without turning around.

Over an hour later, Cecelia appeared in Peyton's office. "What's up?"

Peyton redirected her attention from her computer screen and said, "Hey, Dale wanted me to talk to you. Apparently, Jared caught you and Simon today. So, Dale said you are on probation, and you need to focus on your job. You can't be doing that kind of thing at work."

"Oh, sure," Cecelia replied. "I'll be sure to focus on that." As Cecelia walked away, Peyton knew the situation was not over.

The next morning, Dale called her once again into his office. "So, you need to talk to me about what Cecelia has on you."

"What she has on me?" Peyton questioned, although she knew exactly what he was referring to.

"Cut the crap, Peyton," he said. "I already know."

"Look; we were drunk. I'm so sorry. I don't even remember Chris being there or most of the night. I blacked out and really can't remember any of it. We were just having some fun. And now she's twisting things and has those awful pictures."

"Well, unfortunately you are her supervisor now. I think this whole thing is fishy, but Cecelia is a problem," Dale replied. "I know how hard you work, and I've noticed she has basically stopped working, not to mention her more recent activities. I also don't condone blackmail. I'm going to back you on this, but you need to straighten up. I'm going to fire her, but you need to make sure you separate friends and work. Clear?"

"Yes, sir," Peyton replied. "Thank you so very much."

"Sure; send in Cecelia, please."

Peyton shuddered upon reliving those events. She wanted nothing more than to put that behind her. But now, it was all too real and she needed to get away. Maybe even away from Corbin, considering she was so damaged. She couldn't tell him about the South Dakota visit.

60

FRANKLIN

Franklin opened the heavy front door and walked into the over-bearing foyer covered in extravagant maple and art. "Ann, Ann? I'm back," he hollered. "How are things? Emily doing okay?"

Almost instantly, a stately woman in light-blue medical scrubs appeared. "Shh, Franklin; she's finally sleeping, or at least I hope she's down this time."

"Sorry; I know I have a big voice," he said, a few decibels lower. "I can't help it."

"Well, you can help it; I know you can. So better to say you choose not to," Ann replied. "I've known you and your family too long for you to lie to me."

Humbled by her directness, Franklin said, "You're right, Ann. I'm sorry. So, how was she while I was gone? Was it rough?"

"Yes, rough. I don't know how long I can manage her. Her spells are getting much worse," Ann replied. "Hernando found her roam-ing around, mostly naked, in the calving pasture and talking about the cows being her sweet little babies. When he tried to get her back inside, she bit him on the arm, hard enough to draw blood, and told him, 'That's what we do, us Eastmans!' Clearly, she's losing her sense of reality more and more every day."

Feeling guilty, Franklin said, "Well, you are correct. Why would she bite Hernando? What do you suppose that comment meant?"

"I can't even make a logical guess," replied Ann. "I'm a trained medical professional, but the inner workings of the human mind, especially one in her condition, are complicated. My point is you may need to start thinking about, well, alternatives."

"Ann," Franklin held up his hand, "I'm not putting my Emily away. I have enough money to pay you handsomely to take care of her, and that's what you're supposed to do. How did she get out of the house? You need to watch her more closely."

"Franklin, I am only one person. I have to sleep and shower from time to time. Emily is crafty, even though her mind is failing her. I simply cannot be around every second. She is at the point where she requires constant supervision and care."

"Right, right," Franklin said, realizing how much he needed Ann. "You're right. I'm sorry. Maybe you could refer another person to help you so she can have 24/7 care?"

"Okay, I'll give you some names, but can I say one thing?"

"Sure."

"Well, in my opinion, if you spent even a little amount of time with her, it would go a long way. When was the last time you saw her? You stay in your room or on the ranch or doing God knows what. Maybe your wife needs to know you are still around and that you love her. Love does amazing things, you know."

"Right." Franklin felt uncomfortable. "So, you say she's sleeping now? Why don't you go to your room and get some rest? Make sure her door is locked," he said while pouring a Scotch over a few ice cubes.

Sighing in resignation, yet tired and glad to sleep, Ann retired to her room after checking the lock on Emily's door.

Taking a sip of his drink, Franklin was infuriated. How dare Ann tell him what to do and that he needed to see Emily? He didn't want to remember her like this. He only wanted the vision of her in her beautiful yellow sundress covered with purple lilies and butterflies as she ran across the pasture, her beautiful tan arms and legs muscular and strong, ready and willing to embrace him. He loved that she always wore those brown boots with a square toe and tan stitching. Never would he forget the day she had driven the ATV to the branding site, wearing that dress and those boots. She had called him away from the guys, and as she sat straddling the ATV, she rubbed her smooth, soft inner thigh, and said, "I have something better for you to do than burn a brand in a poor baby cow."

"Calf," Franklin had replied. "A baby cow is a calf."

"Jesus…I know that, but they are still babies," she had replied. "And you have greatly missed the point."

She sped away on that green camo ATV. He left shortly after, catching her in the hayloft, where they made sweet, passionate love. And now, his Emily was fading. They were both facing impending death; sure, maybe not in the next few years, but Franklin hated the realization that it was coming one day.

His illegitimate son hated him for good reasons, and Franklin was confused about why he cared. As much as Emily and he had wanted children, fate did not grant them that. After several miscarriages, the doctors highly recommended the efforts stop for Emily's sake. It was too much of a burden to her emotionally and physically. Franklin complied, but once the realization had hit Emily that she would never be a mother, she hadn't been the same.

Years went by with Franklin being primarily unaware, but one day, he realized his wife was no longer mentally present. She talked randomly about blood, cannibalism, and how she had only wanted a family. Franklin realized the burden of carrying his secret all these years was taking a toll on her. The doctors had diagnosed her with Alzheimer's and issued medication that was supposed to help.

Vowing to provide the best care possible, Franklin had hired Ann to care for Emily, but now it seemed more was needed. He didn't care how much it cost; it hurt him to see Emily like this. Her social circle accepted the diagnosis with much more ease than Franklin and dismissed her tales as a crazy woman's ramblings. That was fortunate for Franklin, but it still broke his heart because he had exposed her to his horrible secret.

61

PEYTON

On her way to get her morning cup of coffee, Peyton ran into Spencer outside of the breakroom. She tried to slide past him, but he stopped her with, "Peyton, can I talk to you?"

Knowing she had to respond, she said, "I'm always available. I just need to get some coffee."

"Well, this will only take a second," he replied.

"Okay, what's up?" Peyton asked, annoyed but hiding it professionally.

Spencer put his hand on her arm and said, "Someone is out to get me."

Peyton felt her cheeks flush and calmed the rising bile in her stomach. "What do you mean?"

"I've done some bad things," Spencer said.

"What are you talking about? What bad things?"

"I can't tell you. They wouldn't like it."

"Spencer, what are you talking about?"

"The voices. I hear them all the time," he replied while his eyes darted rapidly from side to side. "They talk to me!"

"Spencer," Peyton said, "maybe you need to get some help? We have an EAP here at Blast. I can give you the number."

"No, no, no, no! Shh, they will hear us! Peyton, I only did what I needed to do."

"Spencer, you're scaring me. I don't know what you're talking about."

"Oh, I'm sure you will find out," he said before darting down the hall into his plum cubicle.

What the hell? Peyton thought as she prepared her coffee. An uneasy feeling was in the pit of her stomach. Something ominous was in the air. She somehow knew people were going to get hurt or broken or worse.

62

CORBIN

I knew what Spencer had been up to and that he was the one threatening Peyton. Shutting me out had been a bad move on his part. I had always been his best friend and confidant. For him to dismiss me so easily meant he needed to be destroyed, not only for my satisfaction, but also to protect Peyton. I wasn't sure of my future with her now, considering the lies, but no one but me would fuck her over. Her liver would be mine, and I would relish the moment she gave it to me. Therefore, Spencer needed to be eliminated.

When I dialed Spencer again, he answered, "What?" I could hear nervousness in his voice.

"What's the matter, Spencer? Cat got your tongue?"

"Hey, I don't want to go to the movies with you. I have some serious shit going on in my head, and I can't deal with you right now. Give me some space, please?"

"Sure. If that's what you think is your best move—to ignore me—then sure, go ahead and do that. But remember, I know you are the one fucking with Peyton. And you will pay."

The phone went dead, but I laughed. Message delivered.

Sitting quietly in my house, I heard the basement calling me. How long had it been since I had played with my thumb dolls?

Grabbing a cold beer from the fridge and the key to the basement door, I ventured back to my old friends. No matter how many I collected, my own thumb was always my favorite. As I sat in the basement, I realized the anxiety Franklin's visit had caused me. I didn't want anything from him, but yet, I did. I was his son. I wondered what it would feel like to go hunting with him and jointly enjoy the fresh warm liver of a rebellious girl dumb enough to get in a car with us. Silly, silly girl.

And then I thought of the beautiful Peyton Alexander. I wanted her more than anything. While I wanted to eat her liver, I also wanted to trust and love her. And have her love me back. My mind wondered what life could be like if someone actually loved me. Walking hand in hand on the beach. Laughing at silly, scary movies. Grabbing a bite to eat that turned into uninhibited sex in the parking lot of the sub sandwich shop. Waking up in the morning to roll over and see her smooth shoulder peeking from beneath the white sheet. As I would slide my arms around her, she wouldn't even wake, but melt into my form. Ah, the perfect world. But she had lied to me, and Spencer had lied to me. Both of them needed to pay. Or could Peyton be saved?

63

SPENCER

Spencer was exhausted, but he could not sleep. Things had gone awry, and he didn't know how to rein them back in. His trip to visit Cecelia had ended with no information that would help him continue blackmailing Peyton. When the Atlanta PD had showed up in the office the following week, his heart had stopped. They were there to visit Peyton, but what was their purpose? He had been to South Dakota and had read about Cecelia's horrible death online. He only vaguely remembered being there, yet knew he had been responsible for something as evidenced by the sense of guilt he could not overcome. He could not put his finger on the problem.

The police talked to Peyton extensively in her glass-fronted office. Spencer sat, his eyes glued to the scene, sweat beads rolling down his forehead. Pam, the old biddy from Accounting, stopped by to talk about pet rescue and a dog she had placed somewhere. Spencer nodded but had no idea where the dog had found his new home, nor did he care. His only concern was what the Atlanta PD were doing in Peyton's office. What were they asking her? What were their questions? Why did he feel so guilty, and why had Corbin threatened him?

Dismissing Pam with a wave, Spencer waited for her departure before grabbing his phone. He knew he shouldn't, but he dialed Cecelia's number. It was answered quickly by a male voice. "South Dakota State Patrol. Who is this?"

Quickly hanging up, Spencer knew he had to leave. He had done something so wrong. He needed to figure things out.

After leaving the office, Spencer sat alone in his basement apartment, shaking. He tried to calm down enough to remember what had happened in South Dakota, but to no avail. He stared at the frozen game screen, his eyes darting, and let his mind drift. Something was off. He remembered feeling this way one other time in his life. He closed his eyes and tried to remember anything, any detail, any bit of information that would help him figure out what was going on. Why were the police at Cecelia's house? His mind drifted as his double dose of anxiety medication calmed his nerves. He had to remember.

Behind his closed eyelids, he saw blurry forms moving about, white, blurry forms, murmuring quietly. Suddenly, a face developed on one of the forms: a brunette woman with thick black glasses sliding down her nose that appeared a bit too small for her face.

"Spencer?" she asked. "Spencer, can you hear me, honey? Do you know where you are?"

"I'm at camp, right? Mommy said I was going to camp for a while," eight-year-old Spencer stated.

"That's right, honey; you are at camp," the woman replied. "Now, try to relax."

"Can we have s'mores later?" Spencer asked.

"Sure, honey," the woman said to Spencer before turning to another white form. "He has no idea what has happened or what he did."

Spencer blacked out for a moment and was awakened by the familiar scene of his mother's kitchen in Carrollton where they used to live. Debbie, the babysitter, was watching him because his parents had arranged date night, something they tried to do once every two weeks. Spencer had never liked Debbie. She was mean to him and didn't let him watch good shows on TV. She made him eat gross things like frozen fried chicken dinners with watery mashed potatoes and squishy peas while standing over him until he choked down the last bite.

"You eat it because I said so! You do what I say because I am the babysitter!"

"But I want a peanut-butter-and-jelly sandwich," the young Spencer begged. "Please?"

"No, you do what you are told." Debbie ended the conversation by turning to empty the dishwasher. Spencer felt his face flush and his eyes rapidly darting. He screamed at Debbie, leaped, and pushed her.

"I said I want peanut butter and jelly! I am sick of you and your stupid rules!"

Debbie fell face forward, her head smashing into the open dishwasher where the long sharp butcher knife had been placed blade side up. Penetrating her right eyeball, the knife slid smoothly into her brain. Spencer chuckled as he pulled the blue chair to the counter and started fixing his sandwich. Debbie lay quietly as life drained from her body and blood coated the clean dishes.

Spencer sat straight up, eyes wide open and sweat drenching his body as he recalled that long-suppressed childhood memory.

"Oh, my God," he whispered into the dim basement. "I killed Debbie. I didn't go to camp. I was put away. How I am just now remembering this?"

And with one dose of reality came the other.

"Shit," he realized. "I know what happened to Cecelia."

And then, in complete clarity, he remembered everything.

He remembered hanging up the phone in disgust after a conversation with Cecelia. He had thought Cecelia was such a promising source. She had originally told him she hated Peyton, and Peyton had ruined her life, but upon further conversation, she wasn't forthcoming in sharing information.

"What do you want from me?" Cecelia had asked early in their phone conversation.

Sighing because he thought the intent so obvious, Spencer said, "I want you to help me ruin Peyton."

"What? All that shit was a long time ago. I don't want to relive it."

"Well, you said you hated her and that she ruined your life," Spencer replied, his anger and confusion growing. He thought he had the ticket to end the arrogant Peyton Alexander.

Cecelia snorted on the line. "Sure, I hate her, but I'm not going to dredge up old shit. I don't know what you want with me, but I don't want to be involved."

"Wait, wait, wait. Can't you help me at all? Don't you have any evidence? I know something happened at Protect Your Home. I talked to them."

"What? You talked to them? What did they say?"

Spencer, sensing he'd hit a sore spot, said, "Well, Cecelia, you share yours and I'll share mine."

"Fuck you." And the call ended.

Little Miss Cecelia needed some convincing.

Spencer arrived at the Sioux Falls airport and headed toward Mitchell in his rented Ford Focus. He wasn't sure what he was going to do, but if he met Cecelia face-to-face, he could convince her she needed to help him. He had become irrationally obsessed with ruining Peyton, and he would not let someone withholding information stand in his way.

Arriving at 1721 S. Main, Spencer knocked on the door since there was no doorbell. A few seconds later, a trashy-looking bleach blonde woman wearing a halter top and sweat pants presented herself at the door. "Yeah? What do you want?"

"Hi, Cecelia," Spencer said. "I've come to talk with you."

Recognizing his voice, Cecelia tried to slam the door, but his white athletic shoe blocked it.

"What the hell?" she said.

He pushed into her double-wide trailer. A small white poodle awoke from his nap and began yipping furiously from the couch.

Pushing her onto the living room floor, Spencer felt his rage rise. "Shut that dog up! I've come for the dirt on Peyton. Tell me now!"

Cecelia back-crawled away from him, assessing the situation, and said calmly, "It's not like that." Reaching the couch, she comforted the dog, who quickly stopped barking and went to check his food bowl.

"You said you hated her, and she ruined your life! Give me what I want."

"Yeah, yeah," Cecelia said. "It's not as easy as that. Things were complicated. I have a kid now. I don't want to go back to that place in my life. I've moved on."

"Interesting," Spencer said, oddly calm, although his eyes rapidly darted back and forth. "Well, here's the thing, Cecelia; you are going to give me the dirt on Peyton Alexander or things are not going to end well. I don't know how I can make it any clearer."

"Fine, fine; I'm your friend." Cecelia quickly evaluated the situation. "Can we bring this down a notch or two?"

"Oh, that's so much better, Cecelia," Spencer replied. "See how easy this can be?"

"Sure." She considered her options. "Let me get up and share what I have."

"That's all I want," he replied.

Tentatively standing, Cecelia walked down the hall toward the bedroom. Spencer followed. As he entered the room, Cecelia moved slowly to shut the door behind him. Immediately alarmed, Spencer spun and looked at the door.

"Oh, don't worry," Cecelia said. "I want some privacy for what I'm about to reveal."

"Okay, sure," Spencer replied.

Cecelia walked to the closet and said over her shoulder, "I have to get into my safe for the information you want. It's serious and I have to keep it locked up. Is that okay?"

"Yes. I want the good stuff. It must be great if you keep it locked up."

"You know it is," Cecelia replied. Her mind was searching for a way to get this psychopath out of her house before Justin got home from school. She noted Spencer's oddly darting eyes and nervous behavior. She had no idea what Peyton had done to this guy, nor did she want to. She wasn't even sure how he'd found her.

Quickly searching her closet while pretending to access a safe, which was actually a storage box, Cecelia's only hope landed on a pair of stilettos she had purchased to entice Justin's father to marry her, which had been a failure. Grabbing the 4" heeled shoe, she placed it behind her back as she turned. Then she approached Spencer, who stood salivating at the bedroom door.

"Hey," she said. "So, I have what you want behind my back. Can we have a little fun with how you get it?"

Spencer, suddenly aroused without understanding why, said, "Sure."

Was it Peyton's impending demise or this woman provocatively approaching him that suddenly turned him on? Regardless, a hard-on was forming in his khaki pants.

Cecelia approached slowly, her hand behind her back, deceitfully concealing the "dirt" this crazy man sought. As she drew near, she noticed the sweat droplets on his brow and how his eyes never stopped darting from side to side. She thought he would explode when she touched him. Smiling seductively, she whispered into his left ear, "How much fun do you want to have?"

Gripping the shoe tightly, she whipped it from behind her back and aimed for Spencer's temple. Landing a little low from her target, the spiked heel grazed off Spencer's cheekbone, leaving a deep red line on his puffy, flushed face.

"Damn it!" Spencer grabbed his cheek. "What the he—" But Cecelia had time to strike again, this time going for his throat. While she was unable to land any fatal strikes, she had worked him away from the door, and luckily, none of his return punches struck home. Spinning toward the door, she managed to grab the doorknob and open the door, but then he was on her.

Grabbing Cecelia from behind, Spencer threw her toward the bed. She crashed into the bedroom wall on the back side of the bed. Jumping up and leaping at him with more spirit than she realized she had, Cecelia smacked hard into him, momentarily knocking him off-guard. Recovering quickly, Spencer violently shoved her backwards, his rage and anger exploding in his ears. Cecelia crashed into the side of the bed and fell, her head smashing loudly into the gray metal nightstand she'd picked up at Goodwill last month. Spencer heard a loud crack as Cecelia made impact with the cold metal.

The rage pulsating through his veins would not allow Spencer to realize the magnitude of what had happened. In the next few seconds, he became aware of the little fluffy dog barking loudly in the room and biting at his calves. Spinning, he kicked the dog into the opposite wall of the hallway. Fluffy—he'd subconsciously named it—hit the wall with a big yip, and then lay quietly.

Bending to see if Cecelia were still alive, Spencer noted she was taking shallow, uneven, rasping breaths. "What a bitch," Spencer said.

Hurrying into the kitchen, he found a long, metal butcher knife in a flimsy, cluttered kitchen drawer. Returning to the bedroom, he slit Cecelia's neck and then Fluffy's for good measure. He had no other choice. If Cecelia lived, she would have him arrested. He had to finish what he had started.

When all was quiet in the house, Spencer rummaged through Cecelia's closet and dresser looking for anything he could use against Peyton. Finding nothing and once again enraged, Spencer kicked Cecelia's dead body in the stomach. "Cunt."

And then he heard the front door open, and a minute later, in a squalling pitch that only a child can make, "Bandit? Bandit!" followed by footsteps running toward the poor little silent mound of bloody fur. Stepping beside the door to hide, Spencer waited until the crying boy turned and saw his mother lying in a pool of dark, red blood by the bed. Holding the ceramic lamp from the dresser, Spencer waited until the boy had knelt down by Cecelia, crying and sobbing hysterically. The shattering blue ceramic crashing into the back of boy's head quickly quieted him. A quick slice through his neck with the already bloody butcher knife ensured his silence forever.

Before leaving the scene, Spencer grabbed a towel from an overflowing laundry basket in the bathroom and wiped down everything he remembered touching. Satisfied with his cleanup, he used the towel to open the door. Stepping into the early evening, he put this disappointing trip behind him.

Now, several days later, Spencer sat shaking in his dark basement with his many unanswered gaming requests beeping in the distance. He had killed Cecelia. And her son. And her dog.

As the stark realization hit him, he felt his body melt into the couch's sunken seat. "Holy shit, I am the fucked up one. I am the bad guy. It's me. It's not them…it's me."

Pacing back and forth in the basement, his mind racing at his new discovery, he became angry at his parents. "How could they lie to me? Camp? That wasn't camp. They should have given me the treatment I deserved, but they lied to me and sent me away."

Moments passed before his anger subsided and he realized his parents had not been the problem. For the first time in his life, he took full responsibility for his actions, all of them.

Picking up his phone, he dialed Piero's Pizza and ordered his favorite—a medium pepperoni and sausage pizza with extra cheese. After the pizza arrived, he grabbed his bottle of anti-depressants and swallowed them by the handful as fast as he could get them down. Enjoying his final meal, he toasted each piece of pizza with a tall glass of vodka before he passed out, never to wake again.

64

PEYTON

Peyton arrived at Blast early Monday morning to prepare the reports needed for the leadership meeting. Tony, the IT Director, entered her office and said, "Hey, want to let you know we haven't heard from Spencer in several days."

"What?" she asked. "You mean he's MIA?"

"Yes," Tony said. "I've called him several times, but he doesn't answer. He didn't request PTO, but seriously, who would vacation with him?" He laughed.

Annoyed by Tony's behavior, Peyton replied, "Tony, that is not appropriate, but neither is his not coming to work, so let's focus there. When was the last time he came in?"

"Well," Tony said, rolling his eyes toward the ceiling, "I guess it was last Monday. So, he's been missing a full week now."

"Wow, you should have told me much sooner. Let me do some investigating," Peyton replied while realizing her threatening texts had also stopped about a week ago. The last message she had received said, "Peyton, oh Peyton…Cecelia is pissed. You will pay."

Knowing Cecelia was dead was comforting to Peyton, but she didn't know what information her harasser had obtained.

As soon as Tony left her office, Peyton called the emergency number from Spencer's personnel file. After the phone rang six times, a woman muttered in a sleepy voice, "Hello?"

"Hello. This is Peyton Alexander. I'm the HR director at Blast."

"Yes."

"Well, Spencer has you listed as his emergency contact."

Suddenly, the voice was awake and concerned, "What? Yes, I'm his mother. I'm his contact. What's going on?"

"Well, I'm not sure yet," Peyton said, "but have you seen him lately? He's not been to work in a while."

"What? No, my son is dedicated. What are you trying to say?"

"I meant no offense," Peyton replied. "We're worried about him. He's a great employee. So, have you seen him recently?"

"He comes to dinner sometimes. He's a good boy, but he keeps to himself, so I don't know what to tell you," his mother replied.

"Well, his address is the same as yours. Do you think you could maybe check on him? Assuming he still lives there."

"He does, but he has his own space in the basement. He doesn't check in with us. We respect his privacy."

"Sure, sure, but could you check on him, please, and ask him to call the office?" Peyton asked.

"Yes. He'll call you soon."

The call ended. Peyton sighed heavily before grabbing some files from her desk to scan. Would this electronic filing project ever come to an end? Forty minutes later, her phone buzzed, showing an incoming call from Spencer's house. Quickly answering, she said, "This is Peyton Alexander. How can I help you?"

A man's voice answered. Peyton could barely understand him through the sobs, "Ms. Alexander, I don't know, oh my God, I can't believe this, but my son is dead…." Hysterical sobbing ensued. Peyton felt her heart pounding behind her ears.

"What? What are you talking about?"

"My baby boy," came the reply with more sobs. "He's gone, dead; I can't believe this." More cries of remorse followed before a deep professional voice came on the line. "Hello, this is Officer Dorsey with the Atlanta PD. To whom am I speaking?"

Rattled and confused, Peyton replied, "This is Peyton Alexander of Blast....uh, Spencer works, worked here. Did someone say he was dead?"

"That is confirmed, Ms. Alexander. Please state your business with this situation."

"Well, I am the HR Director at Blast, where Spencer works; I mean, worked. Can you tell me what happened?"

"We are not able to disclose any details," Officer Dorsey replied. "Blast...did you say you work at Blast?"

"Yes."

"Interesting," the officer replied. "Didn't we visit with you earlier this week?"

"Well, yes, but it had nothing to do with this," Peyton said, and then she felt a rush of guilt and confusion over why she had said that. Authority figures always made her uncomfortable, even when she had done nothing wrong. Damn Catholic upbringing!

"Ma'am, we will be the judge of that," he replied before the call ended.

"What in the world is going on?" Peyton muttered to herself. Spencer couldn't have anything to do with Cecelia; they were states apart. And she had not killed Cecelia, even though the police had questioned her extensively about the reason she was in South Dakota and the incident at the Taco King. Her outburst with Cecelia had been reported to the Mitchell police by the elderly couple and security video from Taco King had led the police to Peyton. Peyton's stomach was in knots as she headed to her leadership meeting, where she barely paid attention, her mind spinning with uncertainties.

After her meeting, Peyton called Corbin, who answered after the third ring. "Hey, what's up?"

"Nothing; well, no, that's not true," she replied. "Spencer is dead."

"What? What do you mean, he's dead?"

"Just that," Peyton said. "He's dead. I'm freaking out a bit."

"Sure, but what happened?"

"I'm not sure. Tony said he's not been to work for a week, and then I called his parents…and Corbin, he's dead!"

"Peyton, that's awful. Do you know what happened? Like was it a car accident or something?"

"I have no idea. His dad called and said he was dead, and then a police officer got on the phone and asked me some questions about their visit here." She suddenly realized she had not shared her story of the police inquisition at Blast because she had lied to Corbin about her trip to South Dakota.

"What visit is that, Peyton?" Corbin hadn't missed the slip.

"Well, I mean, they asked to schedule a visit to ask me questions about Spencer. Sorry, baby; I'm super-upset."

"Sure, understandably. I am, too," said Corbin. "He was my best friend."

"I know; I'm sorry if I'm being insensitive. I don't know what's going on." She allowed her voice to crack slightly. "But could I see you tonight? I don't want to be alone. Please?"

"Sure…. Let me see what I can do and I'll text you later."

Peyton thought he sounded annoyed.

"Thank you, Corbin," she said, but he was gone.

65

CORBIN

When Peyton called me, I already knew Spencer was dead. What I didn't know was who had killed him. A pattern seemed to be forming—mess with Peyton, end up dead.

I had been watching my old friend for several nights, trying to determine what he was up to so I could end Peyton's torment. Regardless of my current concerns over her, I loved her and had to protect her from others. I would figure out my own scenario after I dealt with her enemies.

The first night, I had watched Spencer's house for hours and witnessed no visitors. The Piero's Pizza man arrived at eight to deliver what I knew was a pepperoni and sausage pizza with extra cheese. Typical. Nothing else happened that night.

The second night, I watched patiently from the prickly ivy bushes. I chastised myself for picking such an uncomfortable vantage point. There was no activity that night.

I stayed throughout the night until early morning to see if Spencer went to work that day. He did not. Perhaps he was taking some PTO and had decided to stay home and play video games or work on his trains for a week. What else would Spencer do with his spare time?

Returning on the third night, I waited well past eight. Still no one coming or going from the basement apartment. No pizza delivery. No shadows moving about and reflecting through the windows. Around ten, my curiosity got the best of me, and I quietly approached the basement, noting there were no cameras. Something didn't feel right, and I had a sickening feeling that someone had taken the pleasure of dealing with Spencer from me. Peeking in one of the small rectangular windows, I was not prepared for the scene that unfolded before my eyes.

Spencer's bloated body was lying coldly on the basement floor. His eyes had already gone blank as they stared questioningly into the heavens—as if heaven exists. He was lying in a pool of urine, vomit, and who knows what else. An aggressive mouse was gnawing at a discarded pizza crust near Spencer's right hand, a hand that was already tinted the bluish shade of death.

I had no idea what had happened, but I should not be present. Making sure my tracks were covered, I exited swiftly. Safely away from Spencer's parents' house and his bachelor, basement pad, I returned to my house and went directly into the basement. I was angry that someone had killed Spencer. That had been my job to do.

My recurring thought was why did everyone who crossed Peyton end up dead? I wondered if she had orchestrated his death. Had I been underestimating Peyton all along?

Poor Cecelia, her son, and the poor pup. That was inexcusable. Perhaps Cecelia deserved it, but certainly not her son or the dog. They were innocents. Could my Peyton have done that? Could she also be responsible for Spencer's death? Had she known it was Spencer causing her trouble at work?

I was annoyed with Peyton, but I needed to see her. I needed answers, and I would not make it easy on her. I was tired of the lies and the deceit, but I needed to be coy. She would be on guard if I were too direct. I needed to play her a bit more to find out the truth, if she were capable of delivering the truth.

Grabbing my phone, I called Peyton. After a couple of rings, she said, "Hey."

"So, I can come over. I know you don't have anything to cook; want me to bring something? And not pizza," I said, quickly remembering the scene I'd recently vacated. I wasn't sure I could eat Piero's pizza for a long time.

"Oh, whatever; surprise me," she replied as expected. Why couldn't she say what she wanted? She used to. Or was my annoyance coming through because I no longer trusted her?

Faking a hearty laugh, I said, "Sardines and Vienna sausages it is!"

"You know me so well," she said before ending the call. Rolling my eyes and feeling my annoyance escalate, I needed to be less transparent when she opened the door to greet me. But, man, I hated it when she ended the call without saying goodbye. Another small sign that things might be unraveling.

Stopping at a nearby Mexican restaurant, I placed a to-go order of chicken quesadillas, cheese dip, and a side of pico de gallo with jalapeños. I couldn't go wrong with that choice. Telling the server I'd be right back to pick up the order, I ran next door and picked up some Miller Lite, just in case.

Moments later, I arrived at the beautiful Peyton Alexander's apartment door and softly knocked. She opened the door and stared at me with a stressed, unsmiling face. I instantly felt guilty for any negative thoughts that had crossed my mind, before remembering she had lied to me. But maybe there was good reason. Regardless, I couldn't think about that now.

"Hey, I come bearing gifts," I said, holding up the bag of food and carton of beer. "Let's make your night better than your day."

"Aw, thank you, Corbin." She smiled softly. "This means a lot to me. I'm glad you're here. It's been a day!" Grabbing the food from my hand, she headed toward the kitchen. I would have to drag the information out of her.

I gave her plenty of time to eat her quesadilla. She dipped it directly into the melted cheese dip, then topped it with a bright, green jalapeño. I laughed as she discarded the "ugly" jalapeños, as she described them—the ones partially red, oddly shaped, or with the nub of stem still intact.

Finally, I sat back and said, "So, what about Spencer? Any news?"

"No, nothing. The police didn't come by. I guess they're busy."

"Sure, sure, but you said they wanted to visit with you. Why you?"

"I guess 'cause I'm the HR person. I don't know," she said while scooping up trash and putting it in the plastic delivery bag.

"So, had he been acting normal at work? Did he seem stressed out? Like anyone was out to get him or anything?"

"No. Well, you know, I didn't hang out with him, so I guess I wouldn't know, but to me, he seemed the same," she said.

"Other than the fact that you didn't even notice he hadn't been there for a week?"

"Corbin…it's not like we were pals…."

"Hmm, really." I could feel my anger getting out of control.

"What are you implying?" she asked.

"Well, I recall seeing you and him having coffee together one day after work."

Laughing, she said, "Oh, Corbin, that was to find out about you. It's not like I was interested in him at all. Come on; you have to know that."

"Okay, then why were you in South Dakota when you told me you were in Dallas? And then right after you get back to Georgia, oh, look Cecelia and her family are found brutally murdered. Explain that one." I relished watching the blood wash from her face, leaving her skin ashen as her beautiful jaw slackened slightly.

"What are you talking about?" she continued to lie. "I don't know what you're saying."

"Cut the shit, Peyton," I said. "I know you weren't in Dallas and that you were in South Dakota right before Cecelia and her family were killed. So, tell me what you did."

"Corbin!" She was already pleading. "I didn't do anything."

"Then why did you lie? You know how I feel about that."

"Corbin, I'm sorry. I know it seemed bad, and I should have told you. I apologize, truly." She held her hand to her chest. "I didn't think you would understand why I needed to go to South Dakota, and I honestly didn't want you there. I didn't need to explain things to my dad."

"Hmm, okay," I replied. "We're supposed to love each other, but I need to be a secret from your dad. Okay, well, that's an issue for another day, but first, I need to know: Did you kill Cecelia, her kid, her dog, and now my best friend, Spencer?"

I watched in great enjoyment as my question sunk into her brain.

"What...? No, of course not. How could you...?"

"Well, Peyton, seems like everyone who crosses you ends up dead," I said without mercy.

"What are you talking about?"

"Whatever. Cecelia was blackmailing you, she ends up dead. Spencer somehow found out and was blackmailing you, too. Now he's dead. Just saying, it's a bit of a coincidence."

"What? Spencer? No, I didn't know. What are you talking about, Corbin? Spencer wasn't blackmailing me; it was Cecelia. Someone else was, too, but I never knew who. It was Spencer?"

"That is pretty irrelevant to the questions I have, Peyton." I was mad at her reactions. She was trying to play me like all women in my life had. But I was no longer a fool—I hadn't been since I had happily massacred Jessica.

"Let's start over," I said, knowing my eyes had grown dark. "What happened in South Dakota, and why were you there?"

"Okay, well, I was there because my dad called and asked me to be there. He was recently diagnosed with cancer, and he was going through a bit of a rough time. He wanted me to be near," she said.

"And, why did you lie to me?"

"Because, Corbin, I know you. You would have wanted to come and meet my dad, and it wasn't the right time. I want you to meet him, and he's doing better now, but it wasn't how I wanted to introduce you. I'm very sorry."

"But why didn't you tell me that? I would have understood," I replied.

"Would you have? I think you would have felt rejected, and I didn't want that. I wasn't and am not rejecting you." She placed her soft hand on my forearm like she had done long ago on our first date.

I pushed her hand away, still not satisfied. "What happened to Cecelia? Did you visit her on your trip there? I was there, too; I heard what someone did to her, and Peyton, if you did that…."

"What? You followed me there?"

"No, not at all. I knew Spencer and Cecelia had been talking. I went there to talk to her and find out what she knew," I said, suddenly defensive. "Don't come at me."

"Why not? You've been coming at me. Okay, I'll tell you everything that happened on my trip to South Dakota. And then, you're going to do the exact same thing."

"No, I am going to ask the questions and you are going to answer them," I replied, "this time with the truth, if you can muster it."

"Don't be a dick," she said.

"What did you call me?"

"I didn't call you anything. I said, 'Don't be a dick,' meaning be nice and stop doing what you are doing right now. Yes, I lied to you about Dallas, but that doesn't make me a murderer. Come on, Corbin; think about this."

"Okay, you went to South Dakota because your dad had cancer. Did you see Cecelia there?"

"Yes, I did, but I didn't kill her," Peyton replied.

"Why did you see Cecelia?"

"I ran into her at Taco King. Trust me, I didn't plan on seeing her. She's the last person I wanted to see, ever."

"Why?" I asked.

"Why, what?"

"Why is she the last person you wanted to see? What does she have on you?"

"Corbin, it was a long time ago; please, just drop it. I didn't kill anyone!" She was getting upset, and I was enjoying it.

"You know what? Until you can be truthful with me, I think we are done," I said. Disappointed in the woman I thought I loved, I played a bold card, hoping for a better reaction.

"What?"

"Peyton, why won't you let me in? I don't care what you have done, but I can't stand the lies. Why can't you trust me to support you completely? I love you and never want anyone to hurt you, but I can't protect you if you don't tell me the truth." I thought that was the most eloquent statement I could deliver, but the result was not what I expected.

"Protect me?" she asked. "Protect me? I don't fucking need anyone to protect me. Protect me? You think that is what our relationship is about? Someone to fucking protect me?"

"Yes, protect you. Obviously, you can't do it yourself. Look at the mess you are in now. You've killed several people—and in a sloppy manner. My God, Peyton, you have to be the prime suspect of these murders. You have to be smarter than this!" I was yelling now, but my frustration was unbearable.

"Oh, so now I'm stupid." She was angry. "Is that what you're saying? I'm a stupid girl who needs the protection of a big, strong man?"

"You aren't stupid. You are acting stupidly. There's a big difference."

"Fuck you," she said so calmly that it shocked me. Her face had turned completely emotionless as she blankly stared at me.

"What did you say?"

"Oh, I'm sorry you don't hear well. I said, 'Fuck you,'" she replied.

"Are you sure you want to go down this path with me?"

"You're the one taking us down this path, and no, I don't want to go down it, so again, if you can't believe what I say and you still insist I'm the murderer, then I must say, 'Fuck you.' I can't imagine how you got this in your head, but I'm not going to put up with it. If you don't believe me, get out."

She was serious, but I didn't know if she was the killer. Some part of me wanted her to be the killer. The thought of her covered in fresh blood as she bashed in Cecelia's head gave me a rush I'd never experienced. Could there actually be someone who understood me? Or was she another lying Jessica? I was confused and uncertain how to navigate the situation. Taking a deep breath, and realizing how much I truly wanted Peyton, if she could be honest, I said, "Look; I want to know what happened."

"Fuck, Corbin; I've been trying to tell you that I don't know! Why won't you believe me?" Her temples throbbed with frustration, but her eyes maintained their emotionless reptilian appearance.

"Okay, okay, sorry, but at some point, if we are to be together, I need to know. And to be clear, Peyton, I love you, and I don't care if you did it. I will support you—not protect you—support you, no matter what. I have to know the cards I'm dealing with, okay?" I tried to hold her hand, but she swatted me away.

"You need to go," she stated.

"Peyton! I'm trying to talk to you. I'm okay with whatever the situation is."

"Just go. I don't want you here."

Stepping back, I said, "Peyton, I love you. Please don't do this. Talk to me, please?"

"Get out," she replied, not even making eye contact but staring diagonally at an imaginary spot on the freshly cleaned floor.

I wasn't sure if she honestly wanted me to leave or if I was supposed to make some grand gesture. But without knowing what to do, the only option I had was to acquiesce to her wish. Leaving her apartment, I was confused and still had no answers.

66

PEYTON

As the alarm blared in the distance, Peyton reached over and slammed it into quiet submission. It was Saturday; why was the alarm set? Rolling over and snuggling into her pillows, she recounted her last exchange with Corbin several days ago. She had not heard from him since, even though she had sent him multiple texts and made several calls.

She wasn't sure how she felt about it, but by the feeling in her stomach, she was the one who had acted inappropriately. He had, after all, said he'd be supportive of her, even if she were a murderer. How many guys do you meet who are cool with that? But by the time he had left, she was too angry to be rational. She needed her time and her space. And why would he question her? Okay, she had lied to him, but what was he doing in South Dakota? Oh, yes, trying to protect her. She rolled her eyes. Maybe his words were not perfect, but was he a bad guy?

Picking up her phone, she called her dad.

"Hey, Dad, how are you feeling?" she asked.

"Good. Thanks for calling. How are things with you?"

"Well…not so great. I'm having a really tough time, Dad. I was thinking that maybe I need to move back home."

"Oh, I see," he replied. "So, the South has taught you to give up when times get hard?"

"No, it's not like that. It's just…I don't know; things are complicated right now."

"Let me guess," he said. "You and Corbin are having issues, so you want to run away."

"No…. Well, we are having issues, but I don't need him."

"Oh, my sweet little princess, I know you don't need anyone. You have made that abundantly clear your entire life. But, honey, let me ask you: Don't you ever just want someone?"

Tears formed in Peyton's eyes and rolled down her cheeks as she realized the honesty of that statement. She didn't need anyone, but it would be nice to be wanted and to want someone. She had never felt that way before. All her past relationships had been superficial at best. When she was dating Charles in college, she had thought she was in love. But, as it turned out, Charles "loved" many women at the university and she meant nothing to him. She mourned the breakup, but in retrospect, she hadn't loved him either. She was wanting to fit in and be accepted. That's what girls do to avoid being labeled as different.

"Peyton," her father continued, "I have a suggestion. Instead of pushing everyone away when things get real, how about giving someone a chance? You don't need them. You are amazing all on your own. But let yourself want someone. Let someone in. I don't know this Corbin fellow, but I noticed how happy you were when you told me about him. Maybe, just maybe, he deserves a little break from the fierce Peyton temper and Baby's fire-shooting nostrils."

"Oh, come on, Dad, a Baby reference?"

"Peyton, don't you try to deflect your father, and stop being a jerk," he replied. "I'm not saying Corbin is the one, but give someone a chance. Someone worthy. Now, I love you, but I gotta go. I have a date with an interesting woman from book club."

Peyton hung up, smiling at the phone. "Hmm, look at Dad putting himself out there."

Peyton spent the day doing silly errands and trying to disregard the conversation with her father.

"Corbin was being a jerk, not me!" she tried to justify. "This is all his fault."

After scrubbing and dusting her apartment from top to bottom, Peyton was still uneasy as the evening wore on. She couldn't let this go. After dialing Corbin's number one more time and being sent to voicemail, Peyton realized the severity of the moment. Pulling her hair into a messy bun, she headed for the office.

It had never seemed odd to her until now that she didn't know Corbin's address. They always stayed at her apartment. When she offered to come over, he would smoothly deflect and explain his house was a mess due to his latest home improvement project. He was building a man cave in his basement and had tools and supplies all over. He promised to have her over when the project was complete.

As her computer monitor came to life, she quickly searched past records and found Corbin's last known address from his personnel file. That electronic filing project had paid off. Jotting down his address, Peyton scurried out of the office and entered the information into her GPS.

Arriving at 398 Melbourne Road in Cumming, Peyton saw Corbin's Nissan parked in the secluded driveway. All the lights in the house were blasting into the night. Peyton parked her 4Runner in the drive and approached the front door. Seeing no doorbell, she knocked confidently on the door. The house was bright, but silent. She rapped a few more times, then took a chance and tried the handle. The door opened effortlessly, welcoming Peyton into the warmth of Corbin's home. She walked tentatively inside, calling his name and looking for him.

As she explored Corbin's place, she was surprised that it was barely decorated, almost as if he had recently moved in, minus the moving boxes. The kitchen housed an old yellow Kenmore refrigerator with some Piero's Pizza coupons stuck to the door with a magnetic clip. Compelled to open it, she found only a bottle of ketchup, some pickles, and a few sandwich bags filled with what appeared to be liver.

Gross, she thought. *He likes liver?*

The living room was equally disappointing. A well-worn, fluffy, tan recliner sat next to a metal TV tray that supported a hideous purple lamp, which greatly overpowered the small table. The television, however, appeared to be a state-of-the-art flat screen mounted expertly against the wall.

"Men," she said, smiling.

Returning from the bedroom where she found his clothes carefully organized by type and color in the small closet, Peyton noticed the basement door, a small dark shadow emanating into the penetrating light. Opening the door slowly, she was welcomed by darkness and searched for the light switch.

67

CORBIN

After the exchange with Peyton, I could only retreat to my basement. I don't know how long I was there. I was totally crushed and devastated by the situation. I was willing to accept her for who she was. All I asked for was honesty. I sat in the dark for hours, maybe days, recounting the people in my life who had hurt and betrayed me. I had thought Peyton was different. I needed her to be. I remembered with clarity how Jessica had severed my thumb so easily; I didn't understand how a person could do that to a child.

What would become of Peyton and me? I loved her. She was different, but was she different enough? Or, by nature, were all women simply varying degrees of evil? What would be horrible about having someone in this world who had your back, and okay, sure, someone to protect you? My desire was not of chauvinistic motivation; it was a sincere response I could not banish from my thoughts. I did want to protect Peyton, and conversely, I wanted her to protect me. I would welcome someone I could trust.

Sure, I had lied to Peyton by omission, but I am a serial killer—that's not something you want a lot of people knowing, especially when you're uncertain of their integrity, as I now was of Peyton's. And while I did have an overwhelming desire to consume her warm, delicious liver, I had an equally powerful desire to keep her safe and close. I wanted to be normal and have someone who loved me; oh, and someone who didn't lie to me. Maybe some of us are condemned at birth to always be alone. Maybe we shouldn't focus so much on finding someone who cares about us, but the desire to be loved and accepted for who we are is an undeniable need of this messed-up species. We all pretend we don't care and don't need anyone, but as you sit alone in the dark with only your thoughts and no one around or even thinking about you, you realize that's a bunch of bullshit.

My deep and philosophical thoughts were violently interrupted by a harsh flash of light, followed by Peyton's voice. "Corbin, are you down there?"

Snapping into reality, I instinctually answered, even though I should have remained silent, "Yes." Then I quickly added, "Wait there; I'll come up." I didn't want her in my basement.

But it was too late. Peyton came trotting down the steps and appeared before me. "Hi," she said.

"Hi," I replied, confused how she knew where I lived, not sure I was ready to see her, and most importantly, wondering how to get her out of the basement before she saw too much. "So, let's go upstairs."

"No, we need to talk, now. I don't want to wait a second," she insisted while staring intently into my eyes. I couldn't even look around to see what thumbs might be out, nor could I remember where they all were placed. She simply could not see them. I was not ready for this crossroad with Peyton—the moment when I had to decide to trust her or eat her. *Please, don't let it be now,* I thought over and over.

While steering her toward the stairs, I said, "Let's go upstairs, grab a beer, and talk. Come on."

"No, Corbin, if I don't say this now, right now, I will lose the courage, so you have to let me, please?" She drooped her eyelids before looking up at me like a sad little puppy separated from its mother.

"Fine," I said. "But don't look at the mess down here. I'm still working on my man cave and I have a long way to go."

"I didn't come here to inspect your basement," she said, laughing.

I wanted her upstairs more than anything in the world. Attempting to mask my anxiety, I simply asked, "Okay, why did you come here?"

She took a deep breath and reached out to hold my hands. "So, here's the deal. I'm horrible at relationships. Whenever things get good, and that means scary to me, I pick a fight and push people away. I build this impenetrable wall around myself for protection, but it also prevents any good from getting in. I know this sounds lame, but I want to tell you I'm sorry for the other night. I got angry and shut down, and it wouldn't have mattered what you said; I would have been pissed and twisted your words. I'm kind of a jerk like that. I'm sorry."

I didn't know what to do or say, so I stared at her. I didn't even know what expression was on my face.

"Okay, so, I'm feeling awkward; would you say something?"

"I'm sorry, Peyton. I don't know what to say." I wasn't even clearly aware of what I was saying because I was trying to remember where I'd placed all my thumb dolls. I knew the exact location of my boning knife, however. I never lost track of it.

"Well, does that mean you hate me and want me to leave, or that we can maybe move past the other night?" She was near tears, and while her apology wasn't that emotional, I could tell it took a lot for her to open up even with that limited vulnerability.

"Peyton, I don't hate you," I said. "But I have to be able to fully trust you. Like 100 percent no matter what—complete and ultimate trust. I know it's weird, but I've been burned and hurt too many times, like you, to have it any other way. But complete trust is hard as hell. Complete trust means that no matter what it is, you accept it as part of that person."

"Sure," she said, and I could see the wheels turning in her mind. "So, you're saying you want to know every piece of dirt from my past, and no matter what it is, you will carry no judgment against it? No matter what it is? No matter how horrible or embarrassing it may be?"

"I don't want to only know the dirt from your past. I want to know everything about your past, good and bad. And no, I won't judge you. I am only here to support you, and I'm sorry—I'm going to say it again—protect you. *But*," I held up my finger to silence her, "that doesn't mean you need me to protect you. It means that as partners, we protect each other."

Could I possibly get out of this basement without her seeing anything? So far, I had done a good job of keeping eye contact. I hoped it would continue. I did not want to make this decision tonight.

"Wow," she whispered. "Maybe, Baby won't have to burn you after all."

"What?" I asked.

"Sorry, childhood reference. I'll fill you in at some point." She smiled. "Corbin, I want to be that person for you, but please be patient with me. I'm not used to opening up and letting people in."

"Well, we haven't even scratched the surface of my mental hang-ups," I said, laughing.

"I called my dad today and he straightened me out. He reminded me that I don't need someone, but that it might be okay to want someone. And, guess what? I want you," she said, reminding me of a goofy school girl.

"And I want you," I said before kissing her softly. *My God, if her lips taste this good, what will her liver taste like?* I could not suppress the thought. Ending the kiss, I said, "Now, can we please get out of this gross basement and go upstairs?"

"Sure," she said. "I'd like to go upstairs, but not to have a drink."

I did it! I was going to get her out of this basement without seeing a thing. Whew. Laughing, I put my arm around her shoulder and moved toward the stairs. And then, she saw them.

68

FRANKLIN

Mustering his courage, and mildly comforted that Ann was sound asleep and unable to bask in the glory of him doing exactly what she had suggested, Franklin unlocked Emily's door and quietly entered the bedroom, illuminated only by the nightlight glowing softly by the bedside. Sliding the chair silently next to the bed, Franklin reached tentatively for Emily's hand. It was always a gamble whether or not she would recognize him.

She sighed softly and said, "Oh, honey. I've missed you."

He fought the tears welling in his eyes and wished this moment could last forever, even though he knew from experience it would be short-lived. God, he missed her so. Trying to keep his emotions in check, he softly stroked her hand and said, "I've missed you, too."

"I don't have much time left," Emily said. "And I don't know how long I'll be here this time. But listen to me, darling. You have to let him in."

"Emily, let who in?"

"That boy of yours," she replied.

"Honey, we don't have any children, remember?" he said, instantly regretting the reference to the miscarriages.

"I'm not talking about ours," she replied, more lucid than he remembered her being in months. "Corbin—isn't that his name?"

"What?" was all he could utter.

"Oh, my dear Franklin. I saw the picture years ago, tucked under your desk blotter. I grew bored waiting for you in your office that day. I'm sorry; I shouldn't have snooped. But you've never kept secrets from me; well, except this one, I guess."

"But why didn't you say anything all these years?"

"It wasn't my place. I figured you would tell me when you were ready, but it seems you were never ready. Or were never in the cross-hairs of my shotgun again." She chuckled. "But it didn't change my love for you. I figured there had to have been a reason you didn't want to share that with me."

"I'm so sorry, Emily." Franklin was overwrought with emotion and tears streamed down his face. "It was right after the last…. Anyway, it was a difficult time, and I didn't want to upset you. And then, well, it was too complicated, and…I don't know; I'm so sorry."

"I know, I know," she said, patting his hand. "I wanted to forget it and kept hoping you would tell me, but the years came and went, and well, what difference does it make to me now? But, you, my love, need to know your son. I'll be gone soon."

"No, Emily." Franklin sobbed. "I need you."

"Franklin, I will always be with you in my heart, even as my mind fails me. He's your son. He's family. It's all we've ever wanted. Do this for me."

"Oh, Emily," Franklin begged as more tears slid from his eyes, but the moment was gone.

She snatched her hand away and screamed, "Who are you? Get out of my house, you fucking *freak*!"

Franklin wiped his eyes, stood, and walked slowly to the door. Opening it, he called into the darkness, "Ann?"

69

CORBIN

"Wait," Peyton said. "What is that?" Her eyes fell upon one of my thumb doll scenes—the one depicting the murder of Jessica at the Quick Pick.

"You play with dolls?" She laughed as she approached the table.

"Peyton. Stop. Please."

As she picked up the Jessica stump drizzled in red paint, I knew things would change. She gasped as she realized she was holding a preserved human digit. As "Jessica" fell to the table with a soft thud, Peyton's face conveyed her utter confusion. "What is this?" she asked.

I knew her words indicated a much larger question and that my answer had to be more than, "Um, it's a preserved thumb doll, obviously."

While searching for something to say that might change the foreseeable future so Peyton would not have to die, I started looking around nervously.

"Corbin…these are thumbs? Are these all human thumbs?" she asked while gesturing around the basement.

Sighing because it was happening, no matter how much I dreaded it, I approached her. I didn't want to have to do this, not tonight—well, not ever. But certainly not this soon. Why did she have to come to the basement?

"Peyton." I sighed. I had to remain calm.

Another emotion flashed across Peyton's face, one that left me uncertain of what she was feeling.

"Oh, my God, Corbin! *You* killed Cecelia and Spencer! Are these their thumbs…and fingers…or whatever all this shit is?"

"Shh. No, Peyton; please calm down. I did not kill Cecelia or Spencer."

"Don't you shush me. I need to know what is going on," she said in her corporate tone that I loved. The few times I'd overheard her stand up to Paul, she had used that tone, and I remembered my intense desire for her then.

Softly touching her arm and looking directly into her eyes, my green eyes doing their magic, I changed my tone to be soft and silky, because this time it mattered. "Peyton, I'm sorry. I will explain everything and answer your questions, but please, can we have this conversation as calmly and rationally as possible?"

I felt her muscles relax slightly under my touch and hoped it was working. To keep us on this path, I added, "There is a lot to cover, and I promise, we will cover it all. So, please, be patient and we'll get through this." Knowing the alternative was me having a delicious meal this evening, I didn't see either outcome as a total loss, although I wanted one more than the other.

Peyton allowed the breath she had been holding to rush into the room. "Okay," she said, "but I have a lot of questions."

Smiling earnestly, I nodded. "I'm sure you do. So, ask away."

"Okay, but you promise that you won't lie to me? You will tell me the complete and total truth, no matter how ugly the answer may be?" she asked.

"I solemnly swear."

"Did you kill Spencer or Cecelia?"

"No, I did not kill either one of them," I replied and added for good measure, "nor the kid or the dog."

"Did you have anything to do with their deaths?"

"I did not."

"Why were you in South Dakota?"

I had to continue the direct responses and could not allow her to doubt my answers. "I was in South Dakota because Spencer was blackmailing you and he had been in contact with Cecelia. I went to see what Cecelia knew or what information I could get out of her. But she was dead by the time I got there. And I had no idea at the time that you had been in South Dakota." It was risky, but I had to remind her of that lie she had told me.

"Okay, I see you had to bring that up; well, that's fair," she said. "I was in South Dakota to visit my dad, like I already told you, and I ran into Cecelia, but I did not kill her."

"You've already told me that,"

"Oh, and you don't believe me?"

Sensing that things could easily take a turn for the worse, I brought back the charm. "Yes, Peyton, I do believe you. When we talked before, my feelings were hurt because of the lie. But I'm past the South Dakota thing now. So, next question?"

It worked. The flush in her cheeks disappeared, and she took this moment to look around the basement, taking in every detail. After a few moments, she asked, "These are all thumbs, preserved somehow and made into dolls?"

"Correct."

"And where did the thumbs come from? Are there a bunch of people running around the world missing their thumbs?" she asked.

"Peyton, I'd like to tell you there are thousands of people without thumbs running around, but there are not." This was going to be a rough night, and I wished I had purchased that undercounter refrigerator I'd seen at Sears so I could open a Miller Lite right now.

Wait for it; wait for it, I joked to myself. Seeing the wheels turning and then the lightbulb going off, I wanted to laugh. *My God, I love this woman.*

Her eyes opened wide and she said, "Oh…they are all dead?"

"They are."

"And did you…?" She couldn't finish the question.

This was a critical crossroads for us, and I couldn't lie. Peyton was not an idiot, and if I lied, I would have to kill her. So, I didn't. "Yes, I killed them. All of them."

I was disappointed by the quick intake of her breath; she tried to keep it under control but failed miserably. I subconsciously walked through the steps I would need to take to reach my boning knife tucked safely in a drawer slightly beyond Peyton's right hip. Easily doable.

"Wow." She took a deep breath and exhaled loudly. "You are being honest. Well, I guess that's good."

The flush had returned to her cheeks, and I noticed her pulse beating rapidly in that perfect little V at the base of her throat. Such a beautiful throat.

"Corbin, I need a beer," was all that came next.

Not wanting us to go upstairs because the basement was much easier to clean, I said, "Okay, I'll go get us one if you promise to wait here. And give me your phone."

"Why the hell do you need my phone?" she asked, trying to appear more confident than she was feeling.

"Peyton, come on. Be logical."

Nodding, she handed me her phone and said nothing until I was halfway up the stairs. "Corbin? Would you bring more than one?"

Laughing hysterically inside, I nodded my head. As I got to the top of the stairs, I took a moment to check my pocket for the key. Confirming its placement, I shut the door and clicked the padlock shut. I couldn't take any chances of her getting out of the basement until I knew how things would end. While I wanted to believe things would work out, I couldn't risk Peyton getting to the police.

Tossing several beers into a plastic bucket and dumping clumps of ice around them, I returned to the basement after leaving Peyton's phone on the counter. After I offered her a beer, she popped it open and took a hearty swig.

"Okay, let's do this," she said. "So, you killed all the people who used to have these thumbs attached to their hands. How many people have you killed?"

"I honestly have no idea, but a lot of them." This was Honest Answer Hour, right? "I kept most of their thumbs, but some of them didn't preserve well, so I had to get rid of them. I guess we could count what's left, if the number is important."

"No, that's okay," she said, not seeing the humor in my answer. "Why did you kill them?"

"Well, Peyton…." I hesitated. Could I tell her about my desire? Could she handle it? Or would it matter at this juncture? I was becoming more and more confident in how the evening would end, and well, I was growing hungry anyway.

"It's a long story," I said. "It started with my mother, Jessica. I killed her because she was a horrid, abusive person who didn't deserve to live. And then, later, well, I guess I recognized a craving. I don't know how to explain it, other than that."

"By killing one person, you developed a craving to kill others? That doesn't even make sense."

"No, it's not about killing. I mean, I have to kill them to get what I need." I realized it was a confusing answer.

"I don't understand. What did you need to get? And why did they have to be dead?" Her face was crimson and her heart pounding. I guessed I should be somewhat sympathetic. This wasn't normal boyfriend shit.

I couldn't believe I was going to share this. I thought I would keep this a secret for eternity. What about this woman caused me to talk about my life?

"I killed Jessica for revenge. I saved her thumb because she took mine. But after that, as I got older, I developed a strange and over-powering desire to eat human liver. And, well, the only way to eat human liver is to kill the human." I paused for an emotional check and determined the reaction was pulling the needle far to the "You're going to have to kill Peyton" side of the spectrum.

Continuing, I added, "But I didn't, er, don't, kill good people. I know that doesn't make it right, but I had to find a balance between my obsession and living in society. So I found horrible people, sluts, women who abused their kids or abandoned them, and those were the ones I went for."

"You killed women who reminded you of Jessica," Peyton whispered in realization.

"Well, yes, I guess I did."

"Do I remind you of Jessica?"

Shocked by the question, I went quickly to Peyton. Looking deep into her beautiful hazel eyes, now heavily streaked with green, I said, "Definitely not! Not in any way whatsoever. Peyton, you are kind and beautiful and want the best for the world. You try to be a hardass, but in your heart, you care and are genuine."

I remembered that time we had stopped at a C-store late at night because Peyton had to pee. As we were leaving, a skinny woman, with rotting teeth and sores covering her face and dressed in a skimpy red dress, approached Peyton.

"Hi," the woman had said to Peyton. "I don't want anything. I wanted to tell you I hope you have a good night and that God is watching over you."

Peyton had smiled and hugged the woman, returning the kindness, then had said, "You be safe tonight, okay?"

When we returned to the car, I asked her why she had hugged that woman. Peyton replied, "Because she needed it and people judge her all the time."

Back in my basement, the next question had been asked. "So, Corbin, would you ever hurt me? Do you want to eat my liver?"

Oh, what to do with this one? I wanted desperately to eat her liver, but I also didn't want to harm her. I wanted to protect her. Let's go with honesty. Hell, I am still in control no matter what happens.

"Peyton, I promised you that I would not lie to you," I said. "So, does the thought of eating your liver sound delicious and compelling? Yes, it does." I noticed a look of panic in her face and her body tensed. "But," I added quickly in an attempt to calm her, "I would never hurt you. I love you. You are the first person who ever cared about me or was nice to me. I know I'm totally fucked up, but I would do anything in my power to protect you no matter what and from anything."

I had to say that, even though I was fully prepared with Plan B in the event I felt I couldn't trust her or she would betray me. If she was truly different and loved me, she would need to accept me for who I am. I wanted to trust her, but we, I, had a lot to risk right here, right now.

Pushing away from me, she said, a little too coldly, "Corbin, I'm going to need some time. Let me go home and mull this over and let's see what happens."

"No, Peyton."

Spinning to look me in the eyes, it was clear she didn't like that answer. "You're not going to let me leave? You're going to kill me, aren't you?"

"No, I'm not going to kill you." I tried to sound as comforting as I could. "But I can't let you leave. If you leave, you will never speak to me again. I know you, Peyton. You need to decide right now whether you give us a chance or you don't. I've opened my heart and all my darkest secrets to you."

She wandered about the basement for a moment, taking in all the scenes. She seemed calmer than earlier, which confused me to some extent. Several different thumb displays were going on. One was a party scene where some of the thumbs were sitting at the bar, and some were passed out, naked on the floor. Another depicted thumbs in a Barbie car going to the beach, leaving one bleeding and run over in the road. Sure, it was horrifying, but that's who I am. Hey, at least I didn't have a scene of one thumb eating the other's liver, right? Well, only because a thumb doesn't have a liver.

"I'm curious," Peyton said. "How do you come up with these scenes? Are they real ones? From your past?"

"No, not at all. I never ran over a thumb and left it dying on the road."

Much to my surprise, Peyton let out a bellowing laugh. "Of course, you didn't. Why would you run over a thumb?" She laughed for a few minutes and then started to cry uncontrollably. Then, I understood her attempt at humor was simply masking her fear and hysteria.

Moving closer to her, I pulled her into my chest and held her close. She allowed me to—a good sign. She smelled amazing, with a slight hint of cherry blossom.

"Peyton, I know I'm a horrible person. I deserved what Jessica did to me. And I don't blame you if you want to tuck tail and run.

You should. I am a stupid, stupid boy. Jessica was right. I'm sorry. I'm a fucking freak."

And in that inexplicable moment, I started to cry. I was embarrassed and felt weak, but I couldn't stop.

Peyton melted into me as we held each other, crying. I had allowed her to see the deepest, darkest crevices of my being, and she was still here. Could she handle this? Her anger and fear seemed to have dissipated. I held her close, feeling something I'd always longed for but had never experienced.

After several blissful moments, Peyton pulled away and slipped her hands up to cup my face. "Corbin, no one deserves what Jessica and others did to you. It's not your fault. My God, you were a child. You didn't do anything wrong. She was a sicko! It is not your fault."

Finally, in control of myself, I looked into her beautiful eyes and said, "But I kill people. How are you going to handle that?"

"I'll handle it. But if you ever raise even a pinky finger against me, I'll kick your ass. Rest assured, this liver is staying right here," she said, patting her side.

"You mean, you can handle…this?" I asked while gesturing around the basement. What was this woman saying? I was out of my element and filled with wonderment. What exactly was happening?

"Who am I to judge?" She smiled softly.

"And, Peyton?" An unfamiliar warmth rushed over my body as I looked into her eyes. "I love you."

Her expression was soft, her eyes warm. My heart had slowed to a steady thump, thump, thump. There was hope for the future. Our future. What an amazing woman my beautiful Peyton Alexander was.

Feeling accepted and loved for the first time in my life, and with a hint of excitement for our future, I wasn't surprised or alarmed when my favorite boning knife was sunk into my flesh. What other end could I expect? Betrayed once again.

Swiftly grabbing the knife, I wrenched it free from her. The handle was already covered in warm blood. Placing a hand over the bleeding opening, I was certain it was a flesh wound. The physical pain paled in comparison to the emotional devastation I felt.

"Peyton? How could you?"

She shrieked and attempted to run, throwing objects in my path in a futile attempt to reach the stairs. Resigned to accept the fate Mother had bestowed upon me, I had confirmation that no one could ever love a freak like me. Grabbing Peyton and holding her close, my blood flowing onto her white T-shirt, I gazed upon her lovingly as the reclaimed boning knife slowly penetrated her stomach, darting quickly to pierce her right lung. Tonight, I would enjoy the delicious liver of Peyton Alexander.

I allowed more tears to flow as I watched her fade from this earth. I kissed her softly and was at peace knowing she would always be with me. Whispering softly into her ear, I comforted her in her last moments. "Hi, I'm Corbin. Welcome to my basement."

ABOUT THE AUTHOR

Born in South Dakota, Lorie Yauney grew up in the country where she enjoyed raising lambs, calves, and chickens. She learned to ride horses at a young age and later trained them and competed in local horse shows and rodeos. As a teenager, she defied traditional roles and enrolled in a bronc riding school without her parents' permission. While she was not successful riding bucking horses, she enjoyed the experience and gained a deep respect for the dun mare who always threw her to the ground. Her country upbringing and love of animals contributed to the strong, caring, independent thinker Yauney is today.

Attending college at Chadron State College in Nebraska, Yauney focused on her love for writing. She enrolled in creative writing courses and joined the college newspaper as a writer. After graduating with a degree in business administration and a minor in psychology, she moved to Georgia and started her professional career. Yauney worked for more than twenty years with an independent insurance agency where she broke through the glass ceiling in her role first as Vice President of Human Resources and then as Chief Operating Officer. However, those accomplishments were no longer fulfilling to Yauney—she needed more. She walked away from corporate America to follow her dreams of becoming a writer and a free spirit. Yauney is a strong supporter of the underdog, believing that everyone deserves a chance, even those who are damaged. Judgment, deceit, and greed are not her credo.

Yauney currently lives in Indiana with her two pit bull girls and close to her daughter and granddaughters. Other than writing, she enjoys her tractor, power tools, and bonfires. She empowers and inspires her family as they build campsites and catch fireflies together.

For more information about Yauney, visit www.LorieYauney.com.